# The Last Grand Adventure

ALSO BY REBECCA BEHRENS

*Summer of Lost and Found*

*When Audrey Met Alice*

# THE Last Grand Adventure

## Rebecca Behrens

ALADDIN

NEW YORK   LONDON   TORONTO   SYDNEY   NEW DELHI

ALADDIN

An imprint of Simon & Schuster Children's Publishing Division

1230 Avenue of the Americas, New York, New York 10020

First Aladdin hardcover edition March 2018

Text copyright © 2018 by Rebecca Behrens

Jacket illustrations and interior map illustrations copyright © 2018 by Robyn Ng

For information about special discounts for bulk purchases, please contact Simon & Schuster Special Sales at 1-866-506-1949 or business@simonandschuster.com.

The Simon & Schuster Speakers Bureau can bring authors to your live event. For more information or to book an event contact the Simon & Schuster Speakers Bureau at 1-866-248-3049 or visit our website at www.simonspeakers.com.

Jacket designed by Laura Lyn DiSiena

Interior designed by Steve Scott

The text of this book was set in Bodoni 72.

Manufactured in the United States of America 0618 FFG

2 4 6 8 10 9 7 5 3

Library of Congress Cataloging-in-Publication Data

Names: Behrens, Rebecca, author.

Title: The last grand adventure / by Rebecca Behrens.

Description: First Aladdin hardcover edition. | New York : Aladdin, 2018. |
Summary: In 1967, unhappy with her newly blended family, twelve-year-old Bea agrees to accompany Pidge, her grandmother, to Atchison, Kansas, where Pidge believes her long-lost sister, Amelia Earhart, will meet them.
Includes historical notes, a brief biography, quotations from the Earharts, and resources for educators. | Includes bibliographical references.

Identifiers: LCCN 2017019299 (print) | LCCN 2017036584 (eBook) |
ISBN 9781481496940 (eBook) | ISBN 9781481496926 (hc)

Subjects: | CYAC: Adventure and adventurers—Fiction. | Sisters—Fiction. |
Grandmothers—Fiction. | Earhart, Amelia, 1897-1937—Fiction. |
Divorce—Fiction. | Stepfamilies—Fiction.

Classification: LCC PZ7.B38823405 (eBook) |
LCC PZ7.B38823405 Las 2018 (print) | DDC [Fic]—dc23

LC record available at https://lccn.loc.gov/2017019299

For my sister, Beth

NEVADA

UTAH

CALIFORNIA

GRAND CANYON

LOS ANGELES

DISNEYLAND

SUN CITY

ARIZONA

PACIFIC
OCEAN

# ONE

## Tomorrowland

It was the happiest place on Earth, or at least it was supposed to be. But I was hot, sticky from spilled lemonade, and unable to dislodge the nervous pit in my stomach. The crowds undulated around me, full of laughter and smiles and felt-and-plastic mouse ears. My father actually whistled as we strolled the park, Julie's arm hooked jauntily through his. Sally's sweaty palm pressed against mine as she squeezed with eagerness.

"I want to go to Tomorrowland! It's brand-new!" Sally's voice was high enough to squeak, which fit with the mouse ears she was wearing. I already had a pair, so I'd passed. And I didn't like how Sally wanted to share everything with me—books and records and telephone calls and hairstyles. If I didn't turn the flimsy little latch on my bedroom door at night, I might wake to find her curled up next to me with her head on half of my pillow, an arm hugging my old teddy bear.

"It's not really *new*," I pointed out. "They just changed it up." Twelve years after the park opened, I guess the park people thought they could do better—kind of like my dad with his renovated family. I tugged on my dress, which Julie had bought me. Somehow my stepmother had no problem selecting the right sizes for Sally, but this dress felt too short on me—and unfortunately it wasn't supposed to be a miniskirt length. (Julie said I was too young for those—maybe when I turned thirteen.) The bell-bottomed pants she'd brought home the week before were inches too long. Both were covered in bright fashionable swirls that I wasn't so sure about wearing, even if Julie insisted they were like something Twiggy wore in *Vogue*.

Julie patted Sally's shoulder. "It's new to us," she chirped. My father, still whistling, was oblivious.

I stared at the sign ahead. TOMORROWLAND: WHERE THE DREAMS OF THE FUTURE ARE REALITY TODAY. I felt that sharpness in my stomach again. Didn't any of these people get it? Sure, here the future looked exciting—with a PeopleMover train and clean white buildings and no litter on the street. Everybody singing along to show tunes and eating carnival food. But what about the world outside of amusement parks? What about all the war and disasters and terrible things to worry about?

There is a reason why there are no newsstands in Disneyland: to keep it the happiest place on Earth.

I let go of Sally's sticky hand, and I watched my father and freshly minted stepmother and stepsister walk a few steps ahead of me. My dad swept Sally up onto his shoulders so she could see above the crowds. Julie grinned up at them. I blinked hard. The three of them together was an echo of the only time I'd been to the park before: with my mom and dad, on my seventh birthday. We'd studied the park map and danced in New Orleans Square and laughed for the whole day, at least that's how I remember it. I had watched them stitch our names into three matching pairs of black felt ears—Ken, Sheila, and Beatrice—like we were permanent. Back then, I thought that my family would always be together and that the world was a place you could understand, that there were some things you could count on no matter what, like your parents being in the same home to tuck you in at night.

When I thought about how things had changed since the last time I had been there, I had to wonder what else would be different the next time I came to the park. Or even when I got home. Disneyland was a pit stop on the way to the house of a grandmother I had mostly met through birthday cards and calls on Christmas. I would be spending two weeks there, and suddenly that seemed like a very long time, even though it had been my idea to go.

I started to get that panicked feeling again: as though the

world were spinning like the Flying Dutchman at the playground, or as though the air had suddenly gotten thin. It had troubled me all spring, whenever a scary news report came on air, whenever my mother left town—and especially when my father remarried and Julie and Sally moved into our house. Now the spinning feeling was back, while amusement park cheer surrounded me at Disneyland. And it wasn't because I was on a ride. I wished I had my journal with me, but it was in my suitcase, in the trunk. I rubbed my free palm along the hem of my dress. *It doesn't fit me, and I don't fit this new family.*

I didn't want to go into Tomorrowland and be fooled by its promise. I wanted to dig my heels into the paved walkway and stand still, to stay in the now. Or better yet, I wanted go back. *Here that's actually possible.* I was in one of the few places in the world where you could actually stop time, by turning a corner and entering the past—or at least a pretty good imitation of it.

I took a step backward and the crowds closed in, dropping like a curtain between my family and me. Craning my neck and standing on my tiptoes, I couldn't see a flash of Sally's matching fabric anywhere. They were gone, off into the future. I took another step back, moving away from the gleaming white structures and toward knotty old wooden ones.

Howdy, Frontierland.

It was almost an hour later when my father, red-faced and

huffing, found me cross-legged on a grassy spot of Tom Sawyer Island. The breeze ruffled my hair and I felt as calm as I had in a while, which was odd because normally being separated from my family at an amusement park would terrify me. Because of the too-shortness of my dress, grass clung to the backs of my legs when I shifted them to a more proper position as he hustled down the path in my direction. Julie trailed behind him with Sally.

"Beatrice." He sighed. "Don't tell me you've inherited your mother's wandering tendencies. We've been looking everywhere for you! Do you know how long we had to wait in line for one of those boats over there?"

My father wiped the perspiration off his brow, then rubbed absentmindedly at his beard. That was a change too—he had been clean-shaven my whole childhood, up until he met Julie. It's like as soon as he and my mother divorced, he had to shed everything about our old life—except me—and then add facial hair.

"I'm sorry . . . I got lost." Which was both true and untrue. I had *felt* lost.

"Well, come on. We have only a few hours left, and Julie thought we should eat at the Blue Bayou. After the Pirates of the Caribbean—Sally's been begging for that, haven't you?" He ruffled her hair, like he always used to do to mine, and I felt a pang of something like envy, even if I was too old for stuff like that.

Sally darted over to me. "Be-ah!" That's what she calls me, no matter how many times I tell her it's "*Bee*, like when you say 'the Beatles.'" A huge grin stretched her tearstained cheeks. "We found you!" Despite myself, I smiled: Sally seemed genuinely distraught by my running off. "*Now* can we go get in the line?" Or maybe she was simply mad about missing time on the rides.

I wanted to stay on that fake adventure island, which, ironically, felt like a very safe place to be. But I let my dad grab my hand and pull me up. I think we were both surprised that I had wandered off in the first place. I'm *not* adventurous and independent like my mother. It's just—in that sea of happy people in that fantasy world, I felt like the only one who could still spot the trash cans and utility poles. And nothing made me feel more alone, and unsure.

It was after Sally and I got into another fight—this time over some of my old paper dolls that she had found in my closet and colored on—that I decided to stay with my grandmother, Muriel, out in Sun City. My father had walked into the TV room and Julie had followed slightly behind him, like she wasn't sure if she should be part of the conversation. They were interrupting an episode of *Lassie*.

"Bea, how would you feel about visiting your grandmother? Only for a couple of weeks—to help her settle in."

"But I'm spending next week with my mom." I had been counting down the days until I could head over to her bungalow, although I would need to devise some way to make sure Sally stayed out of my room while I was gone. I kept my eyes glued to the screen, but I could still sense the look my dad and Julie exchanged.

"Sheila—your mother—phoned and said she needs to go to New Jersey first," Julie said. "Something about a new assignment."

My mother is a writer. When I was small, she started writing little things for the newspaper—like household tips and recipes for new casseroles and the latest in home fashions. Then her friend from college, who had a job at *Look* magazine, gave her a few bigger stories—no more serving suggestions involving salads in hollowed-out watermelons. Around the time my parents split up, she started reporting on the really big things, like the Watts riots and troops going to Vietnam. In January, she'd traveled up to San Francisco to report on the "Human Be-In," when a bunch of hippies gathered in Golden Gate Park to . . . I wasn't really sure what they were doing. But now that it was summer, even more young people were flocking there to spread love and music and who knows what else, so my mother went back to witness the "Summer of Love," as people were calling it. Mom had been supposed to come home that week.

Even though I was hardly the only one of my friends whose parents had divorced, in most cases both of their parents were still around. Their mothers packed lunches and set out trays of deviled eggs as a snack when you went over to study after school. Their dads drove over on the weekend and whisked them away to go to the movies or to the beach. My mom flitted around the country with a notebook. When she was home in California, she spent as little time as possible in the tiny bungalow she rented in the nearby hills. I got it that she didn't want to hang around the suburbs, but I still wondered sometimes— didn't she miss me?

Anyway, sitting there and not watching Lassie save the day, I thought about my options. I could stay at my house, which was no longer just mine and Dad's but also Julie's and Sally's. I could watch my stepmother and father coo at each other and my stepsister systematically take over the whole space. She was like the invading armies they talked about on the news. Nothing was off-limits—not even my pajamas. One night I wandered into the bathroom and found Sally brushing her teeth in my favorite pair. I was surprised she wasn't using my toothbrush, too.

Or my other option: go stay in an old-folks' community with a grandmother I barely knew. The next two weeks would be lonely, anyway, in Burbank—my best friend, Barbara, was

already off at summer camp in the mountains. (I w
of bears and wildcats to join her.) I didn't know w
had to offer, other than no stepsisters constantly in your personal space. The only risk was boredom.

My mother always said that she wanted to go wherever the
stories took her, although mostly she just went wherever *Look*
magazine sent her. "Life is so short, Bea," she'd said. "And yet
there's so much to experience in it." Visiting my grandmother's
house wouldn't be an adventure. But it was at least an experience. I liked the idea of being able to tell my mom all about
it when we were together again, instead of only being able to
recount what had happened on *The Doctors*, Julie's favorite
soap opera, which I could overhear even when I was reading in
my bedroom.

From behind my dad, I could see that Lassie was racing to
Timmy's rescue. "All right. But only until my mother comes
back."

Julie's smile stretched so wide, I thought it might split her
pretty face. "That is so kind of you, Beatrice." She retreated
into the kitchen, humming, and I resisted the urge to stick my
tongue out at her back.

My father patted my shoulder awkwardly. "I think you'll
both enjoy getting to know each other."

The only person who seemed sad that I decided to go was

Sally, who grabbed onto my leg and swore she wouldn't let me leave. It felt like I'd grown a barnacle.

Later on, in my room, I looked around and wondered if I'd made a terrible mistake. I love my room. It's full of bookshelves and a big desk, and the Beatles poster that Barbara gave me for my last birthday and all kinds of magazine pages are tacked to the walls: articles that my mom wrote, and photos that I thought were cool, of people and places all over the world. That makes the walls excellent inspiration for daydreaming. My room was *my* space, and sometimes the only place that seemed predictable anymore (so long as Sally stayed out). I was willing to trade it for the couch at my mom's new place, but that was different. Now I was going to leave it for two weeks for the unknown?

I sat on my bed with a pencil and my two journals. One was my worry journal. After my parents separated, I had trouble sleeping. Fears filled my head instead of dreams. My mother gave me a blank notebook and told me that whenever I have a worry, I should write it down. "Sometimes it helps to put your feelings to paper," she said. "Troubles might seem smaller. Or, if they don't, at least you've acknowledged them." She had filled notebooks with writing, which I used to peek at sometimes. She wrote on and on about drudgery, some of it related to household chores (I had no idea what cruel and unusual punishment vacuuming was) and some of it related to my dad. Whenever

I'd come across those entries, I snapped her notebook shut. I hadn't liked thinking of our family as unhappy.

Eventually my mom's tight smiles and my dad's sighs turned to shouting. I started writing down everything that scared me, from the news reports about Russian missiles to the spelling bee at school to my parents' arguments. I think it helped, but I've also filled several notebooks. Looking at the pile of them in my closet always makes me sad—seeing just how many worries I've had to put to paper. And I'm sure some I forgot to write down.

The other journal was my adventure one, and it was blank. My mother gave that one to me before she left on her first trip for a reporting assignment. "This is for you to write down all the wonderful adventures you have—big and small. Scribble down the ones you hope you'll have someday too. Because you *are* an adventurer—it's in your name. Beatrice comes from *viator*, the Latin word for voyager."

The truth was, though, that I was more of a homebody. The night I made the choice to go to my grandmother's, I wrote in my worry journal:

> I'm kind of afraid to leave my house. What if I come back and Sally has overtaken it even more? What if she

11

scratches up my Beatles album? Dad
says Sally reminds him of me when I
was her age. What if he decides he likes
her better? What if my dad and Julie
enjoy me being gone? What if my mother
comes back and then leaves again and
I miss seeing her altogether? What if
my grandmother is strict and we do
not get along? What if her new house
starts to smell like old people?

Then, in my adventure journal, I wrote:

Every adventure has to start
somewhere. I suppose that could
include my grandmother's retirement
community.

# TWO

## Pack a Bag

Sally was going back for her eleventh gumdrop, having decimated the mound of them in the crystal bowl my grandmother kept on the end table. She shot forward from her perch on the bright green sofa to turn up the volume dial on the TV, even though the show was *Bonanza* and neither of us particularly liked watching Westerns.

I busied myself with snapping the latch on my suitcase open and shut, open and shut. Sally laughed at something in a commercial, her mouth open so wide I could see a rainbow of gumdrop remnants stuck to her otherwise perfect baby teeth—another way she was perhaps a better daughter than me. Dad liked to joke that his long hours at the office were to pay for the braces I'd be getting in the fall.

My first impression of my grandmother was not the best. The last time I'd seen her was when we visited her home in Boston when I was five, and I hardly remembered that trip. Based on the calls and cards I'd received over the years, I had no reason not to expect the kind of grandmother you see on television: sweet-faced and soothing, giver of soft hugs and hard butterscotch candies. Someone with the same caring vibe as Miss Nancy on *Romper Room*. My grandma Anna had been like that. Instead, this grandmother was tall, wiry, and highly irritable.

"She's upset about the move, girls," Julie whispered to us. "We need to be patient with her—Muriel has been through quite a lot."

"Oh, have I?" my grandmother snapped in our general direction from the sofa. "Being dragged across an entire continent against my will?"

My father, rolling his eyes, gently took her elbow and led her into the other room. He called back to us, "Why don't you gals go get an ice cream float or something?"

Julie shepherded us out the door and in the car to the nearest soda fountain. While we sat, spooning the ice cream into our mouths before sucking down the soda, Julie offered a vague explanation of my grandmother's sour mood.

"It's hard getting older," she said. I snorted, because of how Julie hogs the bathroom at night to inspect her head for gray hairs. My mother would never do something like that. Her thick dark hair has gotten a few shocks of silvery white—but she keeps it "au naturel," as she calls it.

Julie ignored me and continued talking. "Sometimes older people can't take care of themselves anymore. They have problems with memory—like forgetting to turn off the stove or not paying their bills. That can make them very frustrated. Same with change."

Well, I found change upsetting too. I slurped at my float. "So we moved Grandmother all the way out to California because she didn't pay a bill?"

"Not only that. She didn't remember a conversation we'd had about getting rid of her car, not one word of it. She called in a panic one day because she thought it had been stolen. And then her neighbor called to tell your father that she was expecting some kind of houseguest . . ." Julie shrugged. "She's a little too old to be on her own across the country anymore. If something happened, it would take us days to get to her." But my grandmother had seemed fine to me, albeit a bit cranky. Her silver-gray hair was in a neat bun, and she still wore sharp clothes. She had no problem moving around her home, and my father even had to keep asking her to stop trying to lift boxes herself. "I'd rather make myself useful, instead of ornamental," she'd sniffed. Although while she supervised from the stiff couch, I noticed she was rubbing her hands like they ached.

"Can you do us a favor, Bea, while you're here? Keep an eye on your grandmother. Let us know if she seems particularly flustered or if she says anything unusual. *Especially* if she forgets anything." I nodded, although it would be hard know if my grandmother was acting different than usual, considering I had no clue what her "usual" was like.

By the time we got back from the soda fountain, Dad was raring to go. He took a long look at his mother, who was standing with her arms crossed, watching him shove the last few boxes into a closet. "We'll be back soon," he said, like all of a sudden it bothered him to leave his mother in her stark new house. Which was funny, because he'd been fine with her living across the country, in Boston, as long as I'd been alive.

Dad, Julie, and Sally congregated by the door, gathering their things. Quick, stiff hugs were shared with my grandmother, and longer and softer ones with me. My dad gave me a wistful look and made a comment about how I looked awfully grown-up, and so much like my mother. Which was nice to hear, although I knew how much she frustrated him. Sally sniffled and pulled a knotted bunch of pipe cleaners out of her jumper pocket. She held them out to me. They were very sticky.

"I made them for you," she said. I looked closer and could see that the pipe cleaners were two figures and the knots were helping them to hold hands. Maybe they were supposed to be us.

"Thanks, Sally."

Then they piled into the car. Sally pressed her nose to the rear window, watching me and waving mournfully, as the car pulled away. I felt an unexpected pang of melancholy as they headed back to Burbank, without me.

I settled into the scratchy green sofa. It had the same texture as the slightly hardened gumdrops. My grandmother sat across from me, in an equally uncomfortable armchair the color of Tang. Apparently, she'd brought none of her furniture from the east. It seemed funny to me that the home of an old woman would have mostly new things. The small ranch house was bright and clean and impersonal—sitting in it felt like being in a waiting room at the doctor's office more than anything else.

The clock on the wall tick-tick-ticked, and I itched to turn on the television set. When I was little, I barely watched television programs. I read books, comics, and magazines, and my mother and I sat side by side writing stories. When my parents split up, though, and my mom started going off on her adventures, I watched television more and more. I couldn't see enough episodes of *Leave It to Beaver* and *The Donna Reed Show*. I loved watching those families sit down to dinner. I loved how their problems wrapped up within a half hour. I loved how television families never turned on the set and saw terrible things on the evening news. I got the same soothing feeling watching those TV shows as I used to get when my mother would come in my room at night and smooth my hair off my forehead as I fell asleep.

But I felt like turning on the set might be rude. I was there to get to know my grandmother, after all.

"So . . . how do you like living here?"

"This overpriced waiting room?" Grandmother sniffed. She spoke sharply, and normally that would hurt my feelings, except I had noted the waiting-room feel too. Whether or not she knew it, we were on the same page. "If I wanted to wait out my days in a sterile shoebox of a home, I could have very well done that in Boston."

"Oh. But aren't there lots of activities you can do here? Like golf, and movies at the community center." We'd passed the golf course on our way in, although I only saw three old bald men baking in the sun on the green.

"I have more important things to do." Grandmother didn't elaborate, but she did ease herself up out of her chair.

"Like what?" Not sure of how to address her, I added, "Grandmother . . . Muriel?"

"Pidge, darling. Just call me Pidge." I watched her cross the room to the hall closet, wondering at her instruction. *Pidge? What kind of name is that?* Dad had never mentioned her having a nickname. He only called her "Mother." Julie had told me to watch for my grandmother "saying something unusual"—did that include a strange nickname? Maybe she was worse off than she had seemed. I took a deep breath, to ward off that panicked feeling.

My grandmother pulled a small brown leather valise, a little weathered, out of the closet and carried it back to the armchair. Her hands trembled as she snapped open the clasp. She pulled out a packet of letters—some old and yellowed, others at the top of the pile looking crisper, fresh. She held the letters with both hands, pressing the packet to her chest like she was giving it a tender hug.

"Are those letters from . . ." I trailed off, realizing that I only knew of my late grandfather as "my pop," the way my dad always referred to him. He'd died before I was born.

"Meelie," my grandmother finished, a hint of a smile curling up her lips. It was the first one I'd seen from her all day. "My sister."

I suppose there were many reasons why my grandmother never visited us in California. Oftentimes when my father got off the telephone with her, the conversation was ended by the exasperated smack of the handset into the cradle. If I ever asked her, during a birthday or Christmas call, if she'd like to visit us sometime, she usually told me that it was too costly or she was too busy with her garden. (That excuse, in particular, did not hold water in December.) But the biggest reason was because of who my grandmother's sister was: *the* Amelia Earhart. According to my dad, that's why she told him she had no interest in traveling by airplane to see us, and snippily reminded him that it had been his choice to settle down so far away from her.

It wasn't until I had brought home an Amelia Earhart biography book from school, and was splayed on the dry grass in our backyard reading, that I learned that part of our family history. My mother had walked by to water some of her rose bushes—this was long before my parents split.

"Lost in a book?"

"Yeah, about Amelia Earhart," I had said, not looking up from the pages. The book was open to a picture of Amelia, who looked particularly lovely with her delicate features and the hint of a smile, like she had a good secret. I remember thinking that the image appeared more like a lady from a shampoo ad—except for the close-cropped hairdo—and less like my idea of a lady pilot. I didn't really have a clear idea of what a lady pilot looked like, to be honest. Only the square-jawed air captains and glamorous stewardesses from magazine ads.

"Oh!" My mother had set down her gardening gloves. "You know, you're her grandniece."

I'd dropped the book so quickly the pages fanned out and I lost my place. "What?"

My mother had picked the book back up. "Grandmother Muriel is her sister. *Was* her sister, I suppose. It's something

I've always been curious about—now that's a story I'd love to write—although I've never talked much to Muriel about it. To be fair, I've never talked much to her, period." Mom flipped through the pages with me, stopping on several other photos. "I think you have Earhart eyes," she said, pointing. "Your father said something funny once, about Muriel being convinced for years and years afterward that Amelia would show up one day. Barnstorm your grandmother's house in Boston, I guess, and land in the backyard." My mother's rueful smile showed me she was exaggerating about the backyard part. "But I suspect she's given up that hope as time has passed. At least, she doesn't refer to her sister in the present tense anymore."

I had never had a sibling, and it would be years before I got a Sally. But even so, I had only been able to imagine how sad and strange it would be to have to think about a sister in past tense.

Sitting across from me in that waiting-room living room, Grandmother Muriel—I mean, *Pidge*—was still clutching the letters to her chest. "Can I read them?" I blurted out. I scooted to the edge of the scratchy sofa, ready to reach forward and grab the stack.

She shot me a look that I wasn't expecting to get from a grandmother: the sort of expression that Sally and I would exchange when one of us tattled on the other. Or maybe more like the dagger look I'd give Sally when I caught her eavesdropping on my telephone calls with Barbara. "These are quite personal, Beatrice."

Ashamed, I scooted back into the bend of the sofa. Pidge watched me closely, pinching a letter between her index finger and thumb. "But at the same time, I feel as though it's not fair for me to withhold them from you, given what I'm going to ask you to do."

A chill ran down my back. That sounded ominous. I didn't think she was going to ask me to eat a bowl of ice cream. *What have I gotten myself into?* If I didn't know that my family would be trapped in beach traffic on their way home, I would've risen up from the couch and gone to the phone in Pidge's avocado-and-gold-colored kitchen and dialed my father to request a very early return. *Although I did agree to come stay with her for the sake of "adventure."* I took another deep breath.

"What are you going to ask me to do?" My voice wavered a bit.

"Pack a bag, darling."

# THREE

## Donk and Ellie

Before I did repack my brand-new willow-green O'Nite suitcase—part of a set my mother had given me for Christmas, although I'd only ever used the weekend tote, for sleepovers at Barbara's—Pidge explained it all. Over a dinner that consisted of a fluffernutter sandwich, despite the fact that Julie had stocked Pidge's refrigerator with all sorts of casserole dishes, cheeses, cold cuts, and even a big wobbly gelatin mold from the supermarket, and she'd also filled the bare cupboards with cans of fruit cocktail and vegetables and crackers. But, as Pidge informed me, she "wasn't much for cooking anymore," so she let me loose in her kitchen. Julie would die before I ate peanut butter and marshmallow fluff for dinner. For that matter, so would my mother—although because it had been weeks since I had eaten dinner at her place, I didn't so much factor her into my decision.

I chewed on my sandwich, which I had accidentally-on-purpose overloaded with fillings. Fluff spurted out the sides and got all over my face. Pidge said nothing, and I was glad that she wasn't the kind of grandmother to constantly come at you with a damp napkin.

"My sister disappeared in 1937. You already knew about her, right? That my Meelie was, in fact, Amelia Earhart?" I nodded. "Well, I must say I'm relieved that your father has shared our rich family history with you."

I swallowed hard and hoped that she wouldn't ask if I knew anything else about our "rich family history," because I really didn't and what little I'd gleaned was actually from my mother—Dad only liked to talk about my schoolwork and perhaps the latest episode of *The Fugitive*, and he was almost always at his office, anyway.

"As I was saying: Meelie disappeared in 1937, during her famous around-the-world flight. They searched for a long, long time. Stories spread—that she was held prisoner by the Japanese during the war. That she survived a crash landing and was marooned on a desert island in the South Pacific. That she was really a top secret government spy, flying for covert operations. That she fabricated the whole disappearance just so she could escape to obscurity, and live happily ever after—in New Jersey, of all places." Pidge paused for a moment, looking down at the letters, which she'd carried into the kitchen with us, although she wouldn't let me anywhere near them while I was eating my messy sandwich. "Or I suppose most people believed she died."

I knew that—after finding out that Amelia was my grandmother's sister, I had torn apart the card catalog at the library one afternoon, and I'd checked out every single book on her that I could find. Which were only a few, but I had still read them all. At the ends of each book, the authors suggested that whatever happened, it was most likely that Amelia was long dead. That was tragic and disappointing. But the not-knowing what really happened—that mystery was tantalizing.

Pidge cleared her throat to make sure she had my full attention. "But only *I* know the truth: My sister is alive."

*"Really?"*

Pidge nodded, a faraway look in her faded blue eyes. "Ever since her disappearance, she has been writing me letters. Of course, I've gotten loads of mail from cranks over the years. They tell me that it's Amelia writing, and she needs money—sent to a certain address. Or they spin wild stories of spy games and romance on a deserted island. But I knew, as soon as I received this first letter—one year to the day after she disappeared—that it truly was my sister writing to me."

Pidge paused, picking up the letter on the top of the pile. It was the most faded of them all; the envelope had become so thin that it was translucent and as Pidge struggled to coax the folded paper out, I worried it would rip. "I'll read this one for you. I can't allow you to touch it—it's too delicate." But as her hands shook, I couldn't help but think it would be safer in mine.

July 2, 1938

My Dear Pidge,

I haven't written till now because there is so much I can't say. Not yet. I can't tell you why I've been gone this year, why my leaving was so spectacularly mysterious, and why I can't share with you, or anyone, where I've been. It's a small miracle that I can send this letter, and I am doing so only on the condition that my words are chosen carefully. I pray that this indeed reaches you, and I hope that receiving it offers you comfort, if not my whereabouts. I can only imagine what it's been like for you and Mother. Wondering. Waiting. Worrying. Wishing.

Do you still have your wooden elephant pal, Ellie, to cuddle with? Its donkey pal is by my side right now. (Yes—"Donk" was a stowaway in my flight bag.) I reach for my well-traveled toy during moments when the loneliness is so strong it knocks the wind out of me. And the more time passes, the more I have missed you, sister.

Lately I've been thinking a lot about our childhood, those golden early years at our grandparents' home. Atchison was a slice of heaven: the view down the bluff to the Missouri River, the scent of summer flowers—syringa and heliotrope—and sunbaked grass. Sometimes in my dreams I'm back there with you. Remember how we raced about the yard on brooms, pretending to ride our steeds? Or "Bogie," the make-believe game we invented with our Kansas cousins? All those long days spent hunting rats in the barn and exploring the wonders of the natural world around us—I wish I still had my tattered copy of _Insect Life_. (I sure could've used it, where I've been hiding out these past months!) I'm writing this letter lying on my stomach, the same prone position we preferred for reading sessions in the yard. If I close my eyes, I can picture the late afternoon sunshine imprinting on the grass, shading the pages of a favorite collection of adventure stories. Our whole family loved the smell of a book. Surely you remember all these things, dear Pidge. But writing these recollections warms my soul, which is the only part of me that gets cold these days.

My first memories of <u>flying</u> were actually at home, with you. We'd spin until we were sick on that Flying Dutchman, and we'd coast on the roller coaster that we constructed in the yard. With a dollop of lard on the hastily hammered wooden track, we were off: "Oh, Pidge, it's just like flying!" Years later, I was trying to recapture <u>those</u> feelings up in the air. The joy and freedom we felt as children, flying around in bloomers Mother had sewn. We were so fortunate to have a mother who encouraged us to be rambunctious and curious, knowing we were happier with room to roam.

I was also lucky to have a sister like you, a companion who would follow me in feats of daring along the banks of the river and under the beams of the barn. If only I could tell you right now the adventure I've had this year! Not in a letter, but face-to-face. I can promise you that I _will_ see you again, even if I can't promise you when. Then, the full truth of this last grand adventure will be revealed. Maybe *when the time is right, we should reunite back in Kansas. For now, give Ellie a squeeze for me (if you still have her), and keep this letter safe and quiet. Please—I am trusting you to tell <u>no one</u>. I swear I'll write as soon as I next can.*

*Love,*

*Your sister, Meelie*

The closing words hung in the air between us after Pidge finished reading, her voice wavering on the final lines. At first I couldn't figure out what to say. Then the questions filling up my head started spilling out of my mouth.

"But how do you know this isn't from just another one of the . . . cranks?"

"Easy. How many people would know about Ellie and Donk? Amelia's late husband, George, got all manners of publicity for Meelie when she was flying, and after the disappearance, but the reporters never wrote about her beloved childhood toy—much less her nobody of a sister's wooden elephant." Pidge frowned. "I wish I could recall what happened to my Ellie. Anyway, those memories she wrote about? They belong to me, too. I believe she included them so I'd know it was really her writing. All the letters are full of details of Meelie's exploits that I am already well familiar with. It's a tad egocentric that she turned them into a biography of sorts." My grandmother laughed. "But Meelie always *did* like to write about her accomplishments." Pidge paused. "I will never forget my sister's voice. She has a particular way of seeing the world and of saying things. Trust me: only one person could have written this letter. The same is true for all of them." Pidge patted the stack of letters on her lap.

Her points were convincing. None of those library books I'd read had told much about Amelia's childhood other than that she was born in Kansas. They'd never mentioned her building a roller coaster or loving adventure stories. They hadn't helped me know this Meelie, the one who was someone's sister and had once been a rambunctious kid wearing "bloomers." Pidge's certainty pushed my skepticism aside. I wanted to believe those letters were real, which brought up other questions.

"So, in the other letters—has she told you what happened to her? Where she is? Why haven't you seen her in all these years?"

Pidge's smile drooped slightly. "Well, no, she hasn't told

me those things. There's never a return address, so I can't send her any of my many, many questions. The letters—and she's sent a total of five over the past thirty years, always without a legible postmark—are cagey. Meelie drops in the rare detail of her life since the flight—tantalizing tidbits, like how she said that she's never cold, or that she could use her copy of *Insect Life* wherever she is. Sometimes words are scribbled out, although I don't know who's doing the redacting. Meelie made it clear that she can't risk telling me the whole story until she sees me again, in person, and that I must wait patiently for that time. I tell you, my patience started to run out about twenty-nine years ago." Pidge made a little laugh, but it stuck in her throat.

I laughed too, but Amelia's excuse reminded me of something I once read in a book, a prank in which a girl told her friend to wait patiently on the playground for a boy who never appeared. After that many years—decades, even—wouldn't Amelia be dying to see her sister again? What in the world could possibly make her take so long?

"However, I received one last letter before your father whisked me to California," Pidge said, holding up the crispest-looking one in the stack. "It's time for us to reunite. Amelia said so. On her seventieth birthday—thirty years after she left us all." She smoothed the surface of the letter with her hand, clearing her throat. "Finally, I'll see her again."

"Wow," I said. "When's her birthday?"

"July twenty-fourth. Four days from now." Pidge had a far-away smile.

"Wait." I frowned. "How will she know to find you here? You just moved. What if she goes to Boston?"

"Smart girl! That's exactly why I didn't want to come out here. Now I'm stuck in California, without my car—a prisoner in this old-fart's paradise." Pidge clucked her tongue. "But it's not *Boston* where I need to be. Remember what she wrote in the letter? About reuniting on the banks of the Missouri?"

I nodded, remembering that part. I took my last bite of the fluffernutter.

"In this letter, she gave me instructions to meet her at our grandparents' old house, in Kansas. She was born there, and Atchison always felt like home for Meelie and me. It was where we were the closest. I suppose we're going back to where we started, and there we'll start anew."

"But how are you getting there?" Dad and Julie hadn't said anything about Pidge taking a trip—and I was supposed to stay with her in Sun City for the next two weeks.

"How are *we* getting there, you mean." Pidge placed the letters back in the valise and stood up, brushing dust off her dark slacks. "Remember how I told you to pack that bag?"

"*We're* going? My dad actually said that's okay?" I crossed my

35

arms over my chest. I'd asked him if I could go to San Francisco to meet up with my mother. But he told me that was no place for a kid, and he didn't want me to travel alone. Weren't Pidge and I both too young and too old to go all the way to Kansas? A new thought popped into my head, as welcome as a splatter of raindrops appearing at a parade. Perhaps my father hadn't okayed it.

"He doesn't exactly know we're going." Pidge's eyes sparkled, unable to contain her glee. All this time, I thought my grandmother in Boston must be so proper. I had based that on the Bostonian grandmother in my favorite movie, *The Parent Trap*. I figured that if I ever visited mine there, it would be just like when the Californian twin in the movie shows up after the switcheroo. (I'd even bring my grandmother a birdcage of Popsicle sticks to see her look of confused disdain.) Pidge was already surprising me with her sneakiness.

I thought about the way Pidge's hands shook, and how sometimes she'd get a glazed, tired look in her eyes. And I thought about Julie asking me to stay alert for any forgetful or unusual behavior. *Well, I don't know what could be more unusual than this turn of events.* A knot tugged itself tight in my stomach. Perhaps a secret cross-country trip was not the world's greatest idea. Maybe I should telephone my father and let him know what was going on.

Pidge could sense my unease. "Don't tell me you're an

Earhart who isn't up for a little adventure," she clucked at me.

Truthfully, I was the girl who sneaked away from Tomorrow-land. I left my adventure journal empty and worry journal full. I never ran with scissors and always looked both ways before crossing the street. I liked to hole up in my room and stare at *National Geographic* photos—rather than see the real thing. I preferred my adventures in books and on the television set. Maybe my mother was the *true* Earhart heir—she was the one off gallivanting in the name of news.

But if we went and found Amelia—that would be news. Big news. What would my mom think of that?

She might be mad about how we'd run off without telling anyone—but I just know she'd also be proud. I'd have things written in my adventure journal, finally, to show her. In that letter, Meelie said that she and Pidge were lucky to have a mother who encouraged them to be rambunctious and knew they were happier with freedom. That's exactly the kind of thing my mom would agree with. She was always egging me on to try new things: foods, books, ways of seeing the world around me. If I was certain my mother would love an adventure like this, wasn't that kind of like having permission?

*Was* I up for an adventure? I didn't know. Honestly, I hadn't planned on anything more daring than learning to play shuffleboard.

I slid off my chair and stood up. Pidge made a *"Well?"* face at me. I glanced toward the phone on the kitchen wall. I glanced back at Pidge, and the valise of letters at her feet.

"I just *un*packed my bag," I said. Her mouth sagged downward, and her head started to shake in disgust. "But," I quickly added, with my best attempt at a brave smile, "it won't take me long to toss it all back inside."

# FOUR

## A Joyride with "Snooky"

After dinner, Pidge made three phone calls. The first was to my house in Burbank, where Julie answered. I could hear her voice percolating even from my spot at the kitchen table, feet away from the telephone. In the background, Sally was whining about something. Then I heard Julie shush her, saying maybe she could talk to me later.

"We are getting on just fine. Thank you so much for stocking the pantry—that was very kind of you." A pause, then, "Yes, Beatrice had the noodle casserole and some Jell-O for dinner." Only the Jell-O part was true. I'd eaten it straight out of the mold with a big serving spoon.

"Why I called? Oh, to check in and say hello." Pidge's response wasn't very convincing, given how infrequently she had called before I showed up at her house. "Also, after you all left a repairman came about the telephone wires. Apparently, squirrels have been chewing on them outside. They will need to be replaced." She paused again. "No, there's nothing you need to do—just letting you know in case you try to call us down here. I wouldn't want you to worry your pretty little head."

I smiled. Dad and Julie had made it seem like Pidge couldn't take care of herself out in Boston, but she was proving to be pretty capable at everything from sandwich-making to excuse-crafting. Although I did have to help her open the peanut butter jar. "Blasted arthritis," she'd said, staring at her long, knobby fingers like they were traitors.

Pidge ended the call before I had to get on the line to talk to Sally or my dad. That was probably for the best, considering. She dialed another number and after a few seconds asked, "Yes, I was wondering if there are any tickets left for a train—the *Super Chief*, eastbound, departing tomorrow." A pause. "I see. Only roomettes? No double bedrooms?" Another pause. "Well, I will have to mull that over. Thank you for the information."

Pidge hung up the phone, then riffled around in the top kitchen drawer for something. With a quiet "aha!" she pulled out a worn red address book. She licked her index finger and flipped through to the end, then squinted at the page. "Let's hope this is still right," she said, before sticking her finger in the dial. She leaned against the wall as we waited for the call to go through. "Cross your fingers, darling." I did as told, without knowing why.

Someone picked up. "Neta Snook, please?" A pause. "Oh,

of course. Neta Snook *Southern*." Another pause, during which she turned to me and said, "I forgot her married name." Then, with a smile on her face, "Hello, Snooky! It's a real blast from your past—Muriel Earhart on the line." I could hear excited noises through the phone. "Yes, yes—it's so good to hear your voice too. I'm in California, in Sun City, of all places. Say, do you think you could do me a favor? Tomorrow I need a ride to Los Angeles, to the train station. By seven thirty in the evening." A pause, as she glanced at the wall clock, which showed it was already past nine at night. "I suppose this is short notice. But I seem to remember you loved a joyride. Come on, won't you do an old friend a big favor?" Another pause, then, "Thatagirl!" It occurred to me that Pidge hadn't mentioned me to this "Snooky" person, but I tried not to let that bother me.

After Pidge got off the phone, she told me that we'd be heading out around lunchtime tomorrow. "It's going to be a long trip. So get a good night's sleep, Beatrice."

I headed into the small guest bedroom, where I plopped down on the stiff twin mattress. I was bone-tired, but no matter how hard I squeezed my eyes or how many sheep I counted, sleep wasn't coming to me. I missed the familiarity of my room. My heart and my mind pulsed. I'd never taken a long train trip before. What was it going to be like? Was Pidge packing food for us, or would there be enough to eat on board? What if I got train sick? Rides at amusement parks—like Disneyland—sometimes made my stomach flip and flop and my head spin. Even the gentler ones. On the way to Pidge's, after watching Sally scream with joy as she spun around in the Disneyland teacups, I had felt so embarrassed. That was a baby ride, but it still made me feel dizzy.

And even though I didn't particularly want to be back in our ranch house in Burbank, I wasn't sure how I felt about hurtling hundreds of miles away from my dad, Julie, and Sally. I'd only just gotten to Pidge's—I wished I could settle in before we had to take off, even though I understood why time was of the essence. I reached into my knapsack and pulled out my worry journal, then started scribbling down all the things bouncing around in my head.

What if we get lost or sick or hurt on the way?

What if my father and Julie go bananas when they find out?

What if my mother isn't that impressed?

What if I AM the only Earhart who isn't brave?

*What if Pidge's whole reuniting-with-Amelia plan is crazy?*

But at the same time, what if it wasn't and we did find Amelia? I paused to chew on the edge of my pencil.

*What if I like being on an adventure?*

*And what if this changes my life?*

If I flipped through my journal, so many of the worries written down would be related to change. I never liked it. From little changes, like switching desks in the classroom, to big changes, like my mother moving out—they all had the same effect, making me feel unbalanced and blue. When the world is full of confusion and conflict, it doesn't really help for things to be all mixed up at home, too. My worry journal kind of helped me handle my fears, but it didn't erase those feelings. Sometimes I wished I could freeze everything around me, not forever, but long enough to let myself catch my breath. Especially after Julie and Sally moved in, and I struggled to get a quiet moment alone, except in the bathroom. And even then sometimes one or both would barge in.

After zipping the journal back inside my knapsack, I turned and shoved my face into the hard pillow, which smelled like dust, and tried to sleep. I imagined flying, up high in the air, like I was in Amelia's plane. That's the last thing I remember before Pidge came into the room and started poking me.

"Rise and shine, Beatrice." When I didn't budge, she jabbed harder with her index finger. "Come on. Up and at 'em. We haven't much time before we have to go. You're sleeping away the whole morning."

I groaned, sitting up. "You told me to get lots of sleep!"

Pidge was already dressed in fresh clothes. An excited smile tugged at the corners of her mouth. "That I did, but you've had plenty!"

My grandmother puttered around the house, making sure the windows were shut and giving extra water to the houseplants that Julie had bought to "spruce up the place." I don't know how long they'll last because she watered the ones in the living room twice—she must've forgotten that she'd already doused them. Pidge hummed a song to herself, some jazzy tune. She went into the bathroom and fussed with her thin silvery hair, arranging and rearranging the chignon in a way that she seemed satisfied with, but I couldn't see any difference between before and after. It was interesting—in all the snapshots I'd ever seen of Pidge, she had long hair. Sometimes pulled up in a ponytail or woven into a braid, and as she got older often pinned into a low bun. But she never cut it short. Otherwise, she and Amelia looked a lot alike. I wondered if Pidge kept her hair long on purpose, to make the sisterly resemblance less uncanny.

I stayed put on the sofa, nibbling cinnamon toast. Pidge didn't care if I ate away from the table and without a plate, which was a nice change. Sometimes I felt like Julie was always chasing me around the house with napkins and coasters and doilies for whatever snack I had in hand. She was so particular, unlike my mom. My mother had tried to keep a clean house, but usually lost interest halfway through dusting or vacuuming. I'd find her in the living room, one hand reluctantly pushing the Electrolux and the other turning the pages of a book.

I fanned myself with a magazine from the coffee table. Sun City was far enough from the coast that it was hot—not surprising, considering sun was in its name. The house had air-conditioning—a big selling point of any old-folks' community—but Pidge left it off, offering a box fan to cool the room. I sipped some juice and reached for the newspaper on the coffee table. Every column on the front page was full of bad news. The headlines shouted about a jetliner crashing in North Carolina and the aftermath of the riots in Newark. That's what my mother went to report on. After the riots in Los Angeles two years ago, she'd explained to me that black people were often treated unfairly and had to fight for their rights, for their voices to be heard. "It's about stopping injustice," she said. The article about Newark said that twenty-six people had died and a lot of businesses were destroyed. I swallowed hard. Sometimes I just wished the world were better.

The least scary article was about the hippies up in San Francisco, but even that was laced with worry about the fact that not a lot of the people there had jobs. Which wasn't true—my mother wasn't a hippie, but she had been at the Be-In and *she* had a job, writing about everyone and everything she saw. The last time I spoke with her on the telephone, though, she joked, "I think I might've actually seen more reporters from *Life* and *Time* than hippies." She promised to send me a copy of her article once it was finished.

I set down the paper, trying to blink the headlines out of my mind. Being inside with the news was like wearing too-tight clothing, and I couldn't breathe deep. I didn't want to think about the situation that my mom was running off to. I stood up to take my juice outside, and that's when I noticed the valise of letters, next to Pidge's armchair. I opened the flap and took out the next one in the stack. Pidge had said I had a right to know what I was getting into, so it was fine for me to read them all. I also figured it made a lot of sense for me to know the instructions from Amelia about where to meet her. Just in case anything happened along the way.

Holding that and my juice glass, I walked out the front door and sat down on the white bricks of the stoop. I was wearing another shift Julie had picked out, still too short but not as bad as some of the others. Barbara would tell me not to complain about the shortness—she was always begging her mom to let her buy a miniskirt. But I felt exposed. The stoop was hot underneath the backs of my legs. I stared out at the rows of identical pastel ranch houses. Despite all the Sun City ads showing old people golfing, gardening, walking, and happily waving to one another, no one was outside other than me, at least as far as I could see. It was a ghost town. I carefully unfolded the letter.

*December 28, 1943*

*My Dear Pidge,*

*This whole mess started on this day back in 1920, thanks to ten dollars and a ten-minute flight.*

My life opened up as soon as I went into the air. I wore a helmet, funny-looking goggles, and my best brown-on-brown outfit. (I'm still wearing brown exclusively, thanks to the muddy terrain where I am now.) I was in the front of the biplane, and the pilot was in the back. The forces pinned me in my seat as we took off, but I pushed myself forward to drink in the view. We flew over Los Angeles, the citrus groves ringing the city, and then out over the ocean. I could glimpse Catalina Island and sailboats bobbing below me. Heading back toward the city and

the mountains beyond, I spotted cars inching
below us. They looked like the insects I loved to
examine as a child. Our landing was smoother
than many rides I've had in automobiles. I
didn't want to climb out, but eventually I did,
into swirls of dust on the runway. I pulled back
the goggles and wiped at my face. I couldn't
find the words to describe my exhilaration. I
had just found the love of my life: the feeling of
being up in the clear smooth air.

As soon as we left the ground, I knew I
myself had to fly. I'd die if I didn't.

(Funny to think of that now, with the whole world believing I died because I _did_ fly.)

To my surprise, Mother and Father didn't object when I told them that next I wanted to _learn_ to fly. Perhaps they knew that I was restless and a bit jealous of you, attending college. Of course, I couldn't be taught by a man—sharing all those hours in a tight space wouldn't have been proper. That's when I found Neta Snook.

I asked her to teach me, and she said that for a dollar a minute in the air and payment daily, she happily would. Thanks to "Snooky," a great flier and an even greater friend, I learned to pilot my own life as well as a plane.

I never would've become the aviator I am without her, or without my sister. You sure were help on the ground—stitching up the fabric, checking the tension, meticulously cleaning wires and binding struts. In those early days, I always felt a smidgen safer knowing my sister's hands had passed over the plane before I swung myself inside. We Earhart girls have always been the capable type! It's like I used to say:

A lucky charm is a nice balm for frayed nerves, but the best mascot is a good mechanic.

Today, as I ate fresh coconut and canned meat under a hot sun, I closed my eyes and took myself back to Kinner Field. You and me and Neta, sitting cross-legged on a blanket in the shade. Stuffing our faces with sandwiches and thick slices of chocolate cake while oohing and ahhing at the pilots' stunts. I loved our airfield picnics—so long as they didn't cut into my time in the sky. You often complained that I was too busy for my little sister. I was simply eager

to be independent, in the air and everywhere else.
The runway of life stretched in front of me, with
nowhere to go but into the future.

Snooky once told me: Ask for forgiveness,
not permission. I ask you, now, for forgiveness
for letting adventures take me far away. I
suppose we are part of the same fleet, but I've
taken a different flight path in life. Truly,
that's my only regret. I know you never much
liked me telling you what to do—but please be
patient with me, Pidge. We'll still share some
stops on our itineraries. There's something my

friend Eleanor (Roosevelt, of course) used to say: Women are like tea bags because you never know how strong they are until you put them in hot water. Well, whether or not the water is hot, we women are strong.

The longer I'm gone, the more I must remind myself of that.

Be strong, Pidge. Don't give up on your old sis.

My love,

Meelie

An aquamarine sedan pulled up to the curb and tooted its horn before the car jerked into park. I folded up the letter and tucked it carefully back into the envelope. Amelia—Meelie—felt like she'd have died if she didn't fly, which seemed like a funny way of thinking. Even small risks loomed as potential disasters to me. Still, Meelie wrote she didn't regret her adventures—even the last one, which had made her vanish for the past thirty years. I shivered despite the Sun City heat. *Well, I'm going on an adventure myself now, and with Meelie's old instructor. Maybe she can help teach me how to "pilot my own life."*

I shaded my eyes from the afternoon sun. The driver's-side door opened, and a woman about Pidge's age—or maybe older—bounded out. She had curly dyed-red hair, dark round glasses, and she was wearing a blouse, long pants, and a scarf wrapped stylishly around her neck. She grinned at me, striding briskly up the sidewalk with a pocketbook tucked under her arm. Her lipstick was bright red—I hadn't ever seen an older lady with lips so vibrant before. *Neta Snook.* Thanks to the letter, I felt like we'd already been introduced.

"Well, I don't think you're Pidge, although you've sure got her Earhart eyes."

That caused a smile to curl at my lips. Nobody had ever told me before that I looked like my grandmother. Instantly I felt more at home on Pidge's stoop. The front door opened behind me. "Snooky!" Pidge set down the watering can she was hold-ing (she was watering plants again?) and quickly moved past me. She and the woman embraced each other tightly, laughter resetting all the lines on their faces.

"Oh, how the years have flown," Pidge said, wiping at her eye.

"*Psssh*. You don't look a day over thirty," Neta said.

Pidge rolled her eyes. "You always were full of it, Snooky." They both chuckled.

"So who's this spitting image?" Neta bent down, hands on her thighs, to peer at me in a friendly way.

"This is my granddaughter, Beatrice."

"Nice to meet you, Beatrice." Neta stood up. "I'm Snooky. Are you coming along with us?"

Pidge butted in. "Oh, yes. I forgot to mention that. Beatrice, will you load our bags in the trunk?" She grabbed Neta's elbow and the two old women disappeared inside, leaving me out on the stoop. I got up, smoothed my dress into place, and found our luggage piled inside the door: my suitcase and knapsack, next to a small suitcase for Pidge and the valise. I put the letter I'd read back inside before I loaded the suitcases into the trunk and the knapsack and valise into the backseat. Then I walked back to the front steps and sat down. I tugged at the blades of dry grass. It hadn't bothered me much when Pidge hadn't mentioned me on the phone last night. But silly as it was, now that her friend was here, I almost felt left out. Wasn't there any place in which I fit anymore? Not at my dad's house, and not at my mom's. Somehow I had thought that staying with my grandmother this summer, I might hold more of her attention.

When Barbara visits hers, she gets lavished with cookies and shopping sprees. She is the center of her grandmother's world. That's how I used to feel visiting my grandma Anna's house. I wondered if to Pidge, I was one more hurdle she had to jump over to get back to Amelia.

"Beatrice!" Pidge was calling from inside. "Come in and have a late lunch before we head out." I scrambled up, happy to be remembered.

Neta and Pidge laughed their way through a pot of coffee, and I ate my sandwich quietly, listening. Instead of another fluffer-nutter, I went straight for the good stuff: a sugar sandwich, made of white bread, butter, and sugar. Barbara and I used to eat them every day after school. It's the sort of food neither Julie nor my mother will let me eat: Julie because it's too fattening; my mother because it's too unhealthy. Sometime before my parents split, my mother started reading all these books on nutrition. Margarine and bacon disappeared from the refrigerator, and my sugary cereals fled the pantry. Weird sprouts and crunchy granola took their places. Already I liked how around Pidge, I could eat whatever I wanted and she didn't bat an eye. Although, as I chewed through the second half of the sandwich, it started to taste a touch overly sweet.

I rummaged in the fridge for some milk, still listening to

them talk. Neta had a great laugh—a joyful howl. Their stories were full of references to Meelie, which wasn't surprising, considering she was how they knew each other in the first place.

"I've had this framed in my den for ages." Neta pulled a photograph out of her pocketbook. "I thought maybe you'd want to see it again." Craning my neck, I could see that the well-preserved picture showed an old white airplane—just a tiny one, not like a jetliner—and two girls in front of it. The one on the left wore a long coat, pants tucked into boots, and a hat topped with big goggles. The other had on a jacket and boots, and was clutching a leather glove. She wore a hat-scarf combination that covered the lower half of her face, but you could still see her eyes. They sparkled mischievously, kind of like Pidge's. It was definitely Amelia.

"That's right before her first training flight. January third, nineteen twenty-one. Can you believe it?" Neta smiled and touched the photo with her lacquered fingertip. "I remember the day she showed up at the field. Wearing a leather jacket that she later admitted she'd slept in and purposefully stained, to pass herself off as an experienced aviatrix. Your sister said to me, 'I want to fly. Will you teach me?' Real direct and determined, so I was fond of her right from the get-go." She slid it across the yellow Formica table to Pidge.

"My goodness," Pidge said. "Meelie looks so excited, and so *young*. Weren't you afraid for your life?" She laughed, but kind of sadly.

"I should've been! Amelia was naturally daring, but not always a natural at flying. But I knew, even in those early days, that she was destined for something big. Fame."

Pidge smiled. "Although I have to say, she didn't have a clue what it would really be like, when she had all that attention on her. She told me once that if she could do it all over again . . ." Pidge trailed off, and her lips closed to a purse. "I think nobody could've predicted how wild it all got."

"Was it hard? Being her sister?"

Pidge stared at the photo. "Well, yes. Meelie liked to do things her way, and she liked to tell me how I should do my things too . . . We butted heads plenty. But isn't it hard being *anyone's* sister?" So far, I could agree with that.

Pidge slid back the photograph, clearing her throat. "Enough of this talk."

I was interested in what Pidge had been saying about if Meelie had been able to do it all over again—did Amelia end up regretting her fame? Or her flying? Her letters sounded melancholy at points, and she kept writing that she missed Pidge. But by then they'd moved on to talking about life on Snooky's ranch, so I picked up my plate and took it to the sink to noisily clean it off. Pidge looked up at me, almost like she'd forgotten that I was in the room at all.

"I suppose we should get on the road soon. Say, I have an idea! On our way to the station, let's take a look-see at Kinner Field. It'll be like the old days." I perked up—I remembered that from the letter. Maybe we could have a picnic too.

Neta smiled. "Oh, there's nothing to see now. That area's all built up, and the airfield's long gone."

"What a shame. So many memories there." Pidge stood up, carrying their plates to the sink.

"Here, Pidge. I can take those," I said, reaching for them.

"You call your grandmother 'Pidge'?" Neta asked, raising a penciled-in eyebrow.

"At my insistence," Pidge said, before the blush covered both of my cheeks. "Because I hate the word *grandmother*. It makes me feel ancient."

"I hate to break it to you, Pidge, but we *are* ancient."

"I prefer the term 'well-preserved,' myself. But in any case, I'll race *your* ancient self out to your Thunderbird!" Pidge dashed toward the front door, moving as fast as her legs would allow.

Neta pushed herself up from the table and hurried after her, giggling. She turned to me. "Well, come on, kid! Are you going to let these two old birds beat you?"

Bewildered, I left the plates in the sink and hurried after them. They'd stopped running as soon as they crossed the doorway, taking the front walk more carefully than the carpeted, wide hallways of Pidge's house. So even though I'm not much of a runner, I blasted past them and reached Neta's car first. I pulled the handle to open the door and hopped inside.

"You got there first," Neta called after me. "Don't you want to ride shotgun?"

"No, I'd rather be in back." I slid to the middle of the backseat and immediately readjusted my dress under my legs—the dark seat was burning hot. I watched as Pidge locked up the house, thinking about the dirty dishes still stacked in the sink. At least I hadn't left the water running when I chased after them to the car. Even in the short time I'd been around her, I had noticed that Pidge was a lackadaisical housekeeper. Either that was her forgetfulness, or she simply didn't care about the things in that house. I figured that was the kind of stuff that Julie wanted to know—but I wasn't about to rat out my grandmother.

They climbed into the front seats, and then Neta stuck the key in the ignition. She revved the engine. "Let's blow this Popsicle stand!" The car shot out from the curb, Pidge hollered a hearty "woo-hoo!" and we were on our way.

Neta was short—whether she had been her whole life or whether it was because she was an old lady now, I didn't know.

Her head barely popped above the headrest. She also leaned forward in her seat, squinting her eyes at what was outside the windshield. I hoped she could see properly. But the way she held the steering wheel was pure confidence—like she was a pilot once again, only for a Thunderbird instead of an airplane. "Turn on some tunes, why don't you?" she said to Pidge. "We need music for a joyride."

Pidge reached over and fiddled with the radio dial. The first song that blasted on had a catchy beat and lyrics that made me think about San Francisco: something about incense and peppermints. Incense was the stuff the hippies burned while they grooved or whatever they were doing up at the Be-In. It reminded me of the pictures I'd seen next to my mom's article in *Look* magazine—girls with messy hair and round sunglasses that made their faces a mystery. The long tunics they wore, with all sorts of wild and interesting psychedelic prints. Sandals and macramé. The last time I saw my mom, she was still wearing clothes a mostly normal mother would wear—but her hair was long and natural.

Another song came on, and in this one a woman wailed about wanting "somebody to love." Her booming voice and the loud, pulsing guitars filled the car. I liked it. Not as much as I liked the Beatles, but the singing in particular made me sit up and take notice.

"Yuck—turn the dial, would you? I don't like that cater-wauling." In the rearview mirror, I could see Neta wrinkle her nose. We were cruising down the highway now, much faster than I'd ever seen an elderly person drive. Whenever we hit a traffic light that looked to be turning yellow, Neta would toot on the horn and barrel through the intersection. "Remember this, Beatrice—yellow means accelerate."

Pidge turned the dial and found Frank Sinatra crooning about a paper moon. "Oh, this song I like. It makes me think of dancing," she said. "We didn't go to many dances as children, Meelie and I. Our father couldn't be counted on to take us."

"Couldn't you go without him?" I piped up from the back-seat. Unless it was a father-daughter dance, I supposed.

"No, in those days, fathers had to escort their daughters to dances."

"Your father always seemed like a great guy to me," Neta said. "Sharper than most anyone I'd met. Charming."

"He was those things." Pidge cleared her throat. "But he had some troubles, too. Sometimes it wasn't easy, our childhood." That made me sad. At least I could count on my father to take me places, even if Sally would be coming along now.

"I always wondered why Amelia needed to fly away," Neta said softly.

Pidge turned sharply to look at her. "What do you mean?"

Neta raised one hand off the wheel to wave in a flying motion. "Something compelled her to wander over to the airfield one day! I just wondered what created that yearning to go way up yonder."

Pidge settled back in her seat. "Up, and away."

Neta sighed. "I wish I could ask her now."

"Don't we all."

"Which brings me to a question I *can* ask—Where are you two gals headed this evening such that I have to cart you to the train station?"

Pidge turned to wink at me in the backseat, which I interpreted as "don't say anything about the letters and the real reason why we're skipping town." I kept my mouth buttoned up, curious what cover story Pidge would spin. Would she tell Neta some version of the truth? As I watched Neta's short curls blow around with the breeze, I thought that she didn't seem like the kind of fuddy-duddy lady to pass judgment on us for sneaking out of Sun City. She also might believe us if we told her about Amelia's letters.

"I decided my granddaughter should see from where her family came. We're headed all the way back to Kansas. A sightseeing trip, good for these lazy days of summer."

"An excellent plan. But her father couldn't give you a lift?"

"Oh, no. He's busy working—and her stepmother has another child to take care of."

"My mother's traveling too," I piped up. "From San Francisco to New Jersey." I don't know why, but I felt the need to explain that she hadn't also flown away. So to speak.

"San Francisco, eh? Ain't that something." Neta raised an eyebrow. "Something *groovy*."

"Well," Pidge said, a defensive note in her tone, which I appreciated, "her mother's become a reporter."

We kept passing other cars along the highway, and if anyone dared to shoot past us, Neta would make an exasperated noise and grumble about speed demons. Then she'd gun it to catch up and overtake them. We made a pit stop at a filling station to use the restroom and grab a couple of sodas. When we got back in the car, the conversation quieted down as Pidge and Neta took in the scenery and sang along to their music.

Another yellow light popped up ahead, but this time Neta squealed on the brakes. "Sorry. Don't want to crash."

"Were you ever in one?" I asked, meaning either car or plane. It made my palms sweat just to think about it.

"Oh, yes. In fact I crashed with Amelia in the *Canary*, once."

Pidge butted in, "I helped Meelie buy that plane. Her bright yellow piece of freedom, as she called it. Can you believe we only had to scrimp and save two thousand dollars for it?"

Neta let out a low whistle. "You'd pay a lot more today." She drove through the green light and continued her story. "It was July twenty-third. Amelia had just gotten the *Canary*. On take-off we didn't climb high enough to gain altitude, and there was a blasted bunch of eucalyptus trees at the edge of the runway. She had two choices: nose down and hit the trees, or head up and face a stall. Well, she went up and we stalled, then we spiraled down, down, down. The propeller broke on the way, and she busted the landing gear."

"Were you terrified?" I asked.

"Falling from the sky is a sensation I never learned to like, to put it mildly. Anyway—and you'll appreciate this, Pidge—on the ground I turned to check on Amelia, and she was already powdering her nose. There would be reporters, you see!" They both cracked up. I didn't know if I'd ever be able to laugh about something as scary as a crash.

The Thunderbird stopped at another light. I looked up and recognized the names on the street signs—we were already in Los Angeles. It was strange to be close to home, without any intention of returning there.

I watched Neta in the driver's seat. Amelia had been lucky to have a friend and teacher like her. One of the things Meelie said—that Snooky taught her to ask for forgiveness, not permission—made me feel less guilty about not telling my parents we'd left Sun City.

The Thunderbird jolted through a left turn. "All right, girls!" Neta exclaimed. "I think we're here." Outside the car window was the red-tiled roof and tall arched windows of Union Station. The clock on the tower showed we were cutting it close—it was almost seven. I reached into my knapsack to pull out my Brownie camera and took a picture. Maybe I'd paste it in my adventure journal, once I developed the roll. A picture of where Pidge's and my journey started. It would be good to get something on those blank pages.

Neta pulled the car to a stop directly in front of the entrance. "One benefit to being old—and there aren't many, kiddo—is that nobody bats an eye when you make your own parking space."

We got out of the car, and Neta insisted on helping me lift our luggage out of the trunk. I balanced the load of my O'Nite and my knapsack, plus Pidge's small suitcase, too. She carried her pocketbook and the valise of letters, tucked safely underneath her slim arm.

"I guess this is good-bye," Pidge said to Neta. She pulled a pair of sunglasses over her eyes, but not in time to hide the wistfulness.

"We shouldn't let it be so long before we meet up again," Neta said, walking forward to embrace my grandmother. "Especially now that you live only a hop-skip away."

"We certainly shouldn't." Pidge let herself be wrapped in

Neta's hug, but still held tightly to the valise with one arm. I snapped a picture of them.

"One of these days, I could take you up in the air again," Neta added as she pulled away.

"Flying? Snooky, at your age?"

"Why not? I shocked people by flying as a young girl. Might as well shock them again by flying as an old broad."

Pidge smiled. "Well, you'll *never* get me in the air again—but I'll come to watch."

"It's a deal." Neta came for me then, squeezing me tight. She smelled like both cut grass and strong perfume. She pulled the red scarf from her neck and wrapped it around mine. "It suits you. Take good care of your grandma," she whispered in my ear. "Wherever this adventure takes you." I promised her I would. Even though it had been a long drive, I felt excited. We were at the start of something. An adventure, like she said.

# FIVE

## All Aboard

Pidge and I waved to Neta as she drove away, tooting a cheery good-bye with the horn. Then Pidge hustled me into the station. "One thing about the *Super Chief*, darling—it's always on schedule. That's a blessing or a curse, depending on your own timeliness."

She walked fast into the station, shoulders back and striding like she owned the place. Her wide pant legs swished with purpose. She reminded me of Katherine Hepburn. But at the same time, seeing her in a place full of other adults, I was struck by her frailty relative to them. Her knuckles were white from the grip on her suitcase handle—she had taken it from me, insisting on carrying her own bag. In the crowded middle of an open concourse, she stopped, looking confused. "It's funny. I was here only a week ago, but I don't remember . . . Ah, yes. This way," she said, nudging the back of my right leg with the edge of her suitcase. I scrambled to catch up with her, my bag tangling up my feet.

"Don't we need to get our tickets?" I asked as we hurried past a ticket window.

"That's all taken care of," she said. I wondered how, though. Julie now kept the checkbook and register for Pidge's bank account in our kitchen drawer, and my grandmother was given a cash allowance by my father for expenses not covered in regular bills. Train tickets must be costly—wouldn't they have used up all her spare money? And when had she purchased them, because last night she'd only called to see if seats were still available—unless Pidge had made the arrangements early in morning, while I still slept. *That must be it.*

A whistle blew as we hit the platform. The train was before us in all its shiny, silver, streamlined glory. The front of the engine was painted a bright red with yellow on the "nose," the words SANTA FE emblazoned in proud black text. I tried to count how many cars long the train was, but Pidge was already pulling me toward it.

"I wonder if anyone famous will be on board," I said as we hurried along the platform edge. People used to call the *Super Chief* the "train of the stars" because so many Hollywood celebrities took it east. It had been the most glamorous way to travel, like a grand hotel on rails. A thrill zipped up my spine at the thought of seeing movie actresses like Audrey Hepburn or Julie Andrews. But many stars traveled by air now. Regular people too. My mother would be flying from San Francisco to Newark.

"Perhaps, but don't get starry-eyed about it. Fame isn't all it's cracked up to be." I supposed Pidge would know, being Amelia's sister and all. "They're just people, same as you and me." Pidge stopped suddenly. I skidded to a halt next to her, nearly taking her out with my swinging suitcase. I dropped it at my feet.

"Here. Climb aboard." She gave me a push in the direction of the train steps. An attendant wearing a red cap stood beside the stairs, one who probably should've been helping us, but he was turned the other way and focused on herding a group of passengers. Pidge shoved me again. "Hurry up, buttercup!"

I scrambled up the slippery metal steps and onto the train. Pidge tossed me my suitcase, the valise, then her suitcase, and finally hoisted herself up behind me. "Follow me." She snaked down the cramped hallway. We were in a chair car, so we must've boarded the *El Capitan* half of the train—the coach part, where instead of fancy sleeping cars there were neat and comfortable seats on the high level and luggage shelves below.

"I thought we were taking the *Super Chief*?" I wanted to make sure we were in the right place, and this didn't seem like it.

"Hush," Pidge said. "And hurry."

"But this is the coach—"

She turned around and shot me a withering look. "Just *trust*, Beatrice." I zipped my lips and followed her. The single-minded way in which she dragged me around the train convinced me Pidge knew what she was doing. We climbed up to the high level to get to the end doors connecting cars. At least the other passengers were mostly settled in their seats, so the aisle was clear as we raced down it. I hoped we'd be in our right spot before the train pulled out of the station, because I wanted to sit at the window and take pictures of Los Angeles rolling away from me.

We stopped in a lounge car. Pidge handed me the valise with the instructions, "Don't let this out of your sight. I have to run to the ladies' and powder my nose—you take a seat there." She pointed to one of the tables. I stacked our luggage onto the opposite bench and set the valise carefully on the tabletop, then slid myself right next to the window.

Pidge took a moment to consider me sitting alone in an empty lounge car. "If anyone comes in, tell him or her your grandmother will be right back, and that I have our tickets." I nodded, relieved she was keeping track of them. Pidge walked over to the lavatory door, struggled for a few seconds with the handle, then disappeared inside.

A few minutes after she shut the door, the train let out a loud wheeze. Seconds later, with a rumble and a toot of the whistle, we started moving with halting jerks. I pressed my nose to the window, even though there still wasn't much to see other than the platform and the underbelly of Union Station: all the tracks and wires and mechanical thingamajigs that make the trains come and go. Slowly, we pulled out from the station and into the sunlight, and the red-tiled building faded into the past. Grungy industrial Los Angeles surrounded us—it wasn't quite the picturesque train-pulling-out-of-a-station scene I had hoped for. But it was still exciting. I pulled my Brownie out of my knapsack for a picture. The train's movement was starting to build up to the rolling speed I expected, but it was slow enough that a photo might turn out.

"Excuse me, miss." I pulled back from the window. A train attendant clicked a puncher three times fast in his hand. "Ticket, please?" He looked around the lounge car, seeming to realize that I was in there by myself with two suitcases, a knapsack, and a battered valise—but no adult. His eyes narrowed. "Are you here all alone? This lounge car isn't open yet."

My face flushed. It felt like being called on by the teacher and not having an answer, or being shushed in the halls. Not that I had much experience being reprimanded at school—I was one of the good girls who answered promptly, always turned assignments in on time, and never harmed a library book. The sense of wrongdoing was unfamiliar, and I didn't like it. My heart thrummed in my chest. "No—well, not at the moment, but my grandmother will be right back. We were heading to our spot when she suddenly—*urgently*—had to use the ladies' room." I scrunched up my face in an embarrassed sort of way. "You know, perhaps she had a bit too much prune juice this morning." I was shocked by my little white lie. Pidge wouldn't touch prune juice—from what I could tell, she drank water and coffee, black. The milk, juice, and orange drink in the refrigerator were just for me.

Now it was the ticket collector's turn to look embarrassed—but also concerned. "Do you think she's all right in there? Should I knock and see—"

"No," I quickly interrupted. "It's fine. She's slow—because she's an old lady, after all. Arthritis."

"Alrighty then. But do head to your car as soon as she's done." He tipped his hat to me and hurried on his way, surely relieved to no longer be discussing the aftereffects of prune juice on an elderly woman's digestive system.

I stared out of the window, feeling flushed from my lie. I wondered what was taking Pidge so long, and why she'd left me to deal with the train attendants. It was almost like she was avoiding them. I chewed at a fingernail and stared out the window. I wished she'd hurry up already. I didn't like sitting there alone. I wanted to be settled somewhere. I pulled out my worry journal from my knapsack and started flipping to a fresh page.

The door at the end of the car opened and clattered shut. I looked up to see a girl, about my age, walking toward me. The train jerked and she wobbled, her braids bouncing up in the air. She braced herself against the wall and I grimaced, overtaken with sympathetic embarrassment for her stumble. "You're brave to walk while it's moving," I called over. "That's why I'm staying safely in this seat."

But she didn't seem very embarrassed. "Right? I feel like they should give you *training* wheels to walk in here!" She giggled as she straightened her checked skirt and then stopped at my table. "I hope you're not planning to sit down for the whole trip. Half the fun of being on a train is exploring. I always walk end-to-end, check out every car. I mean, it's a long ride otherwise."

I'd never really thought of a train as something to explore, just a way to get somewhere. "This is my first time on a train." That was the thing about living in California—the car was king.

"Really?" She plopped down across from me. I was impressed. If I ever tripped or something, I hurried away from whomever had seen. "I've ridden them lots of times. My dad's a minister, so he travels around. My name's Ruth, by the way."

"I'm Bea." I smiled. "Nice to meet you." Now that we were next to each other, I could tell Ruth was younger, but closer to my age than to Sally's.

75

"Likewise!" Ruth glanced around the empty car and at the pile of luggage surrounding me. "Are you all by yourself? That's a lot of stuff. Nobody helped you stow it?"

I shook my head. "I'm with my grandmother, but she's powdering her nose." I pointed to the bathroom. "Where's your dad?"

"I dunno, he was right behind me . . ." As soon as she said it, the door clattered and a man walked into the car. He was handsome—a look-alike for Sidney Poitier. She waved him over. "Dad, this is Bea. Bea, this is my dad."

He smiled. "Pleasure to meet you, Bea."

"Nice to meet you, Mister—" I realized I didn't know their last name.

"Reverend Vaughan." I blushed, already having forgotten that he was a minister. I didn't know many, other than the one from Julie's church who married her and my dad.

"He was talking to a porter and I got impatient, so I went on ahead," Ruth said. "Dad, can I catch up with you later? We're having a nice time chatting."

"Sure, sweetie. You have your ticket?" he asked, and Ruth nodded. "I've got your bag. And you're not traveling all alone, Bea, right?"

"Her grandmother is in the ladies' room," Ruth piped up.

"Very well." He tipped his hat to us. "Nice to meet you, Bea."

"Same to you, Reverend Vaughan!" We watched him head down the car.

Ruth turned back to me. "So where are you and your grandma headed?"

"Kansas. Some town called Atchison. I've never been there before." Truthfully, I'd never been much of anywhere.

"I went to Kansas City once, and it was nice. We're headed to Chicago for a week. My father's going to hear another reverend speak there, at a big meeting they have on Saturdays. But we've also got family to visit." Ruth grinned and bounced in the seat a little. "I can't wait to see my cousins."

"We're meeting up with family too." Hopefully, that would be true. "My great-aunt. But I've never met her before."

"So this trip is full of never-befores for you, huh? Let me think of what advice I have for the train . . ." Ruth drummed her fingers on the table, gazing out the window. She turned back to me. "The viewing cars can get kind of crowded during the day, so the best time to visit them is after sunset, when everybody's eating dinner. If you pick up a soda pop, open it *after* you get to your seat so you don't slosh it all over yourself when the train wiggles. Oh, and keep a couple of napkins or a handkerchief on you, just in case you get rattled while taking a sip. And don't be embarrassed to ask if you need help or anything. The train crew is always nice."

"Boy, you're an expert." Those were good tips. Even

though my worry journal was open, and Ruth's pointers were not worries, I scribbled them down. I could always tear out the page later. "Thanks so much."

"I like to write too," Ruth said, pointing to my journal. "Stories. What are you working on?"

I was too embarrassed to tell her the truth—that this journal was full of my fears and failings. So I pretended it was the other, emptier one in my bag. "This is my . . . adventure journal. I'm writing down everything that happens on this trip."

Ruth nodded approvingly. "That's a good idea." I wanted to ask how many times she'd ridden this train—which were her favorite stops, and when we might pass places good for photographs—but another door clattered. I glanced up to see Pidge finally slink out of the bathroom. Seeing Ruth next to me, her mouth pursed with surprise.

"Bea! I see you've made a friend." She walked slowly toward us, balancing her steps with the train's sway.

"Pidge, this is Ruth. Ruth, this is my grandmother, Pidge."

Pidge smiled warmly. "Nice to make your acquaintance, Ruth. That's a lovely name." She checked her wristwatch. "Girls, I hate to interrupt your chat, but I think Bea and I ought to find our accommodations."

Ruth nodded, standing up. "I should catch up with my dad. Hope to see you again. But if not, have a good rest of your trip, Bea."

"I hope so too—and thanks for the advice!" I waved as Ruth walked away. To run into her again, I would have to muster up the courage to go exploring. I shoved my worry journal back in my bag and pressed my hand to the like-new cover of my other one. *Yes, maybe I would do a little exploring on my own.*

Compared to when Pidge had left me at that table, I felt much better about the trip ahead. Almost excited. I slung my knapsack back over my shoulder and started gathering our luggage, when Pidge leaned to whisper to me. "Are we in the clear?"

I frowned. What did she mean, asking *are we in the clear?* "Of what?"

She paused, and for a few seconds the internal debate of whether to tell me something played across her face. I hugged my arms to my chest. *Something's not right.* "To get on our way, without being bothered. I don't want to tip a red cap for lugging a bag I can carry well enough on my own," she replied. "Let's go find our compartment."

I grabbed my half of our things. "What kind of room are we in?"

"I was hoping for a double bedroom," Pidge said. "But we'll see soon enough."

Surely the ticket would tell what kind of accommodations we had, so why was she *hoping?* I ran through the mental list of things about this train trip that seemed off to me. A double bedroom on the *Super Chief* must've cost a small fortune—and based on what I'd seen in her cupboards and kitchen drawers, Pidge saved aluminum foil and washed out sandwich bags for reuse. Whether it was because she was short on spending money or held memories of the Depression, Pidge was frugal. Why wouldn't she have purchased tickets for a cheaper sleeping compartment, or even coach seats? And hadn't someone on the phone told her that only roomettes were left? My heart started to beat faster, like it was keeping time with the hastening sounds of the wheels on the tracks.

We'd boarded the train all on our own, with no help from the crew, and then Pidge had hid out in the bathroom until we started moving. Nobody had actually checked our tickets yet. Didn't a porter usually help you settle in your room? It was too early for turndown service, but in the movies and on TV someone always carried in your bags and showed you how things like the shades and sink worked.

I couldn't ignore the possibility that had been nipping at my mind since we boarded. Maybe we weren't supposed to be on the train at all. I thought about Pidge's phone call the night before. Perhaps she hadn't been calling to find out if there were tickets to buy, but to see if there were *vacancies*—to know if there was a roomette we could sneak into.

*Are we stowaways?*

# SIX

## Champagne Dinner

I sucked in a deep breath. It wasn't enough to trust. I had to know. "Are we supposed to be on this train, Pidge?"

"What kind of question is that? My father worked for the railroad. Of course we're supposed to be on a train." She turned to check that I was still following her. "Please stop worrying already, Beatrice."

Asking me to stop worrying was kind of like asking my heart to stop beating. It happened without my trying. And anyway, she hadn't actually answered my question.

Pidge paused at the door to a new car, peeking through the glass at whatever lay ahead. Then she motioned for me to follow her, and we made our way across into some kind of transitional car between the two halves of the train. "Oops!" A jolt on the tracks sent Pidge stumbling, until I grabbed her shirttail to steady her. She didn't thank me but, once she had her footing, stiffly said, "Come along."

I wanted to stop her to answer my question, but she wouldn't slow down. I followed Pidge through that car, which held all sorts of baggage, and then finally into a sleeper car. From the second we stepped over and the door slammed shut behind us, it was a whole other world. One of brushed steel and plush carpet, hushed conversations behind closed doors and above the clacking rails. Pidge handed me the valise again.

"Hold this for a moment, please." She went up to a door and knocked lightly. After a few seconds, it opened. A glamorous woman, with platinum blond hair and bright blue eyes, poked her head out. The *Super Chief* was already living up to its reputation: She looked so much like a star, I had to squint to make sure she wasn't actually Tippi Hedren. I'd only seen a few minutes of *The Birds*, when it was airing on television while I was sleeping over at Barbara's. She wanted to watch, but I got too scared and made her change the channel.

"Yes? Can I help you?"

"Oh!" Pidge squinted her eyes and looked confused. "My apologies. I think I must have the wrong door."

The woman smiled kindly at her. "Not a problem. Have a pleasant trip," she said, stepping back inside and softly shutting the door.

That settled it. If we actually *had* booked a roomette, we wouldn't be knocking on random doors to find an empty one.

"We *are* stowaways!" I hissed, staying quiet in case the woman could still hear me. "I can't believe you've made me do this!"

Pidge leaned in close to whisper. "Beatrice, let me introduce you to the concept of free will. I didn't make you do anything—I asked if you'd pack a bag. Which you gladly did! You could've chosen to ask for more information about the trip—I simply thought you were being admirably adventurous."

"I was *trusting* you, like you said. And I know all about free will—so maybe I will use it to get off this train at the next stop!" I dropped my luggage and crossed my arms over my chest in a protective hug. I shook side to side, from emotion and the train's sway.

I swallowed hard. What were my options? We were hurtling along the tracks and already far from Los Angeles. Pidge was dead set on getting back to Atchison by the twenty-fourth, so even if I bailed out at the next stop, I doubted she would. Could I leave my grandmother on the train alone? And what would I do then—hitch back home? Track down my mother and ask her to pick me up on the way to her next big story? Call and beg my father or Julie to come get me? As scary as it was to stay on the train with Pidge, none of those options were any less so.

Pidge's tone softened as she quietly said, "Look, Beatrice, I'm sorry. You're right, and I should've been more honest with you." I wondered whether she was actually sorry, or whether she simply didn't want to get slowed down, or stopped, if I hopped off the train and told my father what was going on. "The truth is, I can't let anything get in the way of my making it back to Meelie. But I could sure use your help getting there." She gave my shoulder a tentative pat. "I was scared on a train once, as a girl. And Meelie told me, 'Lots of times when you know what's the matter, you don't need to be afraid at all, do you?'" She paused, biting her lip. "What do you say? Are you willing to help your grandmother out, on one last grand adventure?"

*Last grand adventure.* I recognized that phrase—another one from Meelie's letters. I was supposed to look for adventures in life, right? And now that I knew the "matter" was that we were stowaways—could I stop feeling afraid? And angry?

I took a deep breath and gave my grandmother a reluctant nod.

"Good girl." Pidge walked over to the next room and lightly rapped on the door. This time, no heads popped out. She nodded. "Yes, this will do." I stood in the aisle, my heart pounding. "Beatrice, what are you waiting for?" I watched her slip in through the narrow doorway. "Come inside!" After hesitating a few seconds more, I followed her in.

To my relief, Pidge was right that the room was unoccupied, with no luggage or personal items already inside. Pidge plopped her suitcase onto the rack. "Put your bags down, darling. I don't want you to hurt your back." I shoved my O'Nite next to hers. She placed the valise on the table in between the chairs. We were in a roomette, and I wondered how we'd handle the space when the two chairs would transform into one flat bed. Would we share it? The bed was only meant for one person. I'd barely ever given my grandmother a hug, and now we'd be sharing a space the size of a sleeping bag the whole night.

Although that assumed a couple of stowaways could hide in a roomette overnight. Turndown service from an attendant, at the very least, wasn't likely to happen.

Pidge sank into a chair, a smile of relief spreading across her face. I sat, facing her, in the other one, unable to relax into it. The view from our large picture window was nicer than the one back in the lounge—the outskirts of the city and the occasional citrus grove, with golden, sun-dried hills in the distance. According to the schedule I'd managed to grab inside the station, we should be arriving in Pasadena any minute. I pulled it out of my knapsack and looked closely at the timetable. After Pasadena, we'd be stopping again in only thirty-nine minutes in Pomona. Another stop a half hour after that, in San Bernardino. Somehow, I'd thought that once we climbed aboard the train, we'd be going nonstop to Kansas. But over the course of its almost forty-hour trip, the train would hit a new station every hour or two. Suddenly, it seemed like a long time to be in that small space with my grandmother.

Pidge tried to cheer me up by rambling on about train trips she had taken when she was younger, but I kept my mouth shut. I would go along with her plan, but I wasn't ready to forgive her quite yet. Eventually she accepted my silent treatment and pulled out a newspaper she'd grabbed from the station. I listened to my thumping heart compete with the *click-clack, click-clack* of the wheels on the rails. Pidge had adjusted her reading glasses on the bridge of her nose and spread the paper wide. The headlines were about an emergency UN meeting about the Middle East, and a local soldier killed in Vietnam. I sighed quietly, and reached into my knapsack for my journals. My adventure one didn't want to stay open, because the spine hadn't had enough practice. In shaky script, I wrote:

> We've left Los Angeles and are on our way. But we're not legal passengers of this train. Pidge lied to me about the tickets so now we're stowaways, hiding out in an empty roomette. Already, this trip is more than I bargained for.

It sounded like I was writing in my worry journal. I paused to think of something positive to say—because an adventurer, a "voyager," like the meaning of my name—would probably embrace all this swirling uncertainty. Meelie would. I chewed on the eraser end of my pencil, then added:

But I like the noise the train makes. It's like what my music teacher always talks about: syncopation. The <u>Super Chief</u> is pretty slick inside and the views outside are neat.

I met a girl in the lounge car, Ruth. She was younger than me but has traveled a lot before. I like that on a train you get to talk to people who are from the same place as you but live different lives. And Ruth gave me good tips for exploring the train—I think maybe I'll use them.

Meelie wrote about the strength women have, especially Earhart women. They are a "capable type." Maybe I can become like that too.

When I opened my worry journal, I had to flip through lots of pages to get to a blank one. I wrote and wrote and wrote—about the possibility of getting arrested or being forced to peel potatoes in the train's kitchen, or about leaving Pidge alone if I couldn't be brave (or foolish?) enough to keep going on this journey. I worried about getting stranded in the middle of the desert and having to chew on cacti to survive. And, of course, about the trouble I'd be in if my father found out that we'd absconded from Sun City.

When my hand started cramping, I closed the notebook. Pidge looked up from the newspaper. "Looks like you're a writer too," she said.

"Not really." I shoved both journals back into my bag and pulled out a library copy of *The Egypt Game* in exchange. I'd read it once already, but it was good enough to read again. "I just keep journals."

"If it's pen to paper, you're a writer," Pidge said, turning back to her newsprint.

"Do you write?" Maybe we had that in common.

"Nothing more than correspondence. Amelia, though, she took a leather-bound diary on all her flights, to record everything she saw along the way." I smiled—that sounded like my adventure journal. Or, what I wanted it to be. "She also wrote poetry and her own books, two of them. Well, three if you count the one her husband, George, finished up. But I don't know how many of those words were really hers."

"Why'd her husband finish it? Was she too busy with flying?"

Pidge grimaced. "No—well, in a sense. It was published after she disappeared."

"Oh." I looked away, out the window at the dregs of the daylight, slipping down behind the dusty hills. The sky lit up like tie-dye, swirls of colors from reddish orange all the way to periwinkle. We must've been getting close to the next stop, because countryside groves had led to the kinds of buildings you expect along the railroad tracks in a town: warehouses and workshops, with the occasional garage. I looked again at the timetable. Pomona was up next.

"When does the scenery get really good?" I asked. Pidge had taken a train to get to California, so she'd seen it all before.

"It's beautiful out in the desert. The sandstone buttes are up to a thousand feet high, and in the most interesting shapes. Sometimes they look like tall ships on a sea of dust. Sometimes they look like animals: resting elephants and dancing bears. There are mountains and rivers and plains. We'll have to spend a lot of time in the viewing car. There are windows on all sides, even the ceiling is glass—" Suddenly, Pidge dropped the paper into her lap. She leaned toward the closed door, straining to listen to something in the hall. It was going to be a long trip, if we were constantly afraid of a knock at the door.

But whatever spooked her passed. "I think it's about time we got some supper, Beatrice." She stood up slowly, massaging one of her legs with her hand. "Put down the book. Let's explore a bit."

Exploring actually sounded good—and my stomach was growling. I put my book down on the seat, using the timetable as a bookmark. Pidge struggled with the latch on our compartment's door, so I stepped up. "Here, let me help." When I reached for the handle, she swatted me away. But the look on her face was apologetic when she turned back around.

"I'm sorry, darling. I'm afraid you have to be patient with your Pidge—I'm still not used to my elderly body, or these aching hands." She stepped aside. "I need to remember there's nothing wrong with a little help now and then."

I offered a half smile and reached to push open the door. The train was slowing down for its next stop, and the attendants were busy waiting by the doors to welcome fresh passengers aboard. At least they'd be distracted while we walked past.

"Wait!" Pidge shut the door again. "Why don't you bring the letters along? I hate to leave them here—in case someone comes by." I found it ironic that she was wary of thieves, considering what we were. I reached over to grab the valise—almost any space in the roomette was within arm's reach, no matter where you stood on the small patch of open floor. Even the door to the private toilet. I grabbed my knapsack in addition to the valise and handed Pidge her pocketbook.

Pidge opened the door a crack, peeked out, and motioned for me to follow her. We slipped past the attendants who were helping a few new passengers settle on the train. She refused to make eye contact or respond to one's "Good evening, madam." My face flushed at her rudeness. And wouldn't ignoring the staff make us look more suspicious?

"Evening, sir," I said back. He smiled and tipped his hat at me. Ruth was right—everyone on the train was nice.

Pidge barreled forward. Eventually, we crossed over into the dining car. "Now the trick is to simply act like you're supposed to be here, and then everyone else will think you are too," she whispered. Aside from the picture windows framed by tan curtains, the dining room could've been a real restaurant somewhere. On one side were two-person tables, with four-person ones on the other. All were swathed in crisp white tablecloths, the places set with real silverware and thick linen napkins. A vase with flowers sat as a centerpiece in the middle of each. Half the plush orange chairs were empty.

Pidge walked up to the maître d' and flashed him a big smile. "Table for two, please."

"Madam, do you have a reservation?"

"What? Oh, no." Pidge cast her eyes downward.

"Your attendant should have requested what time you'd like to dine," the man said, crossing his arms. His uniform was as crisp and white as the tablecloths.

"Well, I'm an old woman," Pidge pouted, "and my granddaughter and I are quite peckish. You don't think you could find a spot for us to enjoy a quick supper, do you?" Pidge nudged me, and I puckered my mouth into a matching pout. "I see several empty tables in this room."

That flustered him. "Madam . . . I *suppose*. Right this way," he said, leading us to a table tucked in the back. Pidge gracefully lowered herself into her chair, and I plopped into mine. She unfolded her starched napkin and set it in her lap; I carefully did the same. I caught her eye across the table, and she winked.

"You're catching on," she whispered. Blushing, I stared out the window. We'd rolled out of the station at Pomona and were back on our way east, the twilight outside world passing in a blur of power lines and the occasional lit-up building.

A waiter came by and handed us menus. On the top left corner was a recommendation for the fancy "*Super Chief* Champagne Dinner." A lot of other food was listed a la carte. I started scanning. No fluffernutters, but there was a "De Luxe

Sandwich Dinner." There was also steak, London mixed grill, a roast chicken, and options for chiffonade salad and shrimp cocktail. And plenty of desserts: a chocolate sundae, layer cake, and strawberry shortcake with fresh whipped cream. My mouth began to water.

"I think I might enjoy the champagne dinner," Pidge said, looking up from the menu.

"Really?" That was an expensive $7.50, and it featured a 16-ounce steak.

"I believe in treating yourself while traveling." Pidge carefully wrote it down; there were instructions at the top of the menu that waiters would only take orders written on a meal check. "Now, did you want the children's menu number one, or number two?"

I stared at her, aghast. She was going to order a champagne dinner, and I had to get a hamburger and milk? I was nearly thirteen, and whenever I went out to dinner with my father, Julie, and Sally, I ordered off the real menu. Even if Dad and Julie wouldn't let me order anything but chicken. My mother never splurged on restaurant meals when I stayed with her, but she also didn't cook me a child's dinner—I ate whatever strange health concoction she was eating.

"Well, I want a champagne dinner too," I said, closing my menu. Pidge and I stared each other down for a few seconds.

I spotted a hint of approval in her eyes. But I still didn't think she'd actually order it for me.

"Very well. *Two* champagne dinners," she said, carefully changing the mark on her meal check. She scrawled a note next to it, but I couldn't read what it said.

I sat a little straighter in my chair. I'd never had champagne before—not even at my father's wedding to Julie. There I'd been slumped in a seat next to Sally, who was the most charming, adorable flower girl, all curls and smiles and ruffles. A junior bridesmaid, I was much less adorable because of the hairdo the woman at the beauty parlor had given me that morning: a misshapen beehive, with all my tangles piled on top of my head and shellacked into obedience with almost a full can of Aqua Net. It looked like a style a Dr. Seuss character would wear. Worse, the dress I was wearing—tulle in seafoam green—looked like something you'd see on a baby doll.

Mostly at that wedding, I wanted to be alone, because no amount of deep breaths could quell my nerves. Celebrations are a hard place to be when you feel unsure or lonely—and I felt both. I didn't want to smile for the cameras or help the happy couple cut the cake. I wanted to find an empty bathroom with a stall I could hide in and wait for the night to be over. Or run outside and see if the Santa Ana winds were a match for my Seussical hair hive. But Sally nervously clung to me the whole evening, and I couldn't even get a minute to splash cold water on my face (although I'm sure that wouldn't have gone over so well, as Julie had let me apply a touch of makeup).

I kept thinking that I saw my mom in the crowd of people smiling, dancing, and clinking glasses. Every time a woman with long, dark hair crossed the room, my heart would jolt. It was crazy that I kept imagining her being there, considering the occasion. Her phantom presence made me wonder how my dad could be so happy—grinning as he danced to romantic songs. Didn't he know what a joke all the talk of "forever" was? Even the people who love you sometimes leave. I was only twelve and it had already happened to me.

When Dad and Julie had their champagne toast, a waiter was poised to offer me a quarter-filled flute to drink. But then he saw Sally next to me, in a matching tulle skirt, and he got us two glasses of sparkling grape juice instead. Sally glugged hers down, but I tossed mine into the dirt of a planter. I felt a little bad that I wasn't toasting my dad—but he had everybody else's well wishes.

So I had never had a sip of champagne before, and that fact made me very excited about my dinner on the *Super Chief.* More well-heeled passengers were filing into the dining car—women in fashionable skirts and shoes, men in spiffy suits. Soft music played, and the waiters bustled between the tables.

"After dinner, we'll take a peek at the lounge car," Pidge said, "and the Pleasure Dome."

"The what?"

"Haven't you read 'Kubla Khan' in school?" I shook my head no. "What are they teaching you these days?" Pidge cleared her throat and recited, "In Xanadu did Kubla Khan a stately pleasure-dome decree." She smiled. "Well, that part of my memory hasn't failed me yet—some words I'll never forget. Anyway, that's famous old poem. Coleridge. I'm not quite sure why they used his words to name these fancy lounge cars, other than their domed windows."

"It must be *pleasurable* to see the view?"

"Very true. Did you know that Meelie was also a poet?" Hadn't Pidge already told me that? Sometimes she repeated herself. Pidge cocked her head like she was about to recite another poem, maybe one of her sister's, but we were interrupted by our food. The red-and-white china plates had Southwestern designs on them—mine had a turtle, Pidge's a deer. First out was an eclectic spread of olives, shrimp cocktail, and consommé—and, of course, two slender flutes of champagne. The way the waiters carried the trays of food and drink to the tables without spilling a drop, while the train shifted as it rolled along, was impressive. As soon as the waiter said, "Bon appétit" and slipped away, Pidge took a long sip of the champagne. "I don't know that this is really the *finest*, but it'll do."

I stared at my glass for a few seconds, watching the bubbles dance up the sides. Then I grabbed the thin stem and shakily raised it to my lips. I took a sip—and the taste was familiar. *Ginger ale.* "I don't think I got champagne."

"That's because I asked for a substitution," Pidge said, matter of fact. "You might be my traveling companion, darling, but you're not of champagne age." Watching my face, she frowned sympathetically. "I suppose that's not very fun, though. And I didn't mean to trick you. Let's get you something special." She signaled to the waiter before I could respond. "A Shirley Temple, please?"

I was disappointed, until the bubbly pink drink appeared in a fancy etched glass, topped with a bright red cherry. "Now, cheers to us!" Pidge said, clinking her flute against my glass.

While we were eating our steaks—with fried onion rings, in my case, and mushroom caps, in Pidge's—I noticed an attendant enter the dining car and stare at us for a few minutes. Were they on to us? I swallowed too hard, coughing on my steak. Pidge looked up at me, alarmed. "Have another sip, darling. Wash it down."

I gulped my Shirley Temple. When I looked up again, the attendant had left the dining car.

Pidge wiped at her thin lips with her napkin. "I'm about done—are you?"

I took a few more sips of my drink. I was getting full, but there was the matter of dessert: a strawberry shortcake with fresh whipped cream was awaiting me, whenever the waiter cleared my plate. "No dessert?" I loved strawberries. And I loved being in that beautiful dining room, eating such a grown-up meal while the train powered across the country.

Pidge glanced in the direction of the waitstaff. "Only if you don't dilly-dally."

I'd barely taken my last bite of shortcake when Pidge pushed back from her chair. "Let's go, Beatrice. Others are waiting to eat." She reached for my elbow and practically dragged me to my feet, with more strength than I knew she had. My napkin fell from my lap onto the carpet.

I took one last longing look at the melted whipped cream and strawberry sauce waiting to be licked off my plate. I snatched the cherry from my drink, popped it into my mouth, and followed Pidge out of the dining room. I noticed that the maître d' had stepped away. Was that why we were dashing out of there?

Pidge led me to the adjacent lounge car. It was mostly empty, which surprised me except for the fact that it was nighttime by then and the incredible vistas passengers were promised to see along the rails were hidden by the velvety dark. *Ruth is right about this being the best time to visit.* A few couples sat in cushy chairs, playing cards or making use of the complimentary *Super Chief* stationery at the writing desk. Pidge and I made our way up the stairs to the Pleasure Dome on the upper level. There we reclined in two side-by-side chairs to look up at the stars. It made me dizzy—although maybe that was the fault of the Shirley Temple fizz that lingered in my pleasantly full stomach—to watch the night sky from a whizzing train. But it was so beautiful. The night was clear, and Pidge tried to point out constellations.

"I've never looked at the sky the same way, ever since she left." Pidge paused, interrupted by a yawn. "Now I always see the sky and wonder where Meelie is watching it from. Or if it's even nighttime, wherever she is." She leaned back and stared through the glass, her hand resting over her heart. I started to say something, punctuated with a hiccup, and Pidge made a soft shushing sound. "Let's just drink in the night, shall we?"

I curled up in my seat, staring overhead. Now that I was full, I felt warm and content and somewhat calmer than I had in a long time. Which didn't make much sense, as I was on a secret trip with my grandmother, and we were stowaways on a train, headed to Kansas to see my famous great-aunt who the world had assumed was dead for the past thirty years. But all that aside—right then, at that moment, I was enjoying myself. I was enjoying the uncertainty, even. I smiled up at the heavens.

Meelie. Could she be out there? Was she also on a train—or in a plane—somewhere, making her way to Atchison? I wasn't yet sure I totally believed that.

"Do you really think she's coming back?" I whispered to Pidge. But in the seat next to me, she snored lightly. Her mouth was open, face slack, and she looked much softer and kinder than when she was awake. I shifted in my seat in time with a shake of the train car. The valise was by Pidge's feet. It felt like the right place to pull out the next letter from Meelie.

*May 20, 1952*

*My Dear Pidge,*

*Today I've been remembering the flights that changed <u>everything</u>: my Atlantic crossings.*

*Right now I feel the way I did in the days*

leading up to them—like something big is about to happen.

When George asked me to be the first girl to fly across the "pond," how could I refuse such a shining adventure? But I hesitated to divulge my plans, and so you and Mother found out about the <u>Friendship</u>'s flight from the press! That was rotten of me, and I'm sure it hurt you both to not know what I was up to.

So as the pilots and I waited for the right conditions, I wrote a good-bye letter, just in case. "Hooray for the last grand adventure!

I wish I had won but it was worthwhile anyway . . ." I truly didn't know if I'd make it back. As I've said, the first hour we climbed up into the air was hands-down the most dangerous of my life. I barely moved until we reached altitude. Then Friendship sailed high over the sea, while I huddled in a fur-lined suit in between the fuel tanks, stealing their warmth. It was inky dark outside. I waited for dawn, with my nose pressed against the glass. Gliding over the ocean, from day to night and day again, felt like magic.

I'll never forget the sense of wonder.

Or the fear. The clouds became thick as divinity candy, blocking the ocean view below. Then we realized the radio no longer worked. I stared so hard, searching for land, that my eyes kept tricking me. The Atlantic was an almost unimaginable amount of ocean. According to our calculations, we should've crossed it already. Fuel was desperately low.

When we spotted an ocean liner, I dropped oranges tied up with a hastily scribbled note, begging for the ship to signal our location.

I missed my target and hope sank along with the oranges. I thought about the letter I'd written before taking off. There were so many more things I wished I'd said to my sister before a final good-bye.

But then, we saw tiny fishing boats. Ones so small they couldn't be far from land! I rejoiced. Soon we touched down in a field in Wales—you know the rest of the story.

I was proud of my _Friendship_ flight. But I didn't like that my entire career had been built around being a passenger, so years later

I took on a new adventure to justify all that attention. "Merely for the fun of it" is what I'd say, when asked why I was going to cross the Atlantic <u>all on my own</u>. But it was about more than fun; I had something to prove. And all I wished to do in the world was to be a vagabond—in the air.

For good luck, I took along an elephant-toe bracelet, because elephants always remind me of Ellie and you. I should've brought old Donk, too, to tuck under my arm at tense moments. The flight was dangerous, and it required courage.

The first few hours were uneventful, but at 12000 feet and with moonlight dancing across the sea below, the altimeter failed me. I felt not horror, but awe at being alone with the stars.

Then fear became my companion. A lightning storm—dazzling but terrifying—lit up the sky. Next, a seam of the plane parted due to a bad weld. I started to feel the slightest bit cursed. The plane began vibrating, but I flew on . . . into clouds that built up ice on the windscreen and sent me into a spin, toward the midnight-blue waters. When I righted the plane, I could see the foam of whitecaps. Pidge, disaster was that close.

Despite all the dramatics, I still had to rely on smelling salts to stay alert as the hours stretched. I flew low because I decided I'd rather drown than burn, if it came to that. Oh, how I hoped it wouldn't. Just when it seemed all might be lost, I spotted green. Ireland! Truly it was pure luck and divine providence that saved me that day—along with my own skill.

Lacking an airfield, I landed in a large pasture. Fortunately I didn't run over any innocent cows. I exited the plane with circles under my eyes and records freshly broken. Once the news hit stateside, I was flooded by telegrams: from the president, the Lindberghs, the British prime minister. Lady Astor's thankfully said I could borrow her nightgown (I'd packed very light). The only telegram I kept, though, was yours. WE KNEW YOU COULD DO IT AND NOW YOU HAVE STOP CHEERS CONGRATULATIONS MUCH LOVE MOTHER AND MURIEL. I never told you how much having my sister's support meant to me, Pidge—it meant the world. Truly.

Those two record-breaking flights were the most important, surely, of my career. One started my adventures, the other proved they were my _own_. I went up in the air because I love life and all it has to offer, every opportunity and adventure it can give. But that pursuit has kept me away, and alone, for far too long. When I return, I hope for some _shared_ adventures. After all, I can think of few things more important than my one and only sister.

Yet you won't be a "little sister" anymore.

I'll need to learn from you how things are nowadays. Pidge, please share your eyes with me. (I wish I'd spent more ink sharing mine with you, because in the air and on the ground wherever I landed, I saw wondrous things. But a typical big sister, I'd mostly nag you in whatever missives I sent during my flying days.) I truly look forward to seeing how you've piloted your own life, where your "flight path" has led you, and all the tricks you can teach me.

My love,

Meelie

I placed the letter on my lap. How funny that Meelie had hidden her travel plans from her family, just like Pidge and I were doing. Would my family be hurt when they found out? And I hadn't expected Meelie to describe being scared on her trips. I always kind of thought that brave people didn't feel afraid when they were doing their daring things. It made me feel better about my own nerves.

The train rattled and Pidge shifted in her seat. I folded the letter back into thirds and slipped it into its envelope. I reached for the valise next to Pidge's left foot, accidentally bumping her heel in the process. She let out a startled snort and sat up in her seat, groggy. "Playing footsie with me?"

"No, that was the valise. The train moved."

She rubbed at her eyes, which still held the haze of sleep. Pidge bent down and lifted the valise into her lap, toying with the latch. "Have you been reading them?"

I nodded. "Two more."

"Tomorrow you should finish the rest. It's hard for me to reread them all now, with my elderly eyes. And it's hard on my soul. If I didn't know that I'd be giving Meelie a hug again on Monday—I don't think I could bear to remember all those moments from our past. I can think of few things more important than my one and only sister." *Didn't Meelie write the same thing?* It was sweet that they felt the same way about each other—maybe bittersweet, considering how long they'd been apart.

Pidge reached over and patted my hand. "Use the letters to get to know Meelie. Before you have the pleasure of meeting her yourself." She smiled at me. "Also, I'm very pleased that you're a curious girl."

I smiled back, although hearing her praise also made a lump rise in my throat. I swallowed hard and looked skyward, thinking about Amelia's words. A pale moon shone down on whatever terrain was outside the Pleasure Dome. I could still hear the chatter from the dining car and hushed conversations of people in the lounge below us, but stargazing through the glass I felt like Amelia might have on the *Friendship*. In a way, I could see why she liked feeling alone with the stars. I felt a sense of wonder too. But I was also kind of happy that Pidge was next to me.

She yawned and nudged me. "Beatrice, I think we should probably find our bed."

"I suppose we should." Which would be its own adventure, considering our situation.

# SEVEN

## *Hide-and-Seek*

P idge stood at the door to a sleeper car, pressing her fingertips into her temples while trying to remember if it was the right one. "Yes—the 'Palm Leaf.' I think this is ours." I hadn't even noticed that the different sleeper cars had names. Maybe Julie was wrong about Pidge's forgetfulness problem.

The Palm Leaf's hallway was empty, so nobody saw us huddled outside our hideaway. It took Pidge a few tries to pry the door open and at first, I was worried that an attendant had locked us out. But it was simply that Pidge couldn't work the handle. I shifted on my feet, remembering when she'd swatted away my help earlier. Finally, she got it open on her own. "These aging hands," she clucked.

The roomette looked the same as we'd left it—our luggage piled on the rack, the curtains open to the moonlight, the chairs facing each other like we'd interrupted a conversation.

Hopefully that meant the porters still thought the room was empty.

"Should we make up the bed?" I yawned. Sleepiness had hit me all of a sudden, traveling through my body fast. My eyelids drooped and my feet ached to be off the floor.

"Yes, but I don't suppose we know how." Pidge rubbed again at the pale skin of her forehead.

"I'll figure it out."

Pidge smiled. "Good girl. We Earhart girls have always been the capable type." That sounded familiar—had Pidge told me that before? Or was that in a letter? She leaned back against the door, closing her eyes as she waited.

Right then, I really wished our adventure were a little more ordinary and we had someone to make up the bed for us. I took a deep breath and inched over to start fiddling with the chairs. It took some poking and prodding and indelicate yanking, but eventually I got them to slide into a bed shape. Pidge came up behind me with an armful of sheets and blankets she'd found in the closet cupboard by the door.

"Let's not be fussy, just arrange these good enough for us to sleep on," she said, spreading a sheet over the chair-bed and dropping a blanket at the foot of it.

"Are we going to fit all right?" The sleeping space was even narrower than I had expected.

She twitched her mouth from side to side in a long *hmm*. "It'll be cozy, that's for sure."

I reached into my knapsack for my toothbrush and paste, then pivoted to the tiny sink to brush the sugar off my teeth. I didn't even change into my nightgown first—I felt modest about undressing with Pidge in the room, and I didn't have the energy to hunt for it in my suitcase. Pidge didn't tell me I had to change out of my dress. Before she slipped out of her slacks and blouse and into a faded pair of women's dotted pajamas, I stepped into the toilet compartment and shut the door. There was barely enough room to stand inside, and it had a weird antiseptic smell, like at the doctor's office. After I came out and washed my hands in the fold-down sink, I climbed onto the far side of the bed, closest to the cold edge of the window. Pidge checked again that the door was latched, then crawled onto the bed next to me. We were so close that the tip of my nose pressed onto her bony shoulder blade. I scooted closer to the window, tugging more of the blanket to cover me.

Pidge fell asleep almost instantly. Her light snores punctuated the clack of the rails. *What if someone checks on the room and catches us while we are sleeping?* I lay awake, turned on my side so I could stare out the window. I wondered what kind of landscape we were hurtling past. I wondered what the people out there were like, what they did for a living. If they were happy.

If they, too, looked up at the stars and missed people. Reading the letters and listening to Pidge talk about Meelie unlocked a feeling I tried not to acknowledge most of the time—I missed my mom.

The rocking of the train made the bed feel like a cradle. It should have soothed me, but instead I missed her more. I squeezed my eyes shut and imagined being little again, with my mom sitting next to me while I fell asleep. She would have read with me for a while—as many chapters as I could beg of *Harriett the Spy* or *The Cricket in Times Square*. Or an old favorite, like *The Runaway Bunny*. Mom would smooth my hair and give me a kiss before turning out the light. How embarrassing is it that I still feel like I'm not ready to sleep without her tucking me in? Every now and then, Sally knocks on my door. When I open it, usually rolling my eyes, she says she wants to say good night. I thought about that for a few minutes. Maybe Sally feels as unsettled as I do with our hastily stitched-together family. Maybe Julie used to snuggle with her more at bedtime before they moved in with us.

In her letters, Meelie seemed to miss her sister so terribly. Part of me wished I were close enough to miss my stepsister like that.

I flipped over, without disturbing Pidge, and imagined what it would be like after our journey, when she and I were back in California—maybe even with Amelia. If we found her, which seemed like less of an *if* than it had this morning, before we left Sun City. Anyway, once my mom got past the whole leaving-without-telling-anyone part, and the stowaway stuff, I knew she'd be enthralled by our adventure. I'd sit down with her at the kitchen table, and I'd show her the pictures I'd taken on the trip. I'd let her read my adventure journal. We could work together on the exclusive she'd write about how Amelia was found again after thirty years. Then, the next time my mom wanted to whisk away to somewhere exotic or interesting or important, maybe I'd come along. I could picture it so clearly: The two of us, wearing matching blue jeans and jackets and dark sunglasses, deplaning in Washington, DC, or Saigon or Moscow. We'd both be clutching reporter's notebooks, and I'd have my camera.

Somehow, despite Pidge snuffling and snoring very close to me, I finally fell asleep. Deeply, although I was not fully rested when I woke up to nudges on my upper back. I peeked my eyes open—it was still dim outside, but you could tell that dawn was approaching. The edges of the sky were eager to turn to light. *Why is Pidge already up?*

"What is it?" I mumbled. I pulled the thin blanket over my shoulders and up to hit my chin, but then my feet poked out at the bottom. I tucked my knees to my chest, now that I was the only person lying on the bed and had the space to do so without sending my grandmother catapulting to the floor.

"Let's go watch the sunrise," Pidge said. "From the Pleasure Dome."

"We've barely slept." I pulled the blanket over my head at the expense of my bare legs.

"Beatrice, get up." The urgency in her voice told me watching the sunrise wasn't a lark.

I considered plugging my ears and trying to ignore her, but Pidge nudged my back again. She yanked on the blanket, and I shivered as it swept over my shoulders and arms.

That's when I heard a knock on the door. Perhaps it wasn't the first one—I had been sound asleep. Panic flashed across Pidge's face as she stood, ramrod straight. "Don't say anything," she whispered to me. I sat up, pulling my knees into my chest and my feet onto the bed.

Whoever it was knocked again. Did the handle jiggle? "Aren't you going to answer it?" I whispered.

Pidge raised a finger to her lips. Her jaw clenched. We waited for another knock, but it didn't come. Maybe it hadn't been a knock at all—maybe we'd only heard a noise from the tracks. The jiggle was the shaking of the train. If someone were going to come confront us for hiding in the roomette, I doubted that he would stop after two or three raps on the door. Perhaps the knocking was like the beneath-the-floorboards thumping in the story "The Tell-Tale Heart," a manifestation of our own guilt for trespassing.

I grabbed the blanket and tugged it around me like a shawl. "Can I go back to sleep?"

"We should stay alert," she said. "You can doze, and I'll sit and watch the sun come up."

Pidge leaned against the window, and I curled up next to her, rolling myself into a cocoon of bedding. But the knocking had unnerved me. I drifted in and out of sleep, catching glimpses of the fiery morning sun popping up over the hills outside. The landscape had changed overnight: gone were California's mountains and citrus groves now that we were in Arizona. I'd expected to see only desert: reddish dirt and those tall sand hills Pidge had told me about. Maybe cacti dotting the otherwise bare landscape. But this part of Arizona was rich with forests. Evergreen trees blanketed the hills in green. Pidge said they were ponderosa pines. Mountains in the distance were capped with snow. The sky was an impossible blue.

The trained stopped in Williams Junction. "This is where the Grand Canyon is. Have you seen it?" Pidge asked.

I shook my head no.

She clucked her tongue. "Wish we had time to hop off and

take a look. It's one of the wonders of the world. There's another train that connects here, takes you right to it."

By then the sun was all the way up, and the view was so nice that I was done with sleep. Still wrapped up in my cozy blanket cocoon, I hopped to the luggage rack and unzipped my knapsack. I took out my journals and my Brownie camera. I hopped back to my spot on the bed and stared through the viewfinder for a few minutes, waiting for the perfect shot. When I depressed the button, the light was hitting the train window in such a way that it cast halos on the edges. It made the thick forest outside look ablaze. The crisp sky was only dotted with cotton-puff clouds, a real change from the shroud of haze in Southern California that we call June gloom.

I was getting hungry, but I was enjoying the view too much to go in search of breakfast. So instead, I wrote. For once, I had more for my adventure journal.

> Last night, I stargazed through the glass ceiling of the Pleasure Dome. I had my first champagne (well, Shirley Temple) dinner, too. My grandmother told me I was a "capable Earhart girl." Just now I watched the sun rise over the mountains as we passed by

the Grand Canyon. This part of the country is beautiful.

I can't wait to see what's next.

In my worry journal, I focused on whether my parents would ground me forever once we got back to California. It's funny, but grounding seemed like a much worse punishment now that I knew that being far from home could be kind of exhilarating.

By the time the train departed Winslow, Arizona, I could hear the slam of other roomette doors and the thumps of people walking down the hallway, probably on their way to the dining car. My stomach growled. "Pidge, is it time for breakfast?"

"It'll be too busy right now," she said. "Why don't I give you a snack instead?" She slowly stood up and hobbled over to her suitcase—maybe the cold air in our compartment last night had stiffened her limbs. I had a few aches from sleeping curled up against the window. Pidge rooted through her pocketbook to produce a package of partially crushed crackers and a brown banana. "Will one of these tide you over? Oh!" She turned to me, a worried look on her face. "You know, digging through here I just realized I forgot to pack my pills. Well, nothing we can do about that."

"Are you going to be okay?" Julie had said to make sure she took her medicine. "What are they for?" Her arthritis, or something else?

Pidge waved her hand dismissively. "Eh, I don't really need them anyway." She reached back in her pocketbook and swiped around. "I also have this," she said, holding up a slightly squished Twinkie.

"Twinkies before breakfast?"

"She of the marshmallow sandwiches dares to judge?"

*She has a point.* I shrugged and took it from her. Although I was starting to crave a healthful meal, even the overspiced black bean stews my mother dreams up or the spaghetti Julie undercooks. Other than the steak dinner last night, I hadn't had a real solid meal since the one I'd eaten at Disneyland.

I finished the Twinkie and wanted to ask if she had another, but I decided I should wait. If I was starving at some later point in the trip, I'd rather not rely on the saltine crackers or the battered banana.

The train rattled along. I itched to change my clothes into something fresh—and into pants. Pidge hadn't worn a skirt since I met her, so I knew she'd approve. But I didn't want to change in front of her and I was afraid if I went into the toilet area to switch outfits, one of my limbs would wind up in the bowl. It was hard to maneuver in there. So I stayed in my wrinkled dress and stared out the window, watching the majestic landscape but from within a thick pane of glass. It looked hot outside, but the air-conditioning kept us an artificial and stale cool. My skin wouldn't stop getting goose-bumpy. I threw Neta's scarf over my shoulders. We had crossed over from Arizona into New Mexico, and now the landscape had the stereotypical desert look I'd expected. Red, dusty sand and clear blue sky as far as I could see. The sun bleached everything. I took out my Brownie camera and took more pictures, trying to figure out how to best frame it so the sky looked as wide and endless as it did in reality.

"You like taking pictures, don't you?"

I nodded. "They can tell stories, sometimes just as well as words." I was thinking of the magazine photos tacked all over my walls at home.

She nodded appreciatively. "My grandfather would like you saying that. He used to tell Meelie and me, 'Your eyes were given to you to see things and I want you to see and remember.' Meelie did a better job than I did of seeing the world. Wondrous things." That reminded me of Meelie's letter, and the idea of sharing your eyes. "I hope her memory's held up better too." Pidge laughed.

"I thought I'd take lots of pictures on this trip—to help me remember it. But I'm almost through a dozen exposures. I should slow down."

"Never!" Pidge shook her head. "We'll just have to stop and buy you more film."

My stomach made a growl so loud Pidge startled. "Maybe I'll go out and get a sandwich and a soda pop," I said, standing up. "I'd like to stretch my legs."

Pidge yawned. "Isn't it nice to relax here, though?"

Perhaps her hesitancy to leave the roomette had something to do with the knocks earlier. But were we really safer from getting caught while we hid inside? Normally, the uncertainty of our situation would make me want to burrow into our space too. But some of Meelie's gumption was rubbing off on me. I didn't want to stay trapped in our compartment. I wanted real food, and a chance to explore the train on my own. "You can stay here," I said slowly. "I am perfectly fine going out by myself to get something to eat."

Pidge studied me for a few seconds. "Pick up lunch for both of us, while you're at it." She fished around in her pocketbook and handed me some money. "I'll eat anything but baloney." I took the money, grabbed my Brownie, and scooted out the door. Pidge peeked her head out, whispering after me, "When you come back, knock three times so I know it's you!"

In the hall, I stopped to smooth down my matted hair and brush at the wrinkles in my dress. I looked a mess—like Sally when she woke up in the morning. Somehow she's able to get her hair standing up every which way, and she always manages to lose a sock in her bed. It makes me laugh to see her stumble out of her room, sleepy and silly, like she got caught up in a Beatlemania mob. I felt an odd pang, like I missed her. If I ever wrote her long letters like Meelie's, that would be a memory I'd include.

I gave up on fixing my hair and wobbled down the car. It felt weird to walk after being cooped up in the cold roomette for so long. I didn't want to go back to the dining room—I wasn't even sure I'd be allowed in without Pidge, and the way the waiter and maître d' stared at us last night was worrisome. I decided to head over to the *El Capitan* half of the train, where I could grab a couple of sandwiches from the lunch counter.

As the train rocked, I swayed into the sides of the hallway. I thought of Ruth's training wheels comment and smiled. Maybe I'd find her again. At the door to the transition car in between the two trains, I stopped. Through the narrow window, I could see where the gap was between the pieces that connected the cars. Below that, the slats of the track whipped by. I knew it was safe to cross over—people did it all the time. Ruth had said she walked the whole length of the train. I'd crossed between cars when we boarded and when we went for dinner the night before. It hadn't bothered me then, when I was walking double-time to keep up with Pidge's determined stride. But now that I was alone, I pictured myself slipping and falling to the track below.

*Think of Meelie up in the air. Flying all the way across the Atlantic. Being scared never stopped her, did it?* I took a deep breath and grabbed the handle. I took another breath, then yanked the door. It was heavy, and I struggled to slide it far enough open to squeeze myself through. My heart pounded as I leapt from one car to the next. The door into the next car was easier to open, thank goodness—I didn't have to wait precariously in the in-between. Once on the other side, I grinned, glancing back through the glass at the car I'd left. The big yellow sign reminded me: RESERVED FOR SLEEPING CAR PASSENGERS ONLY. I wondered why they didn't lock the door if they didn't want people crossing. Then, slightly breathless and strangely proud of myself, I skipped forward.

Moving through the other cars of the *El Capitan* was easier. I took my time walking through the upper level. Didn't Pidge say it was good to be curious? She wouldn't mind if it took me a while to get back. I scanned the car, looking for Ruth's braids. All the seats were full of travelers: men in business suits, college-age kids with long hair and love beads, a few soldiers in their military uniforms. I wondered if they were coming or going from war. I tried to act grown-up as I sauntered down the aisle, or at least like I had Ruth's confidence. People dozed, read newspapers, and stared out the windows while listening to the radio program playing. A few also stared at me, making me tug at my dress and try again to smooth my unruly hair. The train shook, and I bumped into a sleeping woman's seat. "Sorry!" I exclaimed, turning back.

"Bea!" I turned again to see Ruth a few rows ahead, waving at me from a seat near the window. I scurried up to her. She was sitting next to her dad, who was busily writing on a notepad. I wondered if he was working on a sermon or a speech. Ruth had paper out and a pencil in her hand too. "So you did go exploring—good for you!"

I grinned. "Yes—and I took your other advice. Looking at the stars through the observation car last night was wonderful." Ruth beamed. "I'm on my way to pick up lunch. Would you like to join me?"

"Absolutely, I could stretch my legs. Can I get you anything, Dad?"

"A cola would be divine." He reached into his wallet and handed Ruth a few bills. "Nice to see you again, Bea," he said as she stood up to join me.

It was easier crossing into the lounge car with Ruth in front of me, clearing the gap not in a tentative step but with an experienced hop. In the lounge car, we patiently waited at the lunch counter to order our food while I told her about my dinner the night before.

"I didn't realize you're on the *Super Chief*. That's fancy," she said.

My face flushed, knowing the secret of how Pidge and I were on board that train. I grabbed for the cardboard box holding my two turkey sandwiches and two root beers. I didn't know if Pidge would like the soda, but coffee would be treacherous to carry back. "It's nice, sure." I nervously twisted open one of the bottles, thinking of how to change the subject.

"Did you forget? You shouldn't walk around with an open bottle full of soda if you don't want to spill."

"Oh. Well, in that case—do you want to grab a seat for a minute? I don't think my grandmother would mind if I ate with you instead of back in our roomette."

"Sure!" Ruth gestured to an empty table, and we raced over. We both slid right next to the window on opposite sides. I hastily unwrapped my sandwich—I was starving.

"So if you're traveling with your grandmother, where's the rest of your family?"

I swallowed the huge bite I'd taken. "My dad and stepmom and stepsister are back in Los Angeles. My mom's out in New Jersey, I think."

Ruth's eyes widened. "You don't know where she is?"

"It's not like that," I said quickly. "She's reporting for a magazine, and they sent her out there for a story."

"Oh, okay." Ruth looked relieved. "It's funny that both our parents write, but in different ways."

"Yeah, but you're lucky that you get to go along with your dad on his trips," I said.

"Can't you travel along with your mom? At least in the summertime?"

"I haven't really been much a traveler before this, but . . . maybe sometime I will."

"You seem like a natural, honestly." Her compliment brought a blush to my cheeks. "Anyway, you're lucky you have a sister," Ruth said wistfully. "I only have older brothers. But I do have my cousins—I just wish I got to see them more."

"Yeah. It's hard being far away from family," I said. The words surprised me a little. I didn't mean Sally, though. I meant my mom.

I popped the last bite of my sandwich into my mouth. Ruth still had half of hers left. "I guess you were hungry," she laughed. "They don't feed you over on the *Super Chief*? I find that hard to believe."

*Well, not so much if you're a stowaway*, I thought. The train shifted and my Brownie, which was still slung over my shoulder, knocked against the table. I pulled it off and set it down in front of me for safekeeping, and that gave me an idea. "I wonder if we could get a picture of us together."

Ruth brightened. "I'd love that!" Two women were leaving the table next to ours, and I shyly waved at them.

"Excuse me, would you mind taking our picture?"

"Not at all," one said. I handed her my camera and explained where to press.

"On the count of three: One, two, three—cheese!"

"Cheese!" Ruth and I grinned as the lady pressed the button and the flash popped.

"It's nice to make friends on the train," the lady said, handing the camera back to me.

"It certainly is," I agreed, smiling at Ruth. She grinned back at me.

I hated to leave, but Pidge might be wondering where I was. "I should probably head back before my grandmother gets worried."

Ruth nodded, crumpling up her sandwich's wrapper. "Say, I have an idea too: Since we both like to write, could I have your address? I thought we might exchange letters, let each other know how the rest of our travels go. I've become pen pals with other kids I've met on the train."

It would be like sharing our eyes with each other, as Meelie would say. "That's a swell idea! And maybe I could get a reprint of our picture and send it to you."

Ruth's face lit up in a way that reminded me of how Sally looks when I let her into my room to listen to records.

Before we said good-bye at the end of Ruth's car, I pulled out my worry notebook again and ripped out blank pages for us to write our addresses on. It seemed hopeful, to think I wouldn't need that paper to document my worries. We exchanged a quick hug and wished each other well, and then I started the long way back to the *Super Chief*. But when I got to the final door, there was a problem. With that cumbersome box of Pidge's food and what was left of my drink, I wasn't sure how I could pull the heavy handle and keep myself steady as I crossed over to the other side. It was one thing to bravely forge ahead when my hands were free to grip the sides of the streamliner—and another to do it while juggling a box of food and soda bottles, like a tightrope walker at the circus.

I summoned all my courage and pushed my way out of the *El Capitan* into the in between, wobbling as I inched over to the other car.

Then one problem turned into two. The door into the *Super Chief* was locked.

# EIGHT

## *Lamy*

I shifted the box of food to my hip, almost toppling one bottle of root beer, and with my free hand I wiggled the door handle again. My palms were sweaty and slippery. Through the gaps in the walkway, the tracks flashed silver as the train raced along. I winced with every bump and shake. *How am I going to get back inside?* Panic spread through my body like a shiver. The door hadn't been locked on the other side—but maybe that was because the people on the *Super Chief* didn't usually want to cross over to the *El Capitan*. I bet lots of the people cramped in coach seats would love a chance to stretch out below the glass of the Pleasure Dome.

The train rattled, and soda sloshed onto my dress, dripping down to my leg. Ruth had warned me to avoid walking with a full open bottle for that very reason. I pitched forward and bumped, hard, into the cold metal door. I lowered myself to the safety of a crouch—although being nearer to the gaps didn't feel secure at all. I was chewing on my lower lip and thinking of how I could possibly solve my problem when the door swung inward, and I tumbled partway inside, sprawling onto the *Super Chief* transition car. *Thank goodness.* By some miracle, the food wasn't all over the floor. I scrambled to stand up.

"Young lady, what exactly do you think you're doing?" An attendant scowled at me. I scowled right back—until I remembered I wasn't supposed to be there in the first place. My heart skipped a beat, or maybe it was only a particularly strong rattle of the train.

"Trying to get back to my grandmother." I spoke slowly. *Play it cool.* "She's very hungry and needs to eat." I lifted up the box of food.

"And why is she on a different train than you?"

"She's not," I blurted. "I went over to the *El Capitan* for the lunch counter. And"—I anticipated he might ask why I didn't get lunch on my own half—"because I was curious to see what the other train's like."

The attendant studied my face, like he was a human polygraph. Then he sighed, showing I must've passed his test. "Let me help you get settled in the right place." He motioned to the food box. "Hand me that, please?"

I clung to the sides of the soggy cardboard. "Thank you very much, but I think I'm fine now." I'd rather he didn't see where Pidge and I were hiding out.

"I insist," he said, not budging. Reluctantly, I handed him the box, and we walked down the aisle toward the roomette. Maybe it was the train's movement, but my legs were feeling like jelly. I swallowed hard, hoping that Pidge wouldn't be mad when I came back accompanied.

When we got to our door, I knocked three times, softly. Then I knocked again, loudly, hoping that Pidge would pick up on the fourth knock and realize it was a warning. The door rolled open to reveal my grandmother, thankfully no longer in her pajamas, standing with one hand on her hips. "No lunch? Then where have you been all this time? I worried that you got thrown off the train. And did you forget you were supposed to knock *three* times?" Then the attendant stepped into view, holding our food, and Pidge's mouth formed a speechless O.

"I had trouble getting back from the lounge car with our lunch." My voice trembled.

"I'll just set this down for you and be on my way," the attendant said crisply, moving past us and into the roomette. He scanned the sorry state of the tiny compartment, with the linens piled up on the bed and our suitcases half opened and a Twinkie wrapper crumpled on the floor. "Do you need assistance putting up the bed? I apologize no one has been by yet— that's unusual."

I clamped my hand over my mouth to stop a groan. *Unusual.*

He was going to figure out it was because we weren't supposed to be in there.

Pidge cleared her throat. "Oh, it's fine as is—I'm so eager to tuck into my lunch I'd rather not wait a second longer."

He narrowed his eyes as he nodded to her. I stood very quietly in the doorway while he placed the food down. With one last suspicious glance at our room, the attendant backed out to the hall. "Anything else I can do for you?"

"Accept our thanks for your assistance," Pidge said, her voice turning sugarier than the Twinkie.

He tipped his hat in our direction and headed down the aisle. I walked over to the window and sank onto the bed, as much as its firmness allowed for sinking. "Do you think . . ." I started, but trailed off. What was the point in asking? Of course they were on to us now.

She nudged the linens into a heap on the floor and plopped onto the bed next to me, rubbing at her temples. "I guess we'll see. Might as well enjoy this food in the meantime." She picked up her sandwich and unwrapped the wax paper, taking a bite. "Did you already eat?"

I nodded. "I ran into Ruth, so we grabbed a bite together."

"That's sweet." Pidge reached into her suitcase and pulled out another Twinkie. "The last of my secret stash. Here, dessert." She tossed it to me, then patted the blanket we were sitting on. "This reminds me of a picnic at Kinner Field." Despite my nervousness, I smiled. I liked that we were sharing a picnic like she and Meelie used to.

Pidge reached for the unspilled root beer, but struggled to twist off the cap. "Let me," I said. I grabbed the hem of my dress to help me twist and only then realized that it had acquired another large stain, either of root beer or possibly steak sauce, during last night's dinner. The bottlecap popped off and I handed the drink to Pidge.

"I'll change clothes after eating." No point in doing so before, because an errant gob of mayonnaise on my blue jeans would mean I would be down to one clean outfit. I'd packed light.

I had only started to unpeel the Twinkie wrapper when we heard a sharp and official-sounding knock on the roomette's door. Pidge squeezed her eyes shut for a second. "And I was *so* going to enjoy this cold root beer and sandwich." She offered me a halfhearted reassuring smile. "Follow my lead, darling. We're going to act confident. But first—pretend like you are trying to rearrange the bed."

She opened the door to the glowering conductor and launched into speaking. "Oh, perfect—I was hoping that nice attendant would send someone by. My granddaughter and I have tried like the dickens to make up the bed. Could you possibly help us? My back is aching something terrible, and I need a rest." Pidge all but batted her eyes at him, in some kind of old-lady charm offensive. I tugged at the sides of the chairs and blew my hair out of my eyes and tried to seem like I was not desperately nervous.

"Ma'am, could I have your name, please?"

Pidge paused, lips parted and eyes squinting. I could almost see the wheels turning in her head, spinning a plan.

He cleared his throat. "Because, well, no matter what your names are, we have a problem. This roomette is unoccupied," he huffed.

"Nonsense—the train of the stars never has a vacancy!" Pidge laughed, but it came out strained. "Anyway, clearly it *is* occupied, by my granddaughter and me. We are on our way to my hometown for a trip down memory lane. My . . . daughter-in-law booked the tickets. Oh, dear. Where did I put them?"

"Oh, no!" I exclaimed. "They weren't in that bag I threw out this morning, were they?" Behind the conductor's back, I winked.

Pidge, pleased, sneaked a wink back. "Perhaps my daughter-in-law has the ticket numbers written down, back at home."

The conductor was not buying what we were selling. "Ma'am, I hate to accuse you in front of your granddaughter, but I think you knew very well that there were no tickets, and that's why you ran out on your check at dinner last night."

I looked at Pidge, horrified. It had never occurred to me that we hadn't paid for our meal. Pidge stammered, "W-well, I—I never! I am so confused about what possibly can be happening here. There must be some mistake . . ." Her voice trailed off and my heart sank like Meelie's oranges in the Atlantic, realizing that Pidge was floundering. Or maybe she really was confused about the dodged bill?

The anger left the conductor's face and he looked more sad, or worse—embarrassed for us. "It pains me to do this, but I have to treat you two like any other stowaways. Please gather your things. We'll help you exit the train at the next station."

My face flushed with shame and guilt, and I felt sick. My chest became tight and airless. *What's going to happen to us?* In a moment, the trip had gone from an adventure to a complete and utter disaster. A quick glance out the window told me we were hurtling through the middle of nowhere—and how would we keep going from there?

It's funny, because I worried about so many things—things that didn't directly intrude on my life, like the war overseas or protests in far-off cities. Or things that were out of my control, like bombs that the Russians could drop on us. Now I felt fear with immediacy, and it made all the loose worries that usually roamed my brain seem, if not silly, then kind of pointless.

For a moment, I thought Pidge might argue with the conductor, try to convince him that he was wrong. She leaned forward, a determined look on her face, and I waited for the perfect excuse to come out of her mouth. But then she relented, resigned to whatever would happen next.

"Well, I'm certainly not going to tip for any help with our baggage."

We found ourselves marooned on the platform at Lamy, New Mexico, watching the train chug away from the station. The silver sides of the streamliner glinted in the hot desert sun. Pidge hugged the valise of letters to her chest, clinging like it was a life raft. I was sitting across the tops of my O'Nite bag and her suitcase, the knapsack and Pidge's pocketbook at my feet. I hadn't had time to change clothes, as it turned out. With my stained and wrinkled too-short dress and our hastily packed luggage—part of a white silk shirtsleeve dangled out of Pidge's suitcase like a flag of surrender—we must've looked like a real mess. It was 2:30 p.m. and the sun was high, and in the few minutes we'd been standing there, unsure what to do or where to go, I already felt like I'd started melting. Sweat beaded at my hairline and I could feel it running down my back. I could even smell the heat—like mud pies in Sally's Easy-Bake Oven.

In our frantic exit, I hadn't time to chug down the remainder of my root beer, and I thought longingly of it sitting in the cool metal roomette, now that my mouth felt dry with anxiety and thirst.

"I suppose we should head inside and get our bearings." Pidge's shoulders sloped, and the sureness in her step had disappeared—but we were walking across hot gravel, and she was wearing dress shoes.

I surveyed our surroundings before heading into the waiting room. There wasn't much to see, other than the rolling tawny hills, dotted with green desert shrubs. In the distance were more mountains. From what I could tell, the town consisted of the adobe-style train station and a dilapidated old hotel. The farther away the *Super Chief* got from us—now just a flash of silver in the distance, snaking away to Kansas—the more I felt like the whole world had left us behind in the desert.

I scurried inside, where Pidge had wandered over to a display rack with lots of pamphlets. No other passengers were in the waiting area, and the ticket window had been rolled to a close, probably since the train had already passed through. Pidge gathered a few brochures and motioned for me to join her at the seats. I dragged the suitcases along with me, scanning for a bathroom so I could finally change. Although I wasn't sure I could handle blue jeans in the middle of the desert. But I didn't see a bathroom—just a lonely pay phone in the far corner and a dust-covered vending machine.

"Good news first, or bad news?" Pidge asked.

"Can I skip the bad news altogether?"

"No, so I'll start with the good. We can hop a bus to Salina, Kansas. It's not too far from there to Atchison."

"So what's the bad news?"

"Bus doesn't leave from Lamy. We have to get to Santa Fe first."

Hearing her say "Lay-mee" distracted me for a minute—Sally sleeps with a stuffed lamb toy, which she calls "Lammy." Her version of Donk and Ellie, I guess. It's so overhugged that its curled fur is going bald. I shook my head to bring myself back to *this* Lamy. "How far away is that?"

"About eighteen miles. So we should get a move on."

I swallowed hard and willed myself not to think more about the left-behind root beer. "So there's another bus to get from here to Santa Fe?"

Pidge shook her head. "I'm afraid we're going to have to start on foot."

My mouth fell open, like when the hinge on my doll's jaw stopped working. "We're *walking* eighteen miles? In the *desert*?"

The look Pidge returned to me was the most unsettling I'd ever seen, because it was honest. She wasn't going to sugarcoat this for me. "Until something better comes along. Frankly, my dear, we don't have other options. Nor time to waste."

"But we have all this luggage." I tugged at the Peter Pan collar of my dress. The neckline felt tight all of a sudden.

"I know. We'll rest a lot," Pidge said, trying to soothe. "We'll be walking along a main road. Hopefully, some kind stranger will give us a lift."

"A stranger? Picking us up out in the desert?" My voice rose with panic.

"Or perhaps we'll find a nice place to stop on the way. You know, Meelie was flying across the country once, with a map pinned to her clothes—and a gust of Texas wind blew it clear out the window. Lost, she ended up landing in a little town in New Mexico. As in, she put her plane down on Main Street. Kind strangers gave her a good meal and a clean bed, and helped her take off in the morning. So Earhart travelers have luck with unexpected stops in this state." She stood up and stared out the window at the long road stretching into the desert. "Do you think you can do it, Beatrice? You have free will. I won't make you—but I don't know what else we can do, other than admit defeat." She held out her hands, palms up, like she was offering to help me to my feet. Pidge smiled at me, and as the skin around her steely eyes folded, I noticed the bags underneath. We hadn't gotten enough rest on the *Super Chief,* sharing that tiny, hard, cold bed and hiding out from the train crew. Now we were going to try to trek to Santa Fe? It did not seem like a good idea at all.

I eyed the pay phone in the back corner and sneaked my hand into my dress pocket, where a few coins lingered with a candy wrapper and some lint. I could walk over to that phone and dial home. I could call my dad and Julie, tell them to come out and collect us. I could call the operator and ask for the number to *Look* magazine and try to track down my mom.

Or I could go along with Pidge's plan, as foolhardy as it was becoming.

I think Pidge knew what I was considering. She didn't say anything but looked deep into my eyes. I saw hope and determination in hers. I remembered what Meelie had written to Pidge, and what Pidge had repeated to me.

*We Earhart girls have always been the capable type.*

I did want to be like that.

I thought about Amelia's story of all the things going wrong during her flight: a bad seam, icy storms, lost bearings. *Maybe snafus are just another part of having a grand adventure.* She kept on going, and we could too. I stood up without Pidge's offered help, and she folded her arms back against her chest—like I'd offended her by not letting her pull me up. But I was the young one, after all. "Can I take a minute to write something down in my journal, before we go?"

Pidge thought it over. "Just one minute. We need to be off the road by dark." The only way that would happen was if we were successful in hitching, or if we found a decent place to stay. But it was already midday on July 22–in fewer than forty-eight hours, we needed to be in Atchison. We didn't *have* a night to spend along the road to Santa Fe.

I pulled out my two notebooks. I did not know which one to write in about the experience of getting kicked off the train. (Nor the sinking feeling I got while watching the *Super Chief* fade away into the desert hills.) Now we were stranded. I pulsed with worry about what we'd find along the road, if we could get where we needed to go. If we'd find ourselves lost without a Lassie to come save us. Yet we were also at the start of another leg of this journey, and anything could happen next–including good things. But I had one minute, and I wasn't going to scribble down my feelings in both notebooks. I had to choose one.

I took a deep breath and went for adventure.

Starting off, I insisted on carrying both suitcases. Pidge shouldered my knapsack and her pocketbook and clutched the valise in her opposite hand. I also insisted that we spare enough change for two ice-cold sodas from the vending machine in the waiting room. I'd seen magazine pictures of Peter O'Toole acting in *Lawrence of Arabia*, so I feared the wild-eyed, desperate thirst you could get in a desert. It was hard to balance the bags and the soda, especially as the sweat beaded on the bottle and made my hand clammy.

Pidge grinned at me. "Weren't you fussing about being cooped up in that nice roomette? Well, now you've got the whole wide desert at your disposal." Comparing the two, I'd take the roomette. It was air-conditioned.

As we took the first steps on our way, Pidge turned back to me. "Beatrice, we have the runway of life stretching in front of us, with nowhere to go but the future." Hadn't I heard her say something like that before? *Maybe when we left Sun City, with Snooky.* It was actually not a runway but a highway, called the Old Lamy Trail. It looked like back in the day it could've been a cow trail—or a wagon one; I wasn't really sure if they ever kept cows in the desert. Scrubby green grass poked up from the dry dirt, in defiance of the blazing sun and heat. Occasionally a shrub dotted the roadside, like a permanent tumbleweed. There were no buildings around, just one long road reaching toward Santa Fe. The bright blue sky domed above us, dotted with high white clouds. I felt like I was at the edge of the world. It was marvelous. "Wait," I wheezed to Pidge, even though she was walking a few steps behind me. I set down the bags and the soda, my arms praising me for ridding the weight. If they felt that noodle-like after ten minutes of walking, I hated to think how they'd feel in an hour. Or several—we had a long, long way to go.

"What is it?" Pidge shifted uncomfortably. Her low heels must have hurt her feet. I was wearing new Keds sneakers, which had been white at the start of our trip but definitely weren't now that we were tromping through the desert dirt. I wasn't wearing socks, and I regretted that. Blisters were budding on both of my heels.

"I'm going to take a picture," I said. "May I have my bag?"

"Good job using those Earhart eyes to *see*." Pidge handed me my knapsack and sat balanced on the suitcase next to me. I rummaged around for my Brownie. I held it up to the sky, searching the viewfinder for the perfect image. I settled on taking a picture of the road unspooling in front of us. Then I took another of the spotted hills in the distance. "Okay, I'm ready."

It took Pidge a minute to force herself up. "I suppose it's not a good sign that I don't want to stand again." I nodded my head, which was starting to throb.

We walked in silence for a while, mesmerized by striking scenery. I felt so tiny and insignificant below the big sky. It was one of those things you can't think about too long or seriously—the vast space above us that goes on and on, seemingly forever. That's unsettling. I wondered how Amelia could have loved being up in those endless clouds, alone in an airplane. She must've loved it, if she made being in the sky the most important thing in her life.

*As soon as we left the ground, I knew I myself had to fly.*
*I'd die if I didn't.*

I wondered if that's how my mother felt about her travels and her writing.

Pidge interrupted the silence. "You come from a long line of walkers."

"You mean fliers?"

"That's a shorter line, of just Meelie. I was talking about your great-grandmother Amy. She was a pioneer in her own right. Do you know what record she set?"

I shook my head no.

"She was, oh, about twenty-one when she became the first woman to trek her way up Pike's Peak. Mother was always active—rode circus horses around and such. She raised Meelie and me in that spirit. She didn't want us sitting at home, pining for boys and sewing. She wanted us in bloomers, building a homemade roller coaster in the front yard." I remembered that detail from the letters.

"That's really neat," I said, wiping the sweat off my brow with the skin near my elbow. I'd have to note that in my journal. It was the sort of thing my mom would love to hear about. It was funny, thinking about all the women trailblazers in my family—except me and, now that I thought about it, Pidge. It's not that she'd spent her whole life sitting at home and listening to the radio, but she hadn't tried to fly around the world or climb a mountain. "Did you ever want to be the first at something?"

Pidge stopped in the road, shifting the valise from one hip to the other. "Well, no. Or maybe not *no*, exactly . . . It's just that Meelie was the one who did things like that. Not me. I was the second-born daughter. The ordinary one." I nodded in understanding. Oftentimes I felt ordinary too. Pidge pursed her lips, thinking. "Although, you know, Meelie never finished her college education. She may have gotten loads of honors over the years, and even taught at Purdue—but *I* was the one who earned a degree the old-fashioned way, sticking it out in a classroom for years."

"Hey, that's something." Pidge's accomplishment was more feasible—one you could do by reading lots of books and having a good attendance record—but less glamorous. Nobody plans a ticker-tape parade for someone who gets a college degree. But it's still something to be proud of.

*What would it be like to live the kind of life that leaves people in awe, like Meelie's?* I thought about telling people—Barbara or Ruth, or maybe even Sally—about the life I was living at that moment. Trekking through the desert on the way to find Amelia. I think they'd be pretty impressed.

"Ow!" I stopped short, dropping one of the suitcases. The soda bottle that was balanced in the crook of my arm slipped out and, in what felt like slow motion, I watched it fall. I winced as it hit the packed dirt on the side of the road and shattered, sending a bloom of soda into the air and onto the ground. I let go of the other suitcase. The second the handle left my palm, it burned with fatigue. The skin was red and tense from gripping it for so long. In a fit of frustration, I kicked at the dirt—only to remember that what had made me stop was something hard and sharp in my shoe.

I bent to check out my Keds. Pidge, next to me, sighed and gently stretched her neck. I yanked off my sneaker and shook it to find a pointy stone lodged in the sole. I plucked it out and threw it angrily next to the broken soda bottle. Instead of making a puddle, the spilled soda had seeped into the parched ground, leaving almost no trace. Now that it was gone, I felt terribly thirsty. I sank down into the dirt and fought against the tears of frustration welling in my eyes. *Don't cry—you don't have any fluids to spare.*

When my throat stopped feeling so clenched, I asked, "How far do you think we've walked?" The sun was getting lower in the sky, casting its light on the puffy clouds. It looked like we were walking into heaven.

"Perhaps a mile, maybe two." Pidge now pried off the cap on her soda and drank two sips. Then she passed it to me, bottle still two-thirds full, and said, "Drink up. *All* of it."

My first swig took half the remaining liquid. It was hard to stop from sucking down the rest immediately after my relieved *ahh*, but I wanted the soda to last. Didn't explorers and pioneers always ration? That was hard to do when the sun was so punishingly hot. Pidge panted next to me. "We're not going to get there before dark, are we?" I asked, feeling a turn in my stomach. This landscape was nothing like the suburban California I knew. There were no houses, no shopping centers, no churches or car washes dotting the road. Not even a streetlight. Just desert plants and dirt under a big open sky—one that could leave you feeling free or vulnerable, depending on the circumstances. In ours, I felt like an ant under a magnifying glass. I thought of Sally stomping on the bugs on our sidewalk and shuddered. I grabbed Neta's red scarf out of my knapsack and arranged it across my shoulders to protect them.

"Not on foot." Then, like an answer to Pidge's statement, I heard a rumble behind me. I turned, shading my eyes to peer down the road. Off in the distance, a car was heading our way. It was the first we'd seen since leaving the Lamy station.

I pointed to the car and said, "Maybe we won't be on foot anymore."

"Pure luck and divine providence," Pidge said. Another oddly familiar phrase.

We were saved—if that car had somebody good in it. My

stomach flipped again, like I was whirling around on the tea-cups back at Disneyland. Our choice was: stay out in the desert to desiccate, or flag down whoever was in that car. I wished, as I watched it slowly drive toward us, that I'd called home when we were in the train station—even if that was not the adventurous thing to do. I could imagine Julie's peppy voice answering the phone, gasping upon hearing our predicament. Then she'd tell me to stay right where I was while my dad figured out how to come fetch me. She'd tell me not to worry and maybe I'd believe her. But it was too late for that, and all I could do was watch the dust kicking up and wait for the car to reach us—and hope for the best.

# NINE

## Margo and the Rolling Stone

As it drew nearer, I could see that it wasn't just any old car—not a beat-up hatchback or a shiny truck—but a woody wagon. They're pretty common where I live, because surfers love them for taking their boards to and from the beach. But despite being around sand—of the desert variety—the sight of one emerging from the horizon was weird. Especially because this wagon's wood sides were covered by a rainbow of paint colors. As it got really close, I could see that there were actual rainbows painted on it and sunbeams, too.

Next to me, Pidge waved her arm out into the road when the wagon was about a hundred feet away. Her pants billowed in the breeze like sails. She stuck up her thumb, turning back to instruct me, "Now, don't forget to smile and look like the kind of passenger someone wouldn't mind picking up." I suppose I did have an anxious look on my face, and my arms were crossed tightly over my chest, like I was giving myself a reassuring hug. I'm sure the smile I forced looked more like a grimace. I felt a twinge of shame, for being such a square. *Come on, where's my inner Earhart?* I uncrossed my arms and waved.

The wagon slowed to a stop next to us. The person inside leaned over to the passenger window and rolled it down. It was a young woman, with tangled, dark wavy hair and big round sunglasses covering her eyes, which made her look kind of like an insect. "You gals need a ride?"

"That we do!" Pidge said, smiling. "We are trying to get to Santa Fe, over to the bus station. Would that be on your way?"

"It sure can be. I'm just tooling around." I heard the crank-jerk as the girl put the car into park, then she swung open the driver's side door and stepped out. She was wearing a long, colorful patchwork dress that reached to her ankles. Silver bracelets up and down her arms tinkled. She floated over to us and swooped the valise out of Pidge's hands. "Here, let me take that." She popped the trunk, then started pushing around the junk inside to make room for our bags. I carted over one suitcase and then the next, cradling them like babies in my arms because my palms were too raw to grasp the handles any longer. The girl was moving blankets, paint bottles, a tent pole, and some unidentifiable piece of macramé out of the way. Once our stuff was inside she slammed the trunk, which was painted

153

with psychedelic splotches and abstract flowers. "Hop on in."

I squeezed my way into the backseat, which was also littered with scraps of paper and brushes and swatches of fabric, pushing aside the stuff so I'd have a clean spot to sit, although my dress was so stained and sweat-soaked by that point that a dab or two of paint smearing on it seemed silly to worry about. Pidge sat down in front, and then the girl plopped into the driver's seat. She turned to Pidge. "I'm Margo. And this," she patted the dashboard lovingly, "is the Rolling Stone. I like to wander, so we don't gather no moss."

Pidge stuck out her hand for a shake. "Muriel," she said. "Back there is my granddaughter, Beatrice."

"You can call me Bea," I piped up. Just because Pidge called me by my full name didn't mean I wanted everyone else to. Pidge raised an eyebrow at me for correcting her but nodded with approval.

"Let's hit the road, Bea." Margo started the engine and the radio came on immediately, blasting a rock song. She fiddled with the dial to turn it down slightly. I stared out the window and inhaled the scents of patchouli and paint, which didn't smell all that bad together. I licked my lips, wishing that Margo had a bottle of soda or a canteen of water that I could drink. But she was already giving us a ride, so I didn't want to trouble her for more.

"Can I ask why you two were traipsing down the desert

highway with a whole lot of luggage? You seemed pretty jazzed to see me coming."

Pidge glanced back at me, as though she wanted to see if I was okay with her telling our story. "We had some trouble with our tickets on the *Super Chief*, and I'm afraid Lamy became our last stop. Quite unexpectedly."

Margo laughed. "I've heard that story before, but never from two nice ladies like you. Usually it's from a couple of freighthoppers."

"To be fair, we *were* kind of freighthopping," I said. Pidge turned her head sharply, but she didn't look mad that I'd confessed. Just surprised. I appreciated that—it's not how my dad and Julie would have reacted. If they wanted me to talk, they'd nudge me and say, "Bea, why don't you tell So-and-so about" whatever was being discussed. Otherwise, it was understood that I'd be seen and not heard. Sometimes, if Julie was relating something incorrectly, I'd try to jump into the conversation and correct her. But that did not go over very well. "Beatrice," she'd cluck, with the skin between her eyebrows pinching up in frustration, "it's not polite to interrupt." But Pidge, she treated me like an almost-equal.

"Are you kidding me?" Now Margo was really laughing. Her thick waves of hair shook back and forth. "You actually made it through the night? Where'd you sleep?"

155

"A roomette—it was empty, anyway."

"That's a gas. I'm surprised they didn't set you two up in the lounge car until your destination. Seems kinda harsh, stranding you in the desert like that."

"I certainly agree," Pidge said.

The radio changed to one of the new Beatles songs: "With a Little Help from My Friends." Barbara bought the record as soon as it came out, and all June we listened to it over and over again in my bedroom. I hummed along, thinking about how lucky Pidge and I were to have gotten Margo's help. If she hadn't been coming down that lonely road, who knows what we would've done. "Why are you driving out here?" I asked. Pidge, up front, nodded. I guess she also was curious.

"I'm a painter," Margo said with pride. "I've painted all over the place—forests in the east, cornfields in the Midwest. Mountains north of here. A friend of mine moved to a pad outside Santa Fe and asked if I wanted to come paint the deepest blues and reddest reds and grooviest sunsets I'd ever see. How could I say no?"

"I was wondering why your car is full of paint."

"I like to be ready whenever the inspiration strikes, so I take my supplies wherever I go. It's a tricky thing—if you wait too long, it'll disappear on you. Then you're left with a canvas and a brush and nothing to do with them."

"Are you going to stay out here in the desert?" I asked. "Like, permanently?"

Margo let her arm trail out the open window. "Not much longer. I'm supposed to start college in the fall. But I'm not sure I'm done wandering yet. I hear it's pretty choice in San Francisco this summer."

"My mother was there!" I exclaimed. "For the Be-In, and she went back this summer to report for a magazine."

"Yeah?" Margo glanced at me in the rearview mirror, nodding. "Sounds like your mom is pretty boss." I smiled. So many people thought it was strange that my mother had her career and spent so much time away. Sometimes I, too, wondered if there was something wrong with her—or me—because she wanted to follow stories so badly it took her away from our home. But maybe it was something to be proud of.

"I agree," Pidge said. Suddenly feeling bashful, I had to turn my head to look out the window to hide the magnitude of my grin.

The Rolling Stone cruised along the desert landscape. The sun was getting low in the sky. Margo's friend had been right: The sunset was really groovy. I riffled around in my knapsack for my Brownie.

"Margo, could you stop the car for a minute?"

"Why's that?" she asked, but while already pulling to a

stop. I liked that she didn't need to know everything before she did something, but kinda went with the flow.

"The clouds. I want to take a picture of them."

"I like the way you think. That sky is far out."

I stepped out of the car and squinted into the sun. I turned the camera horizontally, then vertically, looking for inspiration. Then a beam of sunlight made the glass of my camera sparkle, like there was magic at the edge of the frame. I snapped a picture.

Margo rummaged around in the trunk while Pidge waited inside. Pidge's eyes were closed, like she was trying to sneak a few minutes of shut-eye. How much rest had she been able to get the night before? It couldn't have been more than a few hours. A twinge of worry shot through me. I felt exhausted, and I was five and a half decades younger than Pidge. And she'd been without her medicine for almost a day now.

"Water?" Margo walked up next to me. I shoved my Brownie back into its case and practically tackled her for the jug she was holding out. I unscrewed the cap and took a long, delicious gulp. "Sorry I didn't ask sooner!" Margo said. "Considering where I found you two." She pulled another bottle out of the backseat and handed it up to Pidge, who drank greedily. Then Margo propped a piece of canvas onto the back of the wagon and grabbed a brush. She dipped it into a paint can that had been on the floor of the backseat and started swishing the brush around, covering the canvas in swirls of azure.

"I should put you in this picture." She squinted at me, smiling. With a dab on another brush, she drew a figure standing below the clouds, staring up at the sky. "Bea's sky," she said, admiringly. The painting didn't look realistic, but staring at it still felt like looking at something real. "They're both pretty choice." I blushed.

We waited a few minutes for the paint to dry, and Margo did some kind of stretching thing where she raised her arms up to salute the sun. I took deep breaths, savoring the scent of juniper and sunbaked pine, and watched the clouds. When we got back into the car, Pidge looked refreshed and the glass bottle was empty.

"So I'm taking you to the bus station?" Margo asked.

"That's right," said Pidge. "Trailways, I believe."

"Do you have enough for wherever you're going? Where *are* you going?"

I hadn't even thought about the money for bus fare. "Do we, Pidge?"

Margo added, "If you need me to spot you some cash—I like to help a fellow wanderer. It's good karma."

Pidge shook her head. "No, we'll have enough. And to answer your question: We're on our way to Kansas. Atchison."

"Kansas. Following the yellow brick road?" Margo asked,

sticking the key in the ignition and starting the engine.

"It's where I grew up. I thought it would be good for my granddaughter to lay eyes on the place. Stand on the banks of the Missouri with me. It's beautiful this time of year."

Margo nodded, and it spurred Pidge to keep talking. I wondered how many times Margo had picked up travelers wandering from the Lamy station—or travelers anywhere she and the Rolling Stone went—and got them to spill their stories with an understanding bob or two of her chin.

"We are also planning to meet someone there. My sister." Pidge weighed each word like the man at the deli counter weighed the sandwich meat, to get the perfect amount and not an ounce more or less on the butcher paper. "We've been estranged for a long time. Thirty years this summer. She . . ." Pidge paused for a moment. "My sister wrote me a letter, and it's brought us back together." I ached for Pidge to tell more, the whole story. That it was *Meelie* we were going to find and everything that meant. Margo seemed like the kind of person who wouldn't think we were crazy to go on this adventure but that we were pretty cool. But I knew the details about Amelia were Pidge's to tell, and she closed her mouth tight after that sentence, like she was afraid of any more of the truth spilling out.

"Thirty years." Margo let out a sigh. "That's heavy. But now this trip you two are on makes all the sense in the world."

160

# TEN

## Santa Fe

I t wasn't much longer before the road stopped being so solitary. We coasted down the hills into Santa Fe. I pulled out my camera and a few times called from the backseat for Margo to stop the Rolling Stone, so I could take more pictures.

"Do you know what time your bus rolls out?" Margo asked.

"Late," Pidge replied. "We're in no rush."

"Then you should do some sightseeing before you go. I could take you around, so you don't have to lug those suitcases. There's a market in the plaza on Saturdays, and it's outta sight."

"We'd really appreciate that," I blurted, before Pidge could answer. I didn't want her to turn Margo down, which she might do out of a sense of us being an inconvenience. I liked Margo— and I also wanted to check out the town. What if I never got back to Santa Fe? Like Margo had said, you had to experience things while you had the chance. My mother would agree. Meelie, too, probably.

The buildings in Santa Fe were like nothing I'd seen before—rounded adobe in white, tan, and desert red. They reminded me of something in between a sandcastle and the Mission-style houses you see in California. Some had blue-painted porches or planters of vibrant flowers. Margo had said that a lot of artists lived here, and I understood why. Santa Fe felt like a painting come to life. Pidge's manufactured community was called Sun City, but it felt kind of empty and cold. This was a real city of sunshine, vibrant and warm.

I hadn't been to that many *real* places. Sure, I knew my neighborhood in Burbank, and other places around Los Angeles, but I had seen little of the world yet aside from the pictures tacked on my bedroom wall. It seemed wrong that I'd walked through New Orleans Square in Disneyland but had never seen New Orleans; that before this trip, my only point of reference for the desert and the Wild West had been Frontierland. By the end of this trip, I'd have made it all the way to the middle of the country. I felt a burst of pride. I had Earhart eyes and now I was using them to see.

We drove to the downtown plaza, where an open-air market was still going on, despite it being near sundown. Farmers, artists, and vendors were selling their food and wares, and flute music drifted through the air. Margo stopped the Rolling Stone and we got out to stretch our legs. We'd parked next to a stand selling food, and before I even knew what I smelled, my mouth watered and my stomach begged with a growl. I walked closer to see what was tantalizing me. Some kind of puffy bread, served piping hot on plates. Pidge sidled up to me and took a deep breath. "Are you as hungry as I am?"

"Yes!" I practically shouted.

"What is this?" Pidge asked the woman dishing it up.

"Frybread. Dough we fry in oil—a Navajo recipe."

"It smells delicious. Could we have two pieces?"

The woman nodded and pushed two paper plates toward us. The oil from the bread had pooled in the center of the plate, smears dotting the rest. Pidge handed the woman some money with a shaky hand. I picked up her plate as well as mine.

We found a spot under a tree and sat down to eat and watch the crowd go by. There were Navajo craftspeople, artist types, farmers, hippies, and men in Western wear. After a few minutes, Margo joined us. "Cool, isn't it?"

I nodded, too busy inhaling my frybread to answer, but I agreed that the plaza was bright and beautiful. I wiped some of the oil off my fingers and pulled out my camera again, taking more pictures than I should have—I was nearing the end of the roll and we hadn't bought more film yet—but I couldn't help it. I shot the mountains beyond the city, the beautiful old Spanish churches, and the booths of food and art and jewelry in the plaza. I loved the colorful strings of chiles hanging like Christmas lights. I wanted to take a picture of the frybread to remember how wonderful it tasted, but a picture of half-eaten food seemed like a waste of film. I wished I had a way of capturing the smells—how my nose tickled from the frying food and the spices for sale—but since I didn't, I just took deep, long inhalations with my eyes closed.

We shuffled around the market stalls, after Pidge finally finished taking bites that were much daintier than mine. I didn't know quite what to make of Pidge's waxing and waning properness. She had a somewhat formal way of speaking, she kept her hair neat, and she always ate like someone important was watching. But she also only wore pants, wasn't averse to tramping through a dusty desert, and had set us off on a freighthopping and hitchhiking adventure. Those weren't things I usually thought of as "ladylike," which Julie had called her, unless you took the word to mean something other than mannerly and demure. My grandmother was made of delicate steel. Maybe *ladylike*, and Pidge, both could be all those things: lovely and tough.

We wandered the booths and tables spread with a bounty of trinkets and handicrafts. Margo examined some paintings, Pidge admired clay pots, but the jewelry caught my eye. One artist had beautiful pieces of turquoise laid out on a table, carved in almost every shape I could imagine: animals, stars, trees, people. A figure of a person playing a flute-like instrument. The turquoise was set in silver that caught the sunlight, making the table almost glow. I ran my fingertips over a few of the smooth, polished pieces, admiring how cool they felt despite the desert sun. And then I spotted the perfect one: an elephant on a thin silver chain. I held it in the palm of my hand. It reminded me of Pidge's Ellie. And the bracelet Meelie had worn on her Atlantic flight.

I squeezed the elephant tighter in my palm. "How much for this one?" I asked the man, snoozing lightly, sitting in a folding chair next to the table. He looked kind of like John Wayne.

He snorted as he jolted awake. "What? Oh, let me see . . . five dollars."

That was much more than I had. Five dollars could get you four movie tickets.

"Thank you." I reluctantly placed the bracelet back down, running the tip of my finger along the charm's edge before turning to walk away. But Pidge came up behind me.

"Did you find a treasure?"

I nodded. "I like that bracelet—the elephant. It reminds me"—I swallowed hard—"of Ellie."

Pidge's hand floated down to the edge of the table, either to steady herself or so she could touch the elephant. "Yes. It reminds me of that too."

Sunlight glinting drew my eye a few charms away, to a small silver donkey on a leather cord. "Look—there's a Donk!"

The vendor perked up, seeing that our interest was serious. He picked up the donkey bracelet and held it out to me. "What if I gave you *both* for five?" That was more reasonable—but I also knew that we had bus tickets to buy, not to mention food along the way. And where would we stay when we got to Atchison? Could we sleep in Pidge's old house? Or would we need a hotel—and what about our trip west, home to California? We had to get back quickly. At some point, Dad and Julie would realize that we weren't sitting on Pidge's scratchy couch in Sun City, watching *I Dream of Jeannie* and eating gumdrops. That would be a big problem.

"C'mon, it's a good deal," he said, his voice gruff like John Wayne's too. It snapped me back from my stream of worries. I patted my knapsack, thinking about the two dollars I had stashed inside.

But Pidge had already pulled her billfold out of her pocketbook. She freed four dollars from the sleeve and held them out. "We'll give you four, and that's our best and final offer." She smiled sweetly, so I did the same.

The seller harrumphed and snatched the elephant bracelet up from the table. I thought he was going to take it away, but then he grabbed the donkey and some tissue paper from a stack and wrapped the bracelets up in it. He shoved the tissue bundles into a small paper bag, which he swapped for the bills that Pidge was still holding out. "You ladies know how to drive a bargain."

We had barely thanked him and walked away from his stand before I had the tissue paper torn off and the elephant bracelet looped around my wrist. Pidge struggled to tie the donkey charm around hers. I stopped and took the ends of the leather, winding them into a secure knot. "Happy?" she asked.

I nodded, suddenly shy. This was the first real present I'd ever gotten from my grandmother—not a generic card and check, but a bracelet, with an elephant like the one she'd so loved. It had real meaning behind it, and a memory—of when we found it, together in Santa Fe, on our wild adventure.

Around the time the sun finished hiding itself behind the mountains, Margo dropped us at the Trailways bus station, on the outskirts of town. She seemed unsure about leaving us there. "The bus really leaves tonight? I don't want you crashing here."

Pidge nodded. "It absolutely does, and we're fine waiting for it. You've been so kind to us, Margo, but you should be on your way."

Margo nodded, glancing at the door into the station like she wanted to stroll in there and read the schedule for herself.

But she decided to trust Pidge, or at least take her word for it. "I'm so jazzed that what I thought was a mirage on the road turned out to be the two of you." Pidge held out her hand for Margo to shake, but Margo bypassed it and wrapped Pidge in a bear hug. It was stiff at first, but then Pidge let Margo's paint-stained arms press her close. "In my wildest dreams, I'll be half as cool as you when I'm old." I thought Pidge might be annoyed at being called old, but she smiled.

Next Margo hugged me, and I breathed in deeply the smell of paint and earth and patchouli. "Thanks, Margo." I kind of wished she were going to take the next leg with us. "Wait—could I take your picture?"

"Of course!" Margo leaned against the hood of the Rolling Stone, making a comically dramatic face. I held up my Brownie and waited until she cracked into one of her wide smiles before I took the picture. It might not turn out the best because of the after-dusk light, but at least I knew I'd captured Margo's vibrance.

"I was gonna give you that painting—*Bea's Sky*. But now I want to keep it for myself, to remember you and this beautiful afternoon. Is that okay?"

"Sure thing." I blushed at the thought that Margo wanted to remember me. "Hey, if you do come out to California—maybe you could visit us?"

"That would be real nice." Margo gave me another squeeze. "Write down your address and number for me, okay?" On a scrap of canvas, I did.

She piled our luggage on the curb and got into the wagon, tapping the horn in a friendly toot as she pulled away. Pidge and I stood, watching and waving. It wasn't until the Rolling Stone turned a corner and Margo was gone that I realized how chilly it had gotten. The sun had gone down, and my dress provided about as much warmth as fad paper clothing. Before we got on the bus, I'd change into jeans—although the thought of putting clean clothes on my dusty, sweaty body was kind of disgusting. I hadn't taken a bath since the night before we left Pidge's house. I wondered if I was starting to smell earthy like a desert artist girl too.

Pidge stared off in the direction Margo had gone. Then she wiped at her eyes and bent down to grab the valise. She slung her pocketbook over her shoulder and reached for her suitcase, grimacing. "Aging isn't for sissies," she sniffed, waving away my outstretched helping hand. "Come on, let's head inside." So I grabbed the rest of our things and, shivering, headed in from the desert night.

# ELEVEN

## *Pay Phone Home*

There was a line at the ticket counter but only a few people sat in the waiting room, quietly reading the newspaper or, in the case of one man, dozing in the avocado-colored plastic seats. I lugged my things over to a section of the waiting room that nobody else was in. It sounds silly, because we only knew her for a couple of hours, but I missed Margo. She'd been like sunshine in human form. I wondered if other people she'd met throughout her travels missed her too—if friends whom she'd made covered the country like dots on a map. That was a truth about her life in the Rolling Stone—Margo gathered no moss, but she still left an imprint on the landscape.

Pidge glanced at the line. "Why don't you sit with our things while I go fetch our tickets?" I wanted to go with her to make sure she actually bought them this time, but somebody needed to watch all our stuff, so I sat down. Pidge walked toward the counter. I never took my eyes off her.

A few minutes later, she triumphantly returned. "We have our tickets to Salina," she said, making a big show of tucking them into her pocketbook. Which wasn't necessary, as I'd already watched her hand over the money.

"How long will it take us to get from there to Atchison?" It was already past dusk on July 22, and we needed to be at Pidge's old house in the morning on July 24. That gave us fewer than forty-eight hours, and we were still in New Mexico. My geography wasn't the best, but I knew those states weren't right next to each other.

"It's close," she said, easing herself into the chair next to mine. "Slightly more than one hundred fifty miles. A three-hour drive, more or less."

"Isn't there a bus we can take directly to Atchison?"

"That's where we're going."

I frowned. "I thought you said the bus went to Salina."

"Does it?" Pidge rubbed her temples. She looked very tired. "Oh . . . you're right. It goes to Salina. All the way to Kansas City, in fact, which is closer but we didn't have quite enough for those tickets. We'll have to figure it out once we get to Salina. But I'm confident." She yawned.

*Figure it out once we get to Salina?* My heart sank. If we didn't have enough for a bus ticket to Kansas City, how were we going to have enough money to get us one hundred and fifty miles farther? I felt the coolness of the elephant bracelet pressing on my wrist. Maybe if I hadn't wanted it so badly, we'd have enough to get all the way to Atchison. I hoped my bracelet would give us good luck, like the elephant one that Meelie wore on her Atlantic flight.

Pidge must have noticed me toying with it, because she said, "Now, don't let that spoil your bracelet. I still love mine. Those four dollars wouldn't have made the difference, anyway. Also, I've pinched a few pennies so we can eat once we get there." Something caught her eye across the waiting room. "Say, why don't you take a dime and go phone your father? It's about time we checked in, or he'll get suspicious."

We grabbed all our bags and relocated our camp to the corner where the pay phone was, even though only two people were still waiting with us, and they hardly seemed like the type to steal suitcases from an older woman and her granddaughter. Pidge stood next to me, leaning up against the wall—in case Dad or Julie wanted to talk to her. As I slid the dime into the coin slot, she whispered, "Remember. We're in Sun City. Tell him we've been playing shuffleboard and that the phone line is still having some trouble." I nodded, suddenly unsure about making the call. I wasn't a good liar. I always got nervous and said too much.

The phone rang a few times before someone picked up.

"Hello?" It was Julie. She sounded frazzled, like she was in the middle of making dinner. Which, based on the time, she probably was.

When my parents had been together, we didn't make a big thing about dinner, mostly because my father wasn't home for it many nights and even when he was, my mother's cooking left a lot to be desired. He and I would try to saw through overcooked steak or neatly spoon gloppy potatoes onto our plates while my mother eyed the dishes like they were traitors in her battle to conquer the kitchen. After my parents divorced, if I was with my dad we would go to a restaurant like Pizza Prince, or maybe the Brown Derby for something special. When I was staying with my mom, she would make something simple like spaghetti and sauce from a can, or something complicated involving lentils and avocado that she read about in a health guide. Then we'd eat with our books at the chipped kitchen table, occasionally piping up with an interesting comment about what we'd just read.

But after my dad and Julie got married, Julie seemed to think an old-fashioned family dinner was the thing that would hold—or bring—the four of us together. In science class last year, we learned about mixtures. In a solution, one substance dissolves into another, like salt into water. A suspension is a mixture of a solid into a liquid—but you can separate the solid particles out, like sand and water. Then there are the things that simply cannot mix, like oil and water. You can combine them and shake up the container really well, and maybe for a minute or two it looks like they've come together nicely. But after a time, they'll separate back out. Anyway, Julie seemed to think that if we got enough togetherness we all could become a solution—and perhaps my dad, Julie, and Sally would. But I felt like I was always going to separate out, so I didn't need her to keep trying to combine us.

"Hi, Julie. I'm calling to say hello," I said. "Is my dad there?"

"Beatrice! I tried to phone you this afternoon. So the line is fixed now?"

Next to me, Pidge shook her head emphatically and mouthed, *"Neighbor's phone."*

I cleared my throat to prevent my voice from taking on a white-lie squeak. "There's still trouble with it. I'm actually calling from the neighbor's. We didn't want you to worry," I added for embellishment.

"Hmph. I should call down to the management office and let them have a piece of my mind—or call the phone company. This is not acceptable, considering what it costs . . ." Julie trailed off as I heard the kitchen timer ding in the background. I closed my eyes for a moment, picturing the cupboards and countertops. Julie had redone them after she and Sally moved in, and honestly I liked the new colors better—everything was cream and blue, and real homey-looking. When it was my mother's kitchen, the cupboards were a pea green that made all the food look unappetizing. Maybe that's part of why Mom had hated to cook. As I pictured the kitchen, I could almost smell the food Julie might be making right then. I had a yearning to be sitting in one of the dining room chairs, waiting to eat even if I would rush through the meal so I could hide out in my room with a book. "What's for dinner?" I asked, before realizing what I was saying into the receiver.

Julie laughed. "Chicken Kiev. Why, isn't your grandmother feeding you enough?"

Other than two Twinkies, the turkey sandwich, and the frybread, I hadn't eaten all day. I was subsisting mostly on the memory of a champagne dinner, and I was starving. But I couldn't admit that. "Of course she's feeding me well; I was just curious. Could I speak to my father?"

"One second." I heard Julie place down the phone and call for my dad. In between pangs of hunger, I felt an unexpected one of homesickness. I scanned the bus station waiting room. It was clean and safe, but I didn't want to sit in a hard plastic seat and eat snacks out of a vending machine or the battered banana in Pidge's purse. Now that the brilliant Southwest sun had gone down, the artificial light inside looked dingy and sad. I longed for a bed—*my* bed. In *my* room. Even if Sally would likely be banging on the door and bugging me while I was in it. I took a few deep breaths and tried to swallow the lump in my throat, before my father came to the phone. I didn't want him to hear the longing in my voice—although I wasn't sure he'd notice. He hadn't picked up on hardly any of my feelings since the wedding.

"Hello? Bea?" I turned away from Pidge, not wanting her to see the tears welling at the corners of my eyes. Suddenly, I felt so far away from everything and everyone familiar. Hearing my father's voice made me consider telling him the truth about where we were. I had to clench the elephant charm in my palm, to remind myself of all the reasons not to. Amelia. Adventure. Did I really want to slink back to the safety of home? I knew if I were there, I still wouldn't feel quite right.

"Hi, Dad," I said, smiling to convince myself I was happy. "We wanted to say hello." My voice cracked a little on that sentence.

"Are you having fun?"

"Mm-hmm." The fewer words, the better—until the lump left my throat.

"I took Sally for a spin on your old bike with the training

wheels today. She did great on it! Gosh, she reminded me of you as she wobbled down the street. Here I was sad that I thought those days were over, now that you're almost a teenager." *And now you're happy, because you have* Sally. *Meanwhile, now that I'm past training wheels, you don't know what to make of me.*

"Do you want to talk to your mother?" I whirled to face Pidge and held out the receiver. She tried to shake her head no, but it was too late. The lump in my throat was not going away. She grabbed the phone.

"Hello!" she chirped. Pidge sounded far less exhausted than she looked. "We are having a lovely time, visiting with each other." I tuned out while she talked, looking at the rack of road maps and pamphlets advertising things visitors could do in the area, like check out a dude ranch or pan for gold. I took deep breaths and convinced myself that I was simply tired and hungry. My father wasn't really replacing me. I didn't actually miss home. No way did I miss Sally. I tried to think of every single annoying thing she had done to me in our short history as stepsisters, to shake off my melancholy. Sally ripped a page out of the book I was reading when I wouldn't put it down to talk to her. She listened in on my telephone conversations with Barbara. She convinced Julie to buy her clothes to match mine. She always put the shampoo bottle back on the edge of the bathtub when it was empty—so the next person to try to use it wouldn't realize it was all gone until she was already wet in the tub.

"Beatrice, your father wants to talk to you again," Pidge motioned me back to her. The wave of homesickness had receded, so I picked up the phone and said with extra cheer, "Yes, Dad?" The line went quiet for a moment, and I could picture him scratching his beard. We didn't have that many conversations at home—when my dad got back from work, he liked to watch television programs or have a drink with Julie. If I was at the table doing schoolwork, he'd pat me on the head and ask, in passing, what I'd learned that day. But that was about it. Since I started junior high, my father often got a deer-in-the-headlights look around me. Like an almost-teenage girl was the most mystifying thing in the world to him. It's funny, but now that I was hundreds of miles away in the middle of an adventure, I wasn't sure what to say to him, either.

"I meant to tell you, your mother called earlier today. She wanted to know how to get ahold of you at your grandmother's. Seems like she's coming home soon—oh, hold on. I'm being interrupted. Here, Sally wants to talk to you."

"Wait! When's Mom coming home?" I couldn't wait to talk to her.

"Be-ah!" Sally sounded so excited to speak with me.

"Hi, Sally," I said, my voice as flat as the desert we'd driven through. Of course she interrupted what my dad was saying about my mom.

"Did you watch *Lassie* yesterday?" We usually watched it together.

"No, I missed it. Hey, listen—can you put my dad back on? It's important." But Sally kept chattering on about the episode. The pay phone began making the warning noise that I either needed to add more coins or end the call. I couldn't let it hang up on me midsentence—not when Julie was already fixated on Pidge's supposed telephone problems. When Sally came up for air, I jumped in. "Wow, so glad Timmy is safe. Anyway, I have to go. Good night."

"Bye! I slept in your bed last night," she said right as I was about to hang up the phone.

"What? No! Don't do that. You have your own bed." I rolled my eyes, even though she couldn't see me. Maybe my frustration would still transmit across the wires. "Good-bye," I said, smacking the handset back in the cradle. Only then did I realize I hadn't gotten to hear about my mom's plans. This was the problem with my new household. You couldn't get a word in edgewise.

"Sisters, right?" Pidge said to me, nodding knowingly. I let out a sigh. "I used to say—you can't live with 'em, you can't live without . . ." She stopped herself with a melancholy smile.

My heart panged for her, and I was reminded of something Meelie had written—that she used her letters home to nag Pidge, like a "typical" big sister. Well. Sometimes big sisters couldn't help but nag, when younger sisters did so very many annoying things.

But Meelie felt regret for that. So much that she was filling the precious pages she sent back with apologies and promises to be a better sister when they were together again. Pidge was racing across the country to find her. They'd not always gotten along—but now it seemed like they'd stop at nothing to be together again. I scratched at the dirt crusted on my arm. *Am I a caricature of a big sister? Am I being too hard on Sally?*

"Like I was saying," Pidge continued. "You *can* live without sisters, but I wouldn't recommend it."

# TWELVE

## The People Left Behind

The girl who had been sitting inside the ticket counter, filing her nails, packed up her things around nine. By then we were the only people left in the waiting room. She stopped in front of us, awkwardly, before she fled. "I'm not supposed to let anyone stay in here for the night," she said, and I couldn't tell if it was uncertainty in her voice or pity. "You ladies don't have anywhere to go?"

"Um, no?" I glanced at Pidge—she hadn't told me that the bus wasn't leaving till tomorrow. In fact, I remembered her telling Margo it left tonight.

Pidge blinked at the girl. "The Salina bus isn't coming?"

She shook her head. "That's first thing in the morning, ma'am."

"What?" My grandmother could be hard to read. I'd seen her talent at manipulating other people—including me, probably—which had gotten us this far. But Pidge wasn't faking this. She was really confused, pulling out the timetable like she could convince the girl otherwise and the bus would magically appear. She ran her finger down the times, her brow furrowed with the determination of being right, until she found the listing. "Oh. I—I must have misread the schedule." She sank back in her chair, looking defeated. And worried.

"Well, I can pretend I didn't see you still in here when I left. You don't seem like the type to cause any trouble." The girl bit her lower lip and reached a hand into her bag. "There's hardly anything decent to eat in the snack machine. Here." She held out a packet of aluminum foil. "Take my sandwich."

"Thanks," I said, beating Pidge to action, because I was afraid she'd be too prideful to take it and then I'd be hungry all night. The girl hurried out, like even going into desert chill was preferable to staying in the brightly lit waiting room with sad cases like us.

"Pidge, when does the bus to Salina actually leave?"

She took out the tickets and squinted at them, then studied the timetable again. "Not until six oh five tomorrow morning, I'm afraid." I didn't even bother to ask if we had enough money to find a motel for the night—clearly we would be camping out in the bus station.

Twenty-four hours earlier, if I had found myself in the same situation, I would've been a wreck. I probably would've raced back to that pay phone to call my family and beg them to rescue me from Pidge's crazy plan. But in the span of a day, something in me had changed. Camping out in the waiting room might not be comfortable, but it was a real, unique experience. I didn't entirely know what was ahead of us on this journey. But perhaps the nervous anticipation was part of its fun.

Pidge rubbed at her temples. "Headache. I thought getting out of the sun would fix it, but I guess I was wrong. I suppose it doesn't help that I forgot to pack some of my pills when we took off."

She'd already told me that. "Were those *important* pills?" She'd been without them for two days. Was some of the wear and tear Pidge was showing—circles under her eyes and trembling hands, and her confusion about the bus schedule—because of that?

"Oh, I'll be fine. They're mostly vitamins, I think. I don't *need* them." I wasn't sure I believed her. "More water should cure this headache." She took a sip from the paper cup she'd filled at the bubbler. "You know who really suffered from them," she continued, "was Meelie. She had sinus pain so bad she even had surgery for it. I asked her why she kept going up in the air, because the pressure made it worse. But she said flying was sometimes the only thing that made her feel better—despite the discomfort. Her attitude was always, if you want something, you go all out and get it, no matter the cost. But boy, were the costs high for her."

"Like what?"

"Well, the fact that she's been missing for thirty years, for starters." Pidge chuckled. "Other things too. She lost all her privacy. And she lost any time she ever had for me." Pidge looked down at her hands. "It's hard being someone's little sister, Beatrice. Don't ever forget that."

"It's hard being an older sister too. I mean, not that I really know."

Pidge looked up at me, her expression stern. "Of course you know."

"Sally isn't really—"

"Pish! She's your sister. I don't ever want to hear you say otherwise. I can think of few things more important than my one and only sister."

She'd said that before. Or I'd read it. I nodded, feeling bad for having upset her. But it was different with Sally and me. Right? Using my dirty foot, I slid the valise out from underneath her seat. "Can I read more about Meelie?" We had all night to kill.

"Sure. Read one aloud to me, why don't you? It'll refresh my memory for when we see her. I'm counting the hours." Eyes still closed, Pidge smiled.

I opened the flap and pulled out the next letter, carefully separated it from its tattered envelope, unfolded the thin paper, and began to read.

December 24, 1957

My Dear Pidge,

It's funny how time doesn't heal all wounds. It remedies some, for sure—but the scars of others will ache decades after you thought they had faded. It's Christmastime, although it doesn't feel like it where I am (Santa would be dripping sweat in that red suit). Christmas is about family, and I am lonely without mine today.

Memories of that holiday dance are also making me melancholy. You know the one: the church Twelfth Night party when we were teenagers. We'd so looked forward to it—stringing up the Christmas decorations and making marshmallows for the hot cocoa, which we hoped some young fellas would enjoy after escorting us home. Wearing our nice dresses—did I sew them out of old curtains? I can't remember now, although I do recall once turning old green silk curtains into a rather fine set of dresses for us. (A capable Earhart girl at work again!) We were simultaneously thrilled to go and terrified that once there, nobody would ask us to dance. At least we could count on a waltz with Father, after he escorted us to the church. He was such a fantastic waltzer—and maybe after seeing how effortlessly we floated across the dance floor with him, a boy or two would invite us out for a turn. The clock tick-tocked, occasionally chimed, and we waited. You twisted at the ribbon on your dress and I swatted your hand to stop. By then, we knew all too well what it meant when Father came home that late.

You were already quivering in your seat when we heard his footsteps, stumbling at the door. It had barely swung open—too hard, banging the wall—when you raced up the stairs in tears. I couldn't bear it either, Pidge, but I had a different way of showing it. I tore down our decorations. I threw the marshmallows into the trash. I ignored our father and the stench of drink. Even if it wasn't too late for the dance, we couldn't be escorted by him in such a lousy state. I went upstairs and lay in bed, trying to read. But later I could hear the sounds of the boys passing by our house on their merry way home from the party, and I thought about the marshmallows in the waste bin. My feelings overwhelmed me. I wanted to float up off my bed frame and into the sky. I wanted to be alone with the stars. I wanted to be free from that sadness and disappointment—truly, I wanted to fly away. Even if that meant leaving my sister.

Our family was peripatetic in those days, but while the moving made us disappear from a string of homes, we did not escape from our problems. I know now that I shouldn't have felt shame about Dad's illness, but I didn't know that then. That shame cast a shadow over everything else in my life. From the happy and fearless little tomboy who ran riot across the bluffs and riverbanks, I became "the girl in brown who walks alone." Memories of our early Kansas childhood, truly golden, made the darkened corners of adolescence so much worse. Those were hard years, for us both.

Yet I don't know that I would've done the things I did in my life without the sense of yearning I felt at that tender age. I don't mean to romanticize difficult times. But I

always had hope that something better would

come; another period of happiness _must_ come.

It was up to me to go forth and find it. I knew

I had to dare to live.

I'm sorry if to do so, I left you behind,

Pidge. That's why I'm writing you today.

I've had a lot of time to think—twenty years,

now!—and many of my imagined conversations

have been with you. I don't want to waste too

much time when we're back together again, so

in these letters I've been writing what I need

to say to make things right. Maybe this way we can pick up where we left off. Ride our horses into the sunset. Play a tune on my ukulele. Fall asleep with books in our hands.

For now—on a clear night, go outside and stare at the sky. Wait until after midnight. Stretch out your arms and lean back your head and look skyward. Then don't imagine me alone with the stars—imagine us up there together. Holding hands. Running through the constellations like we raced the fields along the bluff. Breathless and young and *bright-eyed and happy. Remember us like that.*

*And Pidge—my darling sister—remember*

*I love you so.*

*Meelie*

Pidge fell asleep midway through the letter, but I kept reading. Silently, though, because the letter seemed so personal, so private, that it felt wrong to give voice to her words—even in an empty bus station waiting room. I imagined Amelia's voice in my head: direct and strong, like Pidge's. They weren't as different as I'd thought. Like Meelie had said—or had it been Pidge? Their words were blending together in my head—both were the capable type. Meelie had been determined to go forth and find her happiness. Now Pidge was showing the same determination to find her sister. They were both daring.

I put it back in the valise, but that letter nagged at me. Meelie flew away, even though it meant leaving her little sister. She did so because she felt she had to. But what about Pidge? Left behind, left aching for her sister for three long decades. It wasn't fair. I found myself wishing that Meelie had chosen differently, somehow. That she had found a way to be happy without abandoning those who loved her. What Meelie wrote about the Christmas party they'd missed as girls—that must have been what Neta and Pidge had talked about in the car, how their childhood wasn't always easy and their father had "troubles." My heart hurt for Meelie and Pidge.

The thing that bothered me the most, though, was that when I pictured a younger Pidge feeling so sad, I pictured a girl who looked an awful lot like Sally. She and I had been through a lot, too, with our mixed-up family. And now here I was, flying away from her. At least she didn't yet know.

There was one letter left, but I didn't want to read it yet. Not in the dim, quiet waiting room. I put the valise back under Pidge's seat and pulled out my journals. In the adventure one, I wrote about Margo and the Rolling Stone, the tawny sage-scented hills of Santa Fe, and the clear desert sky.

Someday maybe I'll have a life like Margo's—or my mom's. I could crisscross the country searching for inspiration and experiences. In a cool car (but maybe a little cleaner than the Rolling Stone).

194

I can't wait to meet Meelie and
ask her about all the adventures she's
had. The ones we all know about and
the ones the last thirty years brought
her. She must've had more, wherever
she was. It wouldn't be right if Meelie
were living too quiet a life.

In my worry journal, I wrote about feeling hungry (despite
that sandwich) and wondering when the people back home
would realize we were gone and how we didn't yet have a way to
get from Salina to Atchison. Then I wrote something that really
surprised me, like the pen was moving all on its own and taking
my right hand along for the ride:

What if Dad and Julie decide they
like it better at home without me,
because they can make a solution
when I'm not part of the mixture?
Maybe Dad, Julie, and Sally actually
make a great family—on their own.
What would I do then? Mom is gone
half the time.

I stopped writing and chewed on the eraser end of my pen-cil. I had wondered a lot what it meant that my mom's pursuits took her away from me. She must feel about her reporting like Meelie did about flying. Maybe she was just daring to live. Now I knew from the letters that pursuing big dreams didn't mean you didn't care about the things—and people—you left behind.

Still, though, a worry was gnawing at me. I hadn't captured it on paper quite yet.

I know my parents love me. But
does anyone actually miss me right now?

As my pencil put the dot at the bottom of the question mark, the pipe-cleaner figures Sally had given me as a farewell popped into my mind. Sally surely did miss me. And that led me to the elusive worry.

Have I made a big mistake, by making
myself miss out on being Sally's sister?

# THIRTEEN

## Alone with the Stars

Eventually, lulled by the hum of the electricity, I fell asleep. Some time later, I woke with a jolt, perhaps because the wind rattled a door, or the sizzle of a large bug on one of the hot overhead lights had sparked me awake. Or maybe it was because all of a sudden I had sensed that I was alone in that bus station waiting room, mouth parted and eyes closed, buried in a dreamless sleep. I turned to see an empty seat next to me. The door to the washroom was open, telling me Pidge wasn't inside.

My first thought: *Where is Pidge?*

Followed by a barrage: *What if she's sick?*

*What if someone took her?*

*What if she* left *me here?*

Pidge's pocketbook rested in the hard plastic seat next to me. Our luggage, battered and dusty, was still neatly lined up at my feet, including the valise under the chair. *She'd never leave that for long.* A clock on the wall, much like the ones in every room of my school faraway in California, snapped the minute hand forward. The soda machine in the back, near the shuttered ticket window, hummed. Outside, I heard nothing—not a car engine's rumble, nor a train's rattle, nor a dog's bark. Not even the whistle of the wind. This was tumbleweed country, and I wondered for a second why I didn't hear the twang tune Westerns always used for a scene in a ghost town.

I stood up and rubbed my eyes. I didn't have another dime for a call on the pay phone—only the two dollar bills squirreled away in my knapsack for an emergency—and I wasn't even sure whom to call, if I had any change.

A light bulb flickered, and then the spooky theme song of *The Twilight Zone* popped into my head. Didn't horror shows like that always have aliens taking people away—when they were in places like the desert, where nobody was there to witness them? Or it could be something even weirder, like I was in another dimension now. I pressed my hand on the cover of my worry journal, still in my lap. The possibilities of what could have happened while I slept—a crescendo of scary scenarios—filled my imagination. But even though I longed to retreat to the safety of sleep, I had to make sure Pidge was okay.

The door clattered from the breeze, like it was telling me to head outside to find her. *Time to be brave.* Bea *brave.* I ran to it. I was still wearing my short dress—and no sweater. I rubbed my arms and my knees knocked together as I hunched in reaction to the chilly, dry desert air. It was so dark out, with only a few streetlights to lighten the inky night. I scanned the empty parking lot in front of the station. I wanted to call for Pidge, but if anyone was lurking, I didn't want to attract them.

I took a few hesitant steps onto the asphalt and away from the bright safety of the waiting room. I squinted to adjust to the light. I saw something—a figure, past the lot and in the middle of a dirt field. At first I thought I was looking at a scarecrow, because of how its blouse was waving in the wind. But then the cramp in my chest relaxed.

My grandmother was standing in the dark, arms outstretched. Feet planted solidly on the ground in their old-fashioned shoes. Her head was thrown back, and she stared up at the night sky. Starlight, and that lone streetlight, lit her silver chignon so it was shining. At first I wondered if she was sleepwalking. "Pidge!"

"Meelie!" She dropped her arms as she turned. "Meelie, it's you!" Pidge rubbed at her eyes, surprised to see me, like she'd forgotten I was waiting inside. Her smile grew so big. Did she really think I was her sister? How could she think that? I was a kid. And we were still in New Mexico. And it was the middle of the night.

"Pidge, it's Bea. Are you okay?"

"I—oh . . . Of course." Pidge's filthy pants billowed around her legs. "You startled me."

"Why are you out here?" I ran to her.

"I'm just saying hello," she said, her tone hazy. I thought again about those pills she had forgotten to pack. *Was* she getting confused without taking them? I stepped closer, and Pidge squeezed my hand in hers. I squeezed back but lightly—her skin felt frail, like tissue paper tasked with protecting bones. "I was promising Meelie we'll get there in time," she added. "You know, I still like to go flying with her."

Then I realized what was going on: She was *flying*, like Meelie had described them doing as girls, by standing tall and making their arms into wings. And in the last letter I'd read, Meelie had asked Pidge to try to fly again.

Pidge continued, "When I'm outside at night—it's funny, but I stop feeling so brokenhearted about it all. Sometimes . . . the wind picks up in ways that make me feel like she *must* hear me. Wherever Meelie is. I tell her things—like that I wish she'd never left." Pidge held my hand tighter. "I ask her to come back to me, if she's ready. Sometimes I beg her for, at the very least, another letter."

Pidge let go of my hand to point up. Now that my eyes had adjusted, I saw more of the stars and the shades of the night sky—dark violet and midnight blue, with gray swooshes of cloud. The desert wind was cold. I huddled closer to Pidge. "Meelie always talked about that feeling of being alone with the stars. It was beauty, she said, that lured her heavenward. But I don't think that's true. What brought her into the sky was that up there, she felt most content. She went from being the girl in brown who walks alone to being the girl who flies alone. I always wonder, though—was being alone really so much better than being with her sister?" Pidge lowered a trembling hand to her heart. Very quietly, she said, "There were so many people who loved her. I know she enjoyed some of the hullabaloo. But Meelie also loved her privacy. Maybe she simply didn't have enough Amelia for everyone. And she ran out of fuel."

Having all that attention—and having it all the time—must have been hard for Meelie. I thought about what Pidge had said—whether for Amelia, being alone was so much better than being with her sister. I swallowed hard, focusing on how many times in the letters Meelie told Pidge that she missed her and promised they could pick up where they left off. I'd found those words reassuring. "I think she always had enough fuel for you, Pidge," I said, very quietly.

She reached again for my hand and gave it a squeeze. I looked into her eyes to see if she seemed okay. They were ringed with wetness. "It's a terrible thing, to lose someone. Especially a sister. I have missed her every moment since I heard the news. Through everything else in our lives, we always had each other—from those days playing on the banks of the Missouri to her wild publicity tours. Meelie and Pidge were forever. I have to believe," she said, her voice wavering with force on *believe*, "we still are."

"I believe so too." As we stood below the stars, I tried to find Amelia in them. And every shivering part of me tensed with purpose as I sent a plea to her, or maybe just the universe: *Please, please come back to Pidge.*

Pidge rubbed my bare arms. "Come on, now. You're getting cold. Back inside." She started walking back to the station, taking her steps very carefully in the darkness. I hurried to catch up and hook my elbow with hers. The last thing we needed was to have to find a doctor for a twisted ankle—and pay for the treatment. It would be especially true if our path from Salina to Atchison were to involve any walking.

Pidge settled into her seat to nap, while I riffled through my suitcase for warmer clothes. Even if I hated to put them on over my layers of desert grime, I had no choice. I went into the bathroom first and tried to use paper towels and the sliver of green soap to clean off my limbs before shrugging into my blue jeans and a light sweater. I mostly just moved the dirt around, although the paper towel I used to wipe my feet and ankles was blackened by the time I threw it in the trash can. I'd probably have to change back into my dirty dress in the morning, when the sun came up and the desert felt like an oven again—but right then, it was wonderful to stop shivering. I curled up in my seat and put my knapsack under my head like a pillow, waiting for sleep. Until it came, I watched my grandmother rest. I had a funny feeling, like somehow I was responsible for her now. Even though Pidge snored lightly in the chair next to me, she still sat with perfect posture. I studied her face, imagining what Amelia would look like when—not if—we found her on Monday. Would she have the same cropped hairstyle as when she was last seen? Would she still be so slender and elegant? Or maybe during the intervening years—while living some mysterious alternate life—she would've become pudgy and grown out her hair. Would her face be wrinkled and leather-like from all that time up in the atmosphere, near the sun? Did she still wear all brown? If she'd hidden herself in plain sight all these years, she must not look the same. I pictured her and Pidge hugging as two old women. And as I did, a small smile passed across Pidge's sleeping face, like she was dreaming their reunion too.

# FOURTEEN

## On the Road Again

E xcuse me." Somebody kept poking at my elbow, interrupting the incredible dream I was having about pancakes and bacon. "Excuse me." I blinked my eyes open, cranky because I'd been about to pick up a dream-fork and take a big, delicious bite. A young man, who looked vaguely like one of the Beach Boys, was studying Pidge and me with a mixture of concern, pity, and disgust. I smoothed my hair and sat up, nudging Pidge out of her snores.

"Yes?" I asked. Early morning light trickled into the station. I wondered how long we'd slept—and wasn't the bus coming at 6:05? That was around sunrise. I felt a wave of panic at the possibility that we'd missed it. *Then* what would we do? I checked my wristwatch—it was five till six. We were safe.

"Have you been in here all night?"

"Um . . ." I wasn't sure what to say to the Beach Boy. If I admitted we had, would he throw us out before we could get on our bus? Report us to the police for loitering? But it must be obvious that, based on the sleep creases on our faces and rumpled clothes on our bodies, we hadn't just arrived.

"Of course not," Pidge said calmly. "We got here early for the bus because I was worried about us missing it. I guess we dozed off while waiting, though."

The guy looked at Pidge like he wasn't sure whether to believe her, but at the same time, she was his elder and she didn't look overly vagrant-like. "Somebody must have left the door open last night," he said. I guess we'd forgotten to lock it after we came in from "flying."

I nodded. "Yep, it was open." I really hoped we wouldn't be getting anyone in trouble by saying that.

"It happens." He shrugged. "Which bus are you taking?"

"The one to Salina."

"All right," he said. "It'll be here soon. Usually runs on time." He walked back to the ticket counter and took his seat inside. I stood up to stretch. I had an awful crick in my neck, from the unnatural position in which the plastic seat had caused me to sleep. Next to me, Pidge rubbed her eyes. She offered me a wan smile.

"I'm hungry, Pidge." That was an understatement. Since the dream of a breakfast feast hadn't been reality, now I felt the gnawing in my belly. I needed a real meal—not necessarily of a champagne-dinner magnitude, but something more substantial

205

than packaged cookies or crackers. I thought of Julie's Chicken Kiev and casseroles, and I could almost cry. Even memories of my mother's dry vegetarian "meat loaf" were tantalizing.

Pidge gave me a look of pure guilt as she reached for her coin purse. "You poor thing. Get as much as you want from the vending machine. As soon as we're to Salina—I *promise* you we'll stop for a real meal. But I don't think we have time now." As if to make her point for her, a wheezing brake noise outside the doors announced the arrival of a big silver bus. The Beach Boy motioned at me from the ticket counter, confirming it was ours. "Hurry," Pidge said. "Our chariot awaits. But get something chocolate for me. I believe in treating yourself, after a hard night."

The bus chugged out of the parking lot, half full of passengers. I'd watched them all come on board, since Pidge and I were the first to take our seats. There were a few young men in their military uniforms, duffel bags slung over their shoulders. Maybe they were going to Vietnam. Through the window, I could see that their loved ones waited and watched long after they stepped inside, wanting to stretch out that precious last glimpse before they headed away. There were a few college students with long hair, noses buried in books. Suntanned farm workers filled up more of the seats. A young family got on last, brother and sister in the middle of a battle of nudges.

The morning was still fresh, but in the aisle seat next to me, Pidge's eyes had already fluttered to a close. Her sudden grogginess worried me, but then again we hadn't gotten much rest. The circles under her eyes almost looked like shiners. The bus seats, compared to the plastic ones in the waiting room, felt like the cushiest imaginable. I sighed and leaned my head against the smudgy window, staring out at the passing view. I ate my sandwich crackers slowly, savoring each tiny bite. When they were all gone, I licked the tip of my index finger to gather up every last crumb and salt flake in the wrapper. I crumpled it and shoved it into my jeans pocket. Pidge hadn't finished the Hershey's bar I'd bought for her, and I eyed it sticking out of her pocketbook. But I wasn't about to steal food from my grandmother—especially when she was probably as hungry as I was. We'd decided to throw the blackened banana out once it started oozing in her pocketbook. And the saltines had been pulverized.

I watched the soldiers sitting quietly in their seats. One of them was eating a candy bar and when he saw me staring at it longingly, he insisted I take what was left. I gobbled it down. I listened to those kids start squabbling again and their mother's shushing. I pulled out *The Egypt Game* and read a few chapters. I dozed. I started writing a letter to Ruth, which read like fiction considering all that had happened in the twenty-four hours since we got kicked off the train. I studied a state map of Kansas that

I'd picked up inside the bus station, in case I needed to figure out where we were, or how to get where we were going. I learned that the state flower of Kansas was the sunflower and the state reptile was something called the ornate box turtle. I felt a little bad for the ordinary box turtles that they didn't get the honor. I flipped through a hotel brochure and imagined that we'd stayed there the night before: that I'd taken a long, hot bubble bath and washed off the travel grime before falling asleep in a big comfy bed. But the funny thing was, that scenario seemed kind of dull compared to how I'd actually spent the night.

The bus made a stop, and I ran out to use the filling station's grungy restroom. It was only slightly cooler inside the bus than it was under the sun, and my jeans were damp with sweat.

It smelled different outside, more like plants and less like sunbaked rocks. The landscape had changed—the scenic desert mountains of New Mexico had faded into the wide and open plains of Oklahoma, or maybe Kansas. I wasn't even sure which state we were in. Multicolor grasses waved below a big blue sky. I always thought the flat states in the middle of the country would be boring and ugly, but that was wrong. Maybe *I* was bored after being cooped up on the bus, but the views held unexpected beauty. I snapped a picture.

"Beatrice!" Pidge was leaning out of the bus door, waving to me. "Get back on here!" While I'd been staring at the scenery, everyone else had reboarded and the bus was about to leave. I raced up the steps and, blushing, took my seat.

Thick clouds filled up the sky after we started moving again. Occasionally we'd pass a small town or a farm, and I'd see people out working in the corn and wheat fields. I wondered what it would be like to live below such a huge sky, in a small house surrounded by acres and acres of crops and fields. The clouds broke up again to reveal bright blue.

The bus's motion lulled me into a feeling of calm, even though it was now July 23 and in fewer than twenty-four hours we needed to be at the house in Atchison, still far, far away. Next to me, Pidge drifted in and out of sleep. She'd snatched a copy of the Sunday *Santa Fe New Mexican* in the bus station before we left, and in between naps she'd read the whole thing. I checked out the headlines from the front page over her shoulder: stories about the war in Vietnam, a huge earthquake in Turkey, and more riots. I turned to stare out the window. How could the world be full of so many good and beautiful things—the Grand Canyon, the scent of juniper in the desert, Hershey's candy bars, people like Snooky and Ruth and Margo—and yet so full of pain and struggle at the same time? I didn't understand it. I pictured my mother, sitting down in front of her typewriter somewhere while working on her story. Maybe writing was her way of making sense of it all, and why she felt her work was so important.

We were hours into the trip and the bus was getting hotter still. I shifted in my seat. Pidge was snoring. Loudly. A woman catty-corner from us glared in our direction. I nudged Pidge a few times, trying to get her to shift so she'd stop with the snorting and snuffling. Eventually, she coughed, turned her head, and dozed quietly.

Watching the countryside roll by was making me feel slightly dizzy. I reached below the seat in front of Pidge to slide out the valise. There was one letter from Meelie left, and I couldn't wait any longer to read it. I pulled it out, then pushed the valise back under the seat.

*July 2, 1967*

*My Dear Pidge,*

*By the time this letter reaches your hands, I'll already be on my way. Home.*

*I can't divulge all the details now, but here's*

our plan: July 24. I'll meet you at the place I picture in my mind when I hear the word "home," and that's our grandparents' old house on the bluff in Atchison. Get there as close as you can to the sunrise, while the dew is still shining on the lawn.

It will be my seventieth birthday. Oh, remember the summer birthday parties we used to celebrate there, the air thick with the humidity and the scent of the river? Bees, flies, and mosquitoes buzzing around our heads as we sat in the sunshine and sang. Our family, happy together. These memories have also been my home, Pidge. I've spent a lot of time with them in the past thirty years.

Before my return, I must tell you a few things about when I left. It was a whirlwind leading up to my round-the-world flight. I'd flown the Atlantic, I'd flown the Pacific. I had more records than I could count and a message from President Roosevelt congratulating me on showing "even the 'doubting Thomases' that aviation is a science which cannot be limited to men only." I'm smiling with pride, remembering that.

Around that time you planned a dinner party with me as the guest of honor. You meant it as a nice, proud gesture, I'm sure—and a chance to spend time with me before I flew away. I canceled with no explanation. I realized too late the hurt that caused you. I'm sorry, Pidge. Under different circumstances, I would've loved a chance to share a meal with my sister. But I didn't want to sit at the head of the table and have to shine.

I never let myself appear fatigued in public, so perhaps you didn't know that I was exhausted. From both the fame and the flying.

Why did I need to keep going, then? Well, one reason was money. It had cost oodles to do all that vagabonding in the air. The book deal and endorsements from the round-the-world flight would have set me up well for the rest of my life. Who knows what my next adventure could've been. Often I dreamed of a quiet life with books, friends, California sunshine—and my sister. Although I didn't know if that would've been possible, given the level of celebrity I'd reached.

And so I prepared for this last grand adventure. Some of the plans you knew about. Some you didn't and still don't. It took months and months before I was ready to go. We delayed my departure and told everyone (including you) it was because of the weather, but that's not entirely true. In fact, there were very compelling, confidential reasons to create the delay—and change my route. Then when it was time to finally leave,

I crashed on takeoff. That should have been a sign, right?

But I never would've backed out, Pidge, and not just because if I didn't do it then my legacy would be one of failure instead of success. If I've learned anything, it's how important it is to be brave and to try to do the impossible, even when it feels like you can't.

So I made a second attempt. In Miami I said good-bye to my husband while sitting on the wing of my Electra airplane, holding his hand tight in mine. I really didn't believe I wouldn't hold his hand again, Pidge. Even though my plans were secret, my intent was never to disappear the way I did. Plans go awry.

If I could go back, I'd make sure you were on that runway with me. I'd give you a big hug and tell you that I'd see you later and that I was looking forward to my adventure. I'd urge you not to worry, even if it took me a while to get back. A long while.

But you can't change the past. The trip's

all a blur. More than the details, I mostly remember the huge effort, the mounting fatigue, and my deep sense of pride. Lae, in New Guinea, was the last stop before Howland Island (for refueling, although I'm sure I don't need to explain the details of that leg to you—the whole world came to know my itinerary inside and out after I disappeared). We were worried about weight, so my navigator and I boxed up plenty of things to ship back to the states—souvenirs, clothing we no longer needed, some writing. I even threw in my old lucky charm, that elephant-toe bracelet. But you know which two personal items I still kept with me? A jar of freckle cream and Donk, who stayed in the bottom of my flight bag. It was homesickness that made me pack her in the first place, and I didn't want her returning home without me.

Finally we left: two tired Americans, a couple of bags, my wooden donkey, and 1,000 gallons of fuel. Headed to a tiny speck in the middle of the Pacific, with absolutely no margin of error.

What amazes me now is how everyone assumed we'd make it there.

What really happened—consider it "classified." There are still secrets it's important to keep, and I don't want to have sacrificed these thirty years in vain. And things happened that day that took me by complete surprise. But I do want you to know that I _wasn't_ lost, and I didn't topple into the sea. It's true that I sometimes made mistakes (somewhere out there, Snooky is nodding in agreement), but I was a darn good aviator and that day, I was in complete control of my plane. (I hate the thought of people thinking that I, a woman pilot, couldn't handle the task.)

And that brings me to now. While flying that last grand adventure, the thought of "home" was my shining beacon. But home isn't a place for me any longer. It hasn't been for a long time. Now, home is a person: my sister. You. July 24 will come quickly, dear Pidge. We'll have another birthday celebration, back at my birthplace. Maybe *we'll go for a spin in the yard again. "Oh,*

*Pidge—it's just like flying!"*

*I can't wait to see you, sister. Soon.*

*All my love and more,*

*Meelie*

I placed the letter in my lap, wishing there were still more to read. I desperately wanted to know what had really happened on Meelie's last flight. Why didn't she make it to Howland Island? Where did she end up? And why had she been gone so very long?

When things veered off course for us—like the detour through Lamy—I'd felt like the whole trip was, well, up in the air. I was glad we'd never backed out on our plans, just like Meelie. Pidge and I were trying to do the impossible too. Even if I didn't have Pidge's steadfast faith in Meelie's return, I was not going to give up on the way to find her. No matter what happened.

"Here we are, folks, arriving in beautiful Salina, Kansas. Take a moment to collect your things, and please be careful exiting the bus."

Startled, I dropped the letter onto my lap. By my wrist-watch, it was four o'clock—but in Santa Fe. Kansas was an hour ahead. The bus had barely stopped on its way rattling across the plains, and we'd made it to Salina in just under ten hours. We had about fourteen left to make it another 160 miles to Atchison. Somehow.

I wished I could linger with the letter, but we hadn't a minute to spare. Next to me, Pidge was asleep, but no longer snoring like earlier. "Pidge," I said. "Time to get up. We're in Salina." I shoved my book and the letter into my knapsack.

Pidge didn't move, not even to blink open her eyes.

I tapped her lightly, feeling the sharpness of her shoulders through the thin silk. "Pidge!" I hissed. I glanced around to see if any other passengers were watching us—but most were busily gathering packages, with the few continuing on to Kansas City still reading or dozing in their seats. I nudged my grandmother again, harder this time. Concerned, I stuck my hand in front of her nostrils to see if I could feel her breath.

Pidge still didn't stir.

# FIFTEEN

## The Bon Voyage Diner

Pidge!" The urgency in my voice caught the attention of the driver, who was back inside after helping passengers exit with their luggage. He stared at us and then down at his passenger list. I pressed my hand to Pidge's cheek. Her skin was cold and felt clammy, or maybe it was that my palms were starting to sweat. But she *was* breathing. *What's wrong with her?* The bus would be pulling out of the station soon. "Oh, Pidge, please wake up." I closed my eyes and was slammed with a memory from the summer before my parents split up.

I'd known my other grandmother well. Grandma Anna lived nearby—she really was the little old lady from Pasadena—and she often came over to watch me while my mother met up with friends or worked on her writing or simply needed a break. Grandma Anna taught me how to bake meringues. She weeded our rose bushes. She braided my hair. And she told me stories about when my grandfather had fought in the South Pacific and had a pet monkey. I loved Grandma Anna. Sometimes I felt like I was a nuisance for my mother, an afterthought for my dad. But every time my grandma arrived at our house and stepped out of the car with her arms open wide, the look on her face was pure love for me.

I wish I'd had my camera the last time I watched her get out of the car, grinning and waving at me. I wish I'd captured that look. I just assumed that there would be a next visit, and then another. But one day while my mother and I were watching the evening news, the phone rang. My mom got up to answer it and crumpled to the floor. Then my father drove us to the hospital, where I looked at Grandma Anna one last time as she lay in the cold metal bed, still in this world but already having left it. She was breathing, but the rest of her was gone. As my mother wept next to me, I tried to mold my face into the same look of love my grandmother had always shown me. I squeezed her hand, even though I understood she would no longer squeeze back.

Nothing was quite the same after that. My mother slumped around the house for months. My dad said we needed to be patient. Eventually my mother found her way back to happiness, but it was by working all the time. Then the divorce happened, and my father met Julie.

On the bus, I squeezed Pidge's hand and, without really

thinking about it, I shared a Grandma Anna smile with her, one full of love. Pidge's right eye peeked open and then the left. "Shh," she said, smiling back at me sheepishly. *"Just play along with me."*

"Is there a problem?" The driver loomed in the aisle next to our seats.

"Aw, shucks," Pidge muttered under her breath. Confused, I looked back and forth between the two of them like watching a table tennis game.

"I seem to recall you two were disembarking at Salina—and I need to get this bus back on the road. You're making the other passengers late." The driver spoke politely, but I could tell he was annoyed by the way he tapped his foot and had his arms crossed tightly over his chest.

"I'm terribly sorry," Pidge said. "I fell asleep and haven't quite gotten my bearings. I'm a bit light-headed. Where is the bus headed next?"

"Kansas City," the driver said, switching the crossing of his arms.

"Perhaps we could stay on till then." Pidge smiled charmingly. By then, I understood what she was trying to do.

"Only if you bought a ticket for *Kansas City.* Which, I believe, you did not." His arms uncrossed and one swung down to grab the handle of Pidge's suitcase. "I'll help you with your things."

Pidge sighed and stood up, moving about as quickly as a watched pot boils. The driver clomped down the aisle, glancing back at us with an annoyed look. I grabbed my suitcase and knapsack and scurried after him. With her pocketbook tucked under her arm, Pidge followed me. My cheeks flamed with embarrassment as the other passengers watched us leave, but at the same time, I felt a strange sort of pride for Pidge's gumption.

Outside, the driver set the suitcase down and tipped his hat at us, more exasperated than polite. "Afternoon, ladies." He hopped up the steps and the bus door sighed shut after him. The engine rattled and the bus began to roll away. Pidge was staring at our luggage. "Wait," she said. "Wait!"

"What?" I shaded my eyes from the sun, trying to figure out what had her upset. "What is it?"

"They're on board!" was her anguished reply. "My letters!" At first I didn't understand what she was talking about. Letters *she'd* written someone?

Then my hand slapped over my open mouth. Two suitcases, one knapsack, one pocketbook. But no brown valise safeguarding Meelie's letters *to* Pidge. I could picture it perfectly—resting snugly under the seat in front of us.

"Wait, wait, wait!" I tore after the bus, which ambled toward the stop sign at the exit of the parking lot. "STOP!"

The turn signal was on, and it was waiting to pull out into the street.

I waved my arms wildly over my head, hollering, "Stop! We forgot something!"

But it was too late. They pulled away, even though one of the college students riding in the back had noticed my plight and appeared to be yelling up to the driver. I watched as the silver Trailways bus zipped down the street, then took a turn, and faded from our view.

I dropped to my knees. Tears rolled down my cheeks. Those letters were *everything*. And I forgot them.

"Darling, it's all right," Pidge said, gingerly lowering herself next to me. The seat of her light-colored slacks—the only part that wasn't already filthy—would surely smudge on the asphalt, but she didn't care. I wouldn't either. When your last ties to your long-lost sister are gone—who cares about dirt on your pants? "I've lost Meelie before." She looked up at the sky, squinting in the afternoon sun. "Anyway, tomorrow she can retell us everything in those letters, and more."

I sniffed back a few tears, and Pidge patted my shoulder. "I think you're very hungry. Am I right?" I managed a nod. I was *starving*. "Everything seems a lot worse when you're hungry. C'mon, let's go get something to eat. I see a diner across the street. Hear that? No more vending machines."

I smiled at that promise.

Pidge and I dragged our aching bodies and suitcases into the brightly light Bon Voyage Diner. "Bon Voyage" made me think of ocean liners, but the only sea out there in Kansas was one of sun-bleached corn. The waitress gave us a dirty look as we shuffled inside. Looking down at my wrinkled and sweat-stained clothes and Pidge's dirt smudges, I realized how bedraggled we'd become. We both looked like Pig-Pen from the Peanuts comic strip, minus a cloud of smelly dust around us. Or so I hoped. A lot had happened since my last bath.

Still, the waitress snatched menus out of the holder on the side of the host stand. "Two?" Pidge nodded. I caught a whiff of burger frying, a hint of pancake batter—and I thought I might not be able to keep myself from running toward the open kitchen and gobbling everything in sight. She led us past the soda fountain and I saw a girl sipping a strawberry milkshake, and a boy next to her with an egg cream. I wanted to vault over the counter and attack the freezer with a spoon.

The waitress slapped the menus onto the booth and walked away, her shoes squeaking on the linoleum floor. Pidge and I slid in on opposite sides. As soon as I opened the menu, I wanted everything. A hot beef sandwich. Waffle fries. Spinach pie. I'd even eat the diet plates: cottage cheese and canned fruit with Jell-O. Ooh, and a chocolate milkshake, and maybe a slice of lemon meringue pie. With a couple of scoops of orange sherbet on the side. I was practically drooling. But did we have enough money to eat?

"What's our budget, Pidge?"

"Good question, Beatrice." Pidge reached into her pocketbook and pulled out her billfold. I sat patiently as she struggled to open the small gold clasp on it, doing everything I could to not think about the food. *Glorious food.* Finally, I reached out my hand. "Can I help?"

Rather than seem annoyed at me—like she had earlier when I tried to help—Pidge smiled and handed over her wallet. She watched as I snapped it open in one try. "You loosened it, I guess," I offered. Whenever my mom used to struggle to open a jar and my dad had to pop off the lid, he'd claim that she'd gotten it loose for him.

"Nice of you to say that," Pidge said. "Now count the money, darling."

There were a few faded bills in the money sleeve—six dollars. In the attached coin purse, seventy-six cents. "All we have is in here?" Pidge nodded. I reached into my pants pocket and felt a dime. I pulled it out and added it to the pouch. "Six eighty-six." Then I remembered the two dollars stashed in my knapsack, pulled them out, and smacked them down on the tabletop. "Eight eighty-six! Total."

Pidge let out a whistle. "Well, that might be enough to get us to Atchison, if there's another bus." I stared hard at the menu. I could taste that sandwich. I could feel the spoon in my mouth and sherbet on my tongue. Pidge must have seen the desperate hunger on my face, because next she said, "But you are not skipping another meal. I know I can't go much farther on an empty stomach. Let's eat and figure out the damage later."

The waitress squeaked back to us, a scowl on her face. Maybe she could smell the dried sweat on me. "Ready to order?"

"I'd like a hot beef sandwich, with the waffle fries. Also some orange sherbet, please."

"Anything to drink?"

As much as I wanted the milkshake, I said, "I'll have an ice water."

"Okay." She perked up, now that she knew we weren't just ordering a cup of tea and a piece of toast. "For you?"

Pidge shut her menu. "I'll have a chicken-salad sandwich and a water as well."

"Coming right up." She spun on her heels and squeaked away. That was when I noticed the saltines in a small dish at the edge of the booth, next to the window. I snatched a packet and ripped off the plastic wrap, shoving the crackers into my mouth. Heaven. I licked cracker and salt crumbs off my lips and grabbed another. Then another. Pidge watched me, looking both entertained and guilty.

"Here," I mumbled through a mouthful of cracker, spraying crumbs into the air. "Eat some!" I spread a napkin on the table in between us and opened more packets, making a tower of crackers. Pidge picked up one and started nibbling.

"I have an idea," she said. "Of how we can get to Atchison."

I couldn't respond with my mouth full of saltines, so I nodded. Now that I was being fed, I felt up for anything.

Pidge continued, "You know, Meelie and I were quite the horsewomen. When we lived in Kansas and Iowa, we rode all over the place—on docile mares and wilder horses too." I did recall Meelie talking about riding horses together in one of her letters. Pidge continued, "Amelia was as fearless in a saddle as she was in a cockpit." She couldn't see from her vantage point, but when Pidge mentioned "Amelia" and "cockpit," the man sitting in the booth right behind us appeared to lower his newspaper and lean his ear toward her. But maybe I was just being suspicious. Pidge took a nibble at a cracker, unaware. "As a child I thought perhaps she'd race horses someday. Except as slight as she was, she was too tall to be a jockey. Anyway, even after airplanes caught Amelia's eye, she still loved riding." Pidge, reaching for another cracker, seemed to get lost in thought.

"Okay, but how is that going to get us to Atchison?"

Pidge snapped back to attention, losing the dreamy look in her eyes. "What was my idea . . ." She drummed her fingers on the tabletop, or tried to, but her drumming was soft and uneven. "That's it. I remember now. If we could get our hands on a couple of horses, we could ride to Atchison."

I put down the packet I was holding—the last one in the bowl. It was a plan, but I wasn't so sure it was a good one. For starters, I'd never ridden a horse, and while I liked the idea in theory, in practice horses were tall and unpredictable and had very large teeth, even if they only used them to chew hay and grasses. Who's to say they wouldn't accidentally take a bite out of a girl?

Then there was the fact that we would have to *get* horses. Without money, which meant that unless we found a pair of wild ones willing to let us saddle up and ride, we were going to have to come by them by other means. Like theft. Because who would loan a couple of horses to a tired elderly woman and a dirt-covered girl, for a one-way trip across Kansas? Maybe if we stumbled upon a horse-rearing hippie commune. But otherwise, nobody would let us near their stables.

While I was thinking over Pidge's plan and feeling bubbles of nerves stir in my stomach (or maybe that was the half-dozen packets of saltines I'd eaten on a very empty belly), she kept rambling on about Amelia. The man sitting at the next table turned to listen better. He had even pushed his plate of deviled eggs to the center of the table, like he didn't want the sound of chewing to make him miss a word Pidge was saying. *Why is he so interested in us?*

I tried to think of an inconspicuous way of warning her that we had an eavesdropper when the most wonderful thing happened: I heard the squeaks of our waitress's shoes, skimming across the floor from the kitchen to our booth. Her arms were loaded up with trays and plates. With a heaving sigh but in an effortless motion, she lowered everything to our table-top and pushed a plate with a chicken-salad sandwich toward Pidge and everything else to me. A big, hot, meaty open-faced sandwich. Mounds of waffle fries dusted with salt and shining with grease. And a huge bowl of orange sherbet, topped with whipped cream and a bright-red maraschino cherry. All of it followed by two sweating tumblers of ice water.

"Anything else I can get you at the moment?" she asked, one hand wiping her brow and the other reaching for a bottle of ketchup from an empty table.

I was too busy shoving fries into my mouth to answer. They were hot enough to burn, but I didn't care. Pidge shook her head and said, "No, thank you." She took a long swig of her water and let out a happy *ahh*. Then she started taking very deliberate bites of her sandwich, like she was trying to make it last.

"Want a fry?" I asked, holding one up.

"Of course," she said, snatching it. I went back to attacking my food. It all tasted amazing. But the sherbet was starting to melt—the whipped cream mountain was already deflating and swirling into the orange, and the cherry had toppled to the side of the dish. So I had to eat the rest of my meal backward.

I glanced behind Pidge. The man was back to looking at a newspaper. I got a funny idea suddenly—that he was there because of us. Maybe my father and Julie had realized that something was up and sent a private investigator out east to find us. Or maybe Pidge's whole story about meeting up with Meelie was a ruse, and she was really on the lam. Like the guy in *The Fugitive*. I tried to picture the slim and proper grandmother across from me as a jewel thief or a wanted criminal, and I almost choked on a bite when I started to giggle.

But the more I thought about the whole private investigator idea, the more it stopped being so funny. I gulped down the last spoonfuls of soupy sherbet. If my imagination was running away with me, and he wasn't a spy to track us down—well, maybe we should head off suspicions by making another phone call home.

I'd eaten so fast that my stomach was starting to hurt. The bowl of sherbet was licked clean, but I had plenty of fries and sandwich left. They could wait. "Pidge, I thought I might call my dad to check in," I said. "Can I have a dime?"

235

"Smart girl. I suppose it's high time for that." She pulled out her billfold, not bothering with the clasp herself this time but pushing it across the table to me. I took a dime out of the coin purse and stood up. I felt woozy from overeating and like someone needed to roll me over to the pay phone mounted to the wall in the entryway.

I dropped in my dime and dialed for my house. The phone only rang once before someone picked up. "Hello?" Over the static, I could hear the worry in my dad's voice. I wasn't expecting that.

"Hi, Dad," I said. "It's me, Bea."

"Beatrice!" He sighed with relief. "We've been trying to track you down."

*Oh, no*, I thought. *They know we're gone.* I swallowed hard. Was this the end of the adventure? "Really?" I wished Pidge were standing next to me to coach me through the call. I glanced back at our booth. That man was now leaning over the divider and excitedly talking to Pidge. I tried waving my free hand to get her to come over and rescue me, but she was too engaged in listening to him. I guess he wasn't a PI after all.

"Julie called the management office, and they said the phone should be working fine. That there haven't been any repairs for squirrel damage to the line. So why hasn't Pidge answered our calls? You need to tell me what's going on."

So he didn't know that we weren't in California, only that we weren't answering the phone. We hadn't been found out— and we could forge ahead toward whatever adventures awaited us on our way to Meelie. It was up to me, though: I had to figure out how to explain this situation. I curled the phone cord around my index finger. I wasn't like Pidge, so good at thinking on her feet. I didn't know what to say—and the wrong words could send us straight back to Sun City.

# SIXTEEN

## Serendipity

W e've been . . ." I paused, swallowing the uncertainty that made it hard to form the words. I was staring at a faded painting of sunflowers, hanging lopsided on the wall across from the pay phone. *Okay, that's it.* "Uh, we've been working in Pidge's yard a lot. Planting some flowers. Sunflowers," I added. That was the state flower of Kansas, after all. "Like she used to see as a girl, in Kansas?" I was so unsure of whether I was being convincing that my voice trailed up into a question.

"There's a drought, you know," my dad said. Then, his voice softening, "But it's nice that you've found an activity she enjoys."

I let out a big breath. "I enjoy it too." I wasn't talking about gardening, though.

"Why did she tell Julie that squirrels had chewed up the phone line?"

"Um, she thought they had. Someone came from the office

to check it out. But there wasn't a problem after all. You know how she sometimes gets confused . . ." I trailed off. I felt bad making Pidge seem feeble, but I knew she wouldn't care if it meant we got out of this jam. After all, she'd shared Meelie's philosophy on adventuring with me: If you want something, you go all out and get it, no matter the cost.

Dad was in the middle of asking me about Pidge's health when I heard muffled talking in the background. "Hang on, Sally wants to say hello to you."

I was actually relieved for the interruption. I didn't like lying to my father about our whereabouts. "Okay."

"Hi, Be-ah!"

"Hi, Sally."

"While you're gone, I made a surprise for you. In your room. I think you'll like it!"

Her voice bubbled with so much sweet enthusiasm, I couldn't get angry with her, even if the thought of her doing anything in my room aggravated me. "Sally, that's very nice, but you know my room is off-lim–" The phone beeped to let me know the call was almost up. "Listen, Sally–Can you put my dad back on? The pay phone is running out of money." As soon as I said it, I clamped my hand over my mouth. I was supposed to be calling from Pidge's kitchen, not a pay phone! Hopefully Sally wouldn't say anything.

"Fine." I waited for my dad to come back to the line.

"Beatrice? You still there?"

The warning beeps continued. "Yes, but I should get back outside to help."

"Good girl. Anyway, your mother wanted me to give you the number where you can reach her—she'll be flying back to California on Monday." My mother! Maybe I could use just one more dime to telephone her. Maybe I should tell her what was really going on, to shed some of the guilt I felt for lying to my dad. "Let's see, it's . . . where did I write that down? Okay, it's two oh one, five five five, four two oh six." I repeated the numbers in my head, so I could scribble them on a napkin back at the table. My dad continued, "Your mother wanted you to know—" The phone cut off the call. I could only hope my dad didn't try to call back at Pidge's house—where the ringing would go unanswered. It killed me not to hear what my mother had said. But if I called back, I'd have to explain why my calls kept getting cut short, and I couldn't use the squirrel-repairs excuse anymore.

I walked back to the table, slowly due to my overstuffed belly. I felt both proud that I'd talked our way out of being caught and terrible that I'd been lying to my father. Pidge was still talking to that man, which pricked up my nerves. Even though I had just worked hard to keep us going to Kansas, I felt a pinch of doubt about our current situation. Why did adventure and uncertainty have to go hand in hand?

"Beatrice! You will not believe who we have sitting next to us."

"Who?" I asked, narrowing my eyes as I assessed the man. Now that he wasn't eavesdropping, he seemed less suspect. Round and tanned and jolly-looking, he kind of resembled a warm-weather Santa Claus. His plate of deviled eggs had been replaced with a sandwich and a big slab of pie. I grabbed a crayon that was sticking out of the dish with sweeteners, jotted my mother's number down on a napkin, then shoved it into my jeans pocket.

"The name's Roscoe," the man said, sticking out his hand. I gave it a firm shake. "I had to introduce myself after I overheard pieces of your conversation—the bit about Amelia Earhart."

"Why's that?" I slid into my seat and, despite my fullness, started back in on my cold fries and sandwich. Who knew when and from where my next meal would come?

"I once had the pleasure of seeing your great-aunt fly!"

"Really?" I asked, excited. "When?"

"I was stationed in Honolulu, where she left from on her flight to Oakland. First person to cross the Pacific." He whistled slowly. "Boy, was I ever impressed. You know, my wife and I named our daughter, Amy, after her. One of these days I'll teach her to fly."

"That is delightful," Pidge said, smiling with a touch of sadness. "I'm sure my sister would have been proud to hear that."

"Why, thanks." Roscoe paused, opening and closing his mouth like he was trying to decide whether to say something. "I'm . . . awful sorry about what happened. Such a beautiful, brave soul. When I'm up there"—he gestured to the bright blue sky out the window—"I think about her often."

"Yes." Pidge nodded in agreement. "As do I, albeit on the ground." Pidge paused, leaning closer to Roscoe. "In fact, the trip we're on right now is related to my sister."

He raised an eyebrow. "You don't say?"

"We're heading back to Atchison to see the house Amelia and I grew up in. I want my granddaughter to know that part of my—and Amelia's—history. But unfortunately, we've run into a real pickle."

"That's a darn shame. How so?"

"We got on the wrong bus, and now we're stuck here. I'm afraid that I don't know how to get us the rest of the way." Pidge gave Roscoe a look so innocent and pleading, she might as well have batted her eyelashes. Suddenly I understood the real reason why we were conversing with him, and it wasn't Pidge's eagerness to talk to fans of Meelie. She wanted his help to get us home.

Roscoe thought for a minute before his twinkly eyes lit up even more. "This might be foolish, but I'll bring it up anyway.

242

It's a beautiful afternoon to travel and it wouldn't take long to skip you gals over to Atchison."

*Yes!* A smile blossomed on Pidge's face. "Why, thank you so much! We'd love it if you'd drive us there."

Roscoe laughed, shaking his head. "Not drive you—*fly* you! I have a plane, a little four-seater. Golly, I'm so honored to fly the sister and grandniece of Amelia Earhart. What a story!"

The triumphant relief on Pidge's face turned to horror. Solving our problem of how to get to Atchison was going to involve the one thing she said she would never do: Go up in the air.

Roscoe watched Pidge eagerly as she sat in stunned silence. I understood her feelings—it was how I'd felt on pretty much every part of our trip up to that point, having to decide whether to keep doing something that scared me or take the easy way out. So I stepped in to answer for us. "We would love to fly there with you."

We followed Roscoe out to his car—waddled, really, after all that food. He tossed our luggage into the trunk while I clambered into the backseat. Pidge sat down in the front, still silent. Despite all the sunshine we'd soaked up over the past two days, she suddenly looked very pale. From the backseat, I reached up and squeezed her shoulder. She raised her hand to cover mine with a soft pat.

Roscoe drove through Salina, telling us how he moved to town in the '50s to work at the Air Force base, and after it closed he started working part-time at a junkyard selling scrap and also part-time as a mechanic at the municipal airport. His plane was at a small airfield on the outskirts of town, near where he lived with his wife, June. She had a pie-baking business. His son was serving in Vietnam, piloting helicopters. Amy was attending college in town, and "a bit of a women's libber," according to Roscoe. But he said that with pride in his voice. Pidge responded to everything with an anxious grunt or a nod, so I had to chime in from the backseat to keep the conversation going.

Roscoe curled his hand into a fist and tapped his breastbone as we stopped at a crosswalk. "Hrm, danged indigestion. June would not be happy with me—she has me on a diet of cottage cheese and cantaloupe these days. Doctor says I have too much cholesterol. So sometimes after I finish up at the junkyard, I like to swing by the Bon Voyage Diner for a bite. Don't tell June, but there's nothing like their meringue pies. It's okay—my wife sticks to double-crust apple and berry pies. Once in a blue moon, she'll make a cream pie or pumpkin. But not lemon meringue. I keep those slices my little secret. Along with the patty melts and deviled eggs I eat there too."

Pidge offered a smile, but the edges of her mouth twitched

with nerves. "Your secret's safe with us. We've got some of our own. Right, Beatrice?"

From the backseat, I nodded. Why was she speaking about our secrets? Was she going to tell him about why we *really* needed to get to Atchison?

"Oh? Now if it has to do with Lady Lindy, I wish you'd share it with me. But I don't mean to pry."

Pidge nodded and sucked in a deep breath. "I have reason to believe my sister is alive. We're going to Atchison to find Amelia."

We hadn't told Snooky, or Ruth, or Margo, or even my own family. And Pidge just blurted our secret out to a perfect stranger like Roscoe?

Pidge continued, "I thought you should know. If you're flying us there." She nervously pulled and twisted the fabric of her loose pants. "Because this is more than a pleasure trip home to reminisce. It's a reunion—a rescue mission, in a way." My eyes about bugged out of my head. *I can't believe she told him!* Although, maybe Pidge telling Roscoe about our mission was a way of convincing herself that, yes, we *needed* to take this flight. Even if this was the thing that scared her the most.

Roscoe let out a low whistle. "Well, I'll be danged. You know, I always thought she was still alive. There was just no way . . . that close to home, she wouldn't *let* herself not make it all the way back. No, sir. Even if the plane went down in the Pacific, Amelia sure seemed like a woman who'd find her way back into the air. Can you tell me—" He coughed, sounding winded from the excitement of the news. "Can you tell me how you know? Have you seen her? Spoken with her? *Was she turned into a spy during the war?*" His eyes shined bright with the possibilities. "Say, did something happen to her like that plane in World War Two, the one that crashed and marooned soldiers in Shangri-La? Did she live on a desert island? Or in a jungle?"

Pidge shook her head. "I don't know. We've only communicated through letters I mysteriously receive—but they are letters full of things nobody but my sister could've written. She hasn't told me the whole story, only bits and pieces. Some of her words are even scribbled out, perhaps by someone else. I'd show them to you, but we lost them on our way here. Anyway, there must've been something very secret, and very important, to keep her away all those years." Pidge raised her chin in certainty. "There's no way she would've left me alone down here otherwise. Not Meelie. But soon enough, I'll hear the whole story. From her, in person."

Roscoe let out a low whistle. "Wowee. Here I thought I was just going to get myself some surreptitious pie and a sammie. Not help solve the mystery of Amelia Earhart."

*Beep BEEP!* Somebody behind us tapped out a warning that Roscoe had ignored the changing stoplight. He waved his right hand above his head in apology as we continued on. We were out of the town now, driving past acres and acres of green and golden wheat—crops unlike the citrus groves and avocado trees I was used to seeing in Southern California. I liked the look of the neat rows, the hearty stalks still undulating with the breeze and glistening in the late afternoon sunlight. It reminded me of a song we always sang in elementary school, "America the Beautiful," and the lyric about spacious skies and amber waves of grain. Now I could see how Midwestern farmland could inspire the opening lines for an anthem about the whole wide country.

"Well, here we are." Roscoe pulled the car onto a gravel driveway and up to a well-kept barn-like structure.

"Shouldn't we be at the airport?"

"Nope. I keep 'er in the hangar there, and the runway's right out back. Don't worry—we'll find a proper place to land in Atchison. I'm like what they used to call a barnstormer, I suppose. Although it's frowned upon these days—the officials want hobbyist pilots like me to fly in and out of municipal airports."

Roscoe was already out of the car and walking toward the hangar, telling Pidge and me to "have a rest and digest" for a few minutes while he got the plane ready. "Her name is the *Serendipity.*"

247

"How perfectly fitting," said Pidge.

While we waited, I joined Pidge in worrying.

I had been on an airplane once before, when was five and my parents and I flew out to Boston to see Pidge. That trip was the last time I'd seen her before this summer. I don't remember much about the flight—mostly the puffy white clouds like cotton candy. I had wanted to roll down the windows, like we were in my father's car, so I could touch them. My mother had laughed and explained that airplane windows must stay shut, which made me pout. My father had woken me up to see the mountains as we flew overhead, but I'd sleepily told him I'd look after my nap and curled back into my seat, to his great disappointment. I hadn't been afraid to be up in the air, but I don't remember being afraid of much when I was five, other than a neighbor's dog that snarled and snapped as I ran past its tether. Unlike now, when I had journals full of the many things that scared me.

Now that I was about to do it, I realized one of those things was going up in an airplane. I might have been less frightened if we were at the airport in Burbank, where I'd been a few times to pick my father up from business trips. The stewardesses paraded past in their cute uniforms, and the pilots tipped their caps to one another. Skycaps whisked luggage away. The travelers waited calmly in chairs, flipping through magazines and newspapers. They often were dapper and glamorous, people with rich or important lives waiting to go up in the air for a drink and meal and be over another state before they could wipe their mouths.

Anyway, at the Burbank airport there were official people all around, checking tickets and waving the planes here and there. The control tower used its bird's-eye view to keep everything in order. We were in an empty field, with nobody watching. What if something happened? I thought about the stories of Amelia and Snooky at Kinner Field and the times that they had trouble getting off–or staying off–the ground. Hitting a copse of trees, or worse. Who would know to rush into the wheat fields to save us if Roscoe botched takeoff?

I turned to Pidge, to ask if we should really be letting a stranger fly us across the state. Her eyes were closed and her hands were clasped together, like she was praying. I paused, tracing my fingertip along the edge of the backseat window. The clouds were high in the sky, as puffy and pretty as they were on my only other flight. But even though I was sitting in the backseat of a parked sedan, I already felt like I was up in the air, dipping and diving with the turbulence of my nerves. "Pidge?"

She turned to me. Her mouth, tight with fear, attempted a smile. Pidge looked like she needed a long nap and a solid meal—more solid than the sandwich she'd picked at while we sat at the Bon Voyage Diner. "I can't do this, Beatrice. I thought I could do anything to get back, but . . . not fly." She sucked in a breath like she was trying not to cry. "I'm so ashamed. Meelie once wrote that 'courage is the price.' And here I'm so close but I can't pay it."

After all the distance we'd traveled, this couldn't be where our journey ended. "No, Pidge," I said firmly. "You *can*. I'm also scared. But Meelie—and you—have taught me that's no reason not to keep going. I'm willing to be brave for this. You can be too!"

Pidge looked down at her hands, shaking her head. I continued, "Think of that telegram you sent Amelia when she landed across the Atlantic. 'I knew you could do it and now you have.' I know *you* can do this, Pidge. We might be almost out of money, but we can scrape up enough courage, between the both of us."

Pidge wiped at her eye, staring out the window. She took a deep, shuddery breath. Then she reached out and grabbed my hand. Squeezing it hard, she said, "All right. Let's be brave together."

# SEVENTEEN

## Courage Is the Price

Roscoe called us over not long after. His plane, he proudly explained, was a Cessna Skyhawk. It wasn't actually little, just a lot smaller than a jet. Outside, it was white with cheerily painted red stripes. The wings were placed over the top of the cockpit—or whatever the inside of the plane was called, since the front seat with the controls wasn't separate from the backseat. There was a cute propeller on the nose, which gave the plane a human face and, for some reason, made me think of someone sneezing. *Serendipity* looked friendly. That was a good sign. I took a deep breath and tried to take her at her name: a pleasant coincidence, like kismet. The sweat on my palms and trembling I felt inside were hard to ignore, though. To counter them, I focused on Meelie.

I climbed in, staying clear of the front seat because of all the dials, controls, and pedals. What if I bumped something and messed it up? Even though we were still on the ground, I buckled up tight. Pidge was about to follow me into the back-seat when Roscoe stopped her.

"Say, why don't you sit up front? Then I can tell all my pals that I had 'Earhart' as a copilot." He winked.

Pidge looked back at me. "Is that all right with you, Beatrice?"

It was probably for the best. Whether from nerves or excitement, I felt like I might throw up, and I didn't want to do that all over Pidge's pants—even if they were already covered in stains.

She sat down in the left front seat, and Roscoe finished up checking on things outside of the plane. I heard him bang a few parts, punctuated by his whistling. My stomach made a gurgle so loud that Pidge glanced back at me. I forced a smile. *Bea, brave.* I tried to imagine how wonderful it would feel when we were on the ground again—in Atchison. At long last and with time to spare.

Pidge leaned back, holding up her arm to show off her bracelet. "A lucky charm is a nice balm for frayed nerves." I grinned and raised my hand to show mine. "Although the best mascot is a good mechanic," she added. "You know, I used to work on my sister's planes, in the early days." Hadn't she already told me that? Or perhaps Meelie had written something similar. Pidge's stories and the letters blended together in my head.

Roscoe finally arranged himself in the pilot's seat. "Buckle up, gals," he said, in between breaths. He had a slight wheeze I hadn't noticed earlier. "That patty melt is not agreeing with me today," he said sheepishly. "Or perhaps the eggs." He let out a small burp. "Or pie." Pidge's cheeks flushed with embarrassment for him, or maybe nervousness.

Roscoe fiddled with some knobs and controls, and then the chortle of the engine started. The smell of airplane fuel filled my nose. I squeezed the elephant bracelet around my opposite wrist, and stared out the window at the ground. Suddenly I didn't want to leave it. But at the same time, I did. I thought of every beautiful thing that Amelia had said about flying. She had seen wondrous things in the air. She'd given her whole life to it—so being up there must be magical. I took deep breaths. *Courage is the price.* I was ready to pay it.

Then we were taxiing down the bumpy bare field, racing past tall stalks of wheat. I peeked into the front and saw Pidge clutch the edges of her seat, the skin of her knuckles white as the bones beneath. I felt us speed up and I squeezed my eyes shut, silently begging *please let us be safe please let us be safe please please please.* Then the rumble of the ground below the wheels stopped, and the bumping turned to the smoother shakiness of liftoff. I pried my eyes open and stared out the window at the fields waving good-bye below us, farther and farther away with every rickety second. The plane banked a few times, and the force of it either pushed me back into the seat or slid me from one side to the other.

"Wahoo!" Roscoe yelled back to me, grinning. The noise of the engine was loud. He was saying things into the radio—maybe to a control tower somewhere? But unless he leaned back in my direction, it was too noisy for me to make anything out. Pidge's head was turned so she could stare out the window. Her eyes glistened with tears. She closed them, and stopped clutching her seat to wipe them away. When she opened her eyes again, she caught me watching her.

"It is beautiful up here," she said, shouting so I could hear. "You should be looking out the window." She pointed out at the view. "Beatrice, I feel like I'm already with her." The tears came back to her eyes. I reached my hand up to grab hers, and I squeezed it. That stopped the lump in my throat from leading to tears of my own, but just barely.

I let go and turned to my window, pressing my nose to the cold glass. We were not as high as I had thought we'd be, and the clouds weren't below us. There weren't really any clouds, in fact—the evening was clear. The angle of the sun had fallen, and golden light cast into the plane. I looked down at houses, roads, trees, and fields. A small blue lake, glittering. I could see children playing at one edge, with a raft that looked like a doughnut. We passed over a big red barn with white trim.

I saw farm stands and mail trucks and land that looked like a patchwork quilt, with its neat square areas of different-colored crops. It was beautiful—overwhelmingly so. I'd never seen the world like this, from the viewpoint of a bird or a plane or a superhero. It was a funny thing—despite all the ugliness of war and injustice, up in the air, the world still looked like a perfect place, a utopia. Wondrous. *This must be what Amelia felt when she flew.* I could see how it made the hard things in life—like her dad's sickness—fade away, at least temporarily. I closed my eyes and imagined being alone up there. It was terrifying, but also exciting. I did feel kind of free. If we saw Amelia, *when* we saw her tomorrow—I would have so much to ask. I opened my eyes again.

At the controls, Roscoe took one hand away from the thing that steered, and rubbed at his chest again. Maybe he'd gotten a mosquito bite. I turned back to the window, not wanting to miss any more of the views.

I was in the middle of snapping a picture with my Brownie when the plane made a sudden jolt. I quickly looked to the front seat, but Roscoe seemed calm at the controls, and Pidge was still gazing out her window with rapture. I turned my attention back to world below us and marveled at the steeple of a small white church. A bird flew by the right-side wing. It was so close I could see its feathers.

Then the plane made a sudden dip.

I shrieked and slammed my hands down onto the seat, pressing to steady myself. *What is Roscoe doing up there?* Maybe he was stunting, some kind of maneuver to impress us. A figure eight or a loop-the-loop. The plane leveled off, and I leaned forward. "What was that?" Pidge had turned and was blocking my view of Roscoe. At the same moment, we realized what was going on, and our mouths dropped slack.

Roscoe's face was red as a ripe tomato. Beads of sweat had formed at his white hairline. His right hand was still clutching one of the controls; his left was clutching his chest. He let out a wheeze and struggled to get the words out. "I–think–I'm–sick." Then the plane took another dive, us screaming along with it.

# EIGHTEEN

## Brace Position

M y first thought, as we plummeted, was actually of Sally. I pictured her back in my bedroom, playing with my old dolls. Reading my other journals. Scratching up my favorite records. Replacing my Beatles poster with one of the Monkees, and pulling down all my magazine photos. Curling up on my bed with my books and smearing things on the pages. But I wasn't angry, imagining her like that. Sally would spend the rest of her life thinking about the stepsister she'd lost. She'd be like Pidge—years would add lines to her face but never erase the sadness behind her smile. Maybe someday she'd make a pilgrimage like ours, to this spot in Kansas where she lost her sister—or the closest she had to one. Unlike Pidge, Sally would know what had happened to me. But somehow I wasn't sure that would make any of it easier, and I felt a deep sadness for her.

But those thoughts of Sally filled my head for only a few

seconds. Then my attention snapped back to what was happening in the front seat. By then Roscoe had let go of the controls with both hands and was doubled over, grabbing at his midsection. *Serendipity* moved on her own, not downward, but unsteadily forward in the air. The wind, or something, buffeted the plane. "Take the controls!" Roscoe grunted, in between moans. Then he turned his head and threw up, all over his shirt and the window. I screamed again, and thought I would be sick myself.

But Pidge was in action. She'd unbuckled her seatbelt and had scooted over to grab the steering things. The donkey bracelet dangled from her wrist in between knobs. "Roscoe, stay with me. Tell me what to do to get us on the ground!" Her voice was sharp and frantic but strong. Without looking back at me, she yelled, "Beatrice, get in a brace position—put your head down and hug your knees." In response to my whimper, she added, "I promise you, darling, that I will keep you safe!"

Pidge could barely open her billfold. How was she going to control a plane with her shaky hands? I tried to unbuckle and move up to the controls to help her.

"Get back in your seat and buckle up!" she screamed at me. "Brace position. Now!" I obliged. With my head between my knees, I couldn't see outside of the plane, nor the chaos up front. I could only feel *Serendipity* bucking like a bronco.

258

I could hear Pidge shouting questions at Roscoe and him grunting answers. I closed my eyes and mouthed all the prayers I could remember and squeezed my elephant charm. I tried not to think about Amelia's plane over the ocean, thirty years ago.

From the front seat, I heard Pidge crying out. "Oh, Meelie. Get us out of this mess, please. Meelie, I need you, sis. Don't let me be alone up here. Help me remember what to do."

Roscoe was still moaning in between commands. But the movements of the plane became a little smoother, even as I felt the pressure of us heading quickly toward the ground below. For what felt like an eternity I cowered in my seat, not knowing what would happen.

Roscoe exclaimed, "That's it, that's it . . ." A huge thudding bump rocked the plane. Smaller bumps continued, like we were kernels inside a movie-popcorn machine. My seatbelt hugged me to the seat, but every part of my body rattled, from my toes to my teeth. My ears ached from the change in pressure. Bile rose in my throat.

The plane stopped. I jolted forward, then the seatbelt tugged me back.

The sudden calm was overwhelming. It still felt like we were moving—and in my seat, I was: breath panting, heart pounding, body shaking like a leaf. I slowly unfurled from my brace position. Were we on the ground? Were we okay? Or was this how the afterlife started?

All was quiet from the front of the plane. I rubbed my eyes and looked out the window. We were on a small dirt road in the middle of a cornfield. Clouds of dust swirled around us. Trembling, I unbuckled my seatbelt. *"Pidge?"* I tried to whisper and barely made a sound. I coughed and cleared my throat. "Pidge?" My voice came out shaky and craggy.

I tried to stand up, but my knees buckled. Hunched over, I climbed toward the front seat. Roscoe was passed out in his, throw-up covering the front of his neatly pressed shirt. But he was breathing. Pidge sat next to him, still clutching the controls. Her eyes were open. She blinked.

"Pidge! Are you all right?"

She gingerly let go of one of the steering things. "I–I think so. I might've bopped my head." She pushed the strands of hair that had escaped her chignon back from her face. She blinked again, like she had just woken up. There was a reddish smear on her cheek, but I think it was from her lipstick, not blood. "It's very odd," she said, her voice getting dreamy. "Meelie's first crash happened on this day in 1921. July 23." She paused. "You know, she was up there just now. Helping me."

That coincidence was odd, but this wasn't the time to reminisce. "We need to call for help." I reached around Roscoe's belly and found the radio. I pressed the buttons, which thankfully were clean, at random. "This is the plane *Serendipity.* We've crashed. I mean, crash-landed. Or emergency-landed. Whatever it's called—the pilot is sick. Send an ambulance, please!" The staticky sounds suggested the radio was on, but I had no idea if anyone had heard our call, or if they would know where we were. "I'm going to get out and run for help." If we were on a road—it had to lead to people somewhere.

Pidge nodded. "Good girl. Hurry." Her voice was soft and tired.

I opened the door and tumbled out of the plane. I didn't know whether to go left or right, so I took off in the direction of the setting sun. My legs and arms ached from all the bumps and shaking, but as I looked at them, I saw no cuts or scrapes. How in the world had we survived that rough landing unharmed? How in the world had Pidge gotten the plane down? *It's like Meelie really was looking out for us . . .* My head spun with anxiety, relief, and disbelief.

"Hey! You there!" I whirled around, unsure of where the voice was coming from. A boy in overalls stood on the gravel, shading his eyes and staring at me. "Are you from that airplane?"

"Yes! And we need help!" Suddenly exhausted, I dropped

to my knees. He took another look at me, then turned and ran in the other direction.

I couldn't move another inch. The whirling in my head was getting worse. I lay down in the dirt, and I closed my eyes.

I opened them to see a kind-faced woman staring down at me. "You poor, poor thing." As I started to sit up, she put out her hand to stop me. "Shh. Take it easy, all right? Go slowly. You had a real shock." She held out a cup of water and helped me grasp it to take a sip.

"My grandmother is in the plane. The pilot is sick. They need help, badly."

"Help is already there, sweet pea. They're bringing them back to the house. Take a deep breath. When you're ready, let's help you up."

I did as she said. When I sat up, the world spun. I had to remind myself that I was safe on the ground.

With her arm around my waist to support me, we slowly walked down the road to a ramshackle farmhouse. A few men in overalls and caps—farmers, I guessed—stood talking to a couple of uniformed police officers. A stretcher was being loaded into an ambulance with Roscoe strapped onto it. But I could tell he was alive.

"Where's my grandmother?"

The man standing nearest to me pointed to the open door. "Helen, take her on inside." The woman, who must have been Helen, gave my shoulders a squeeze as she led me through the doorway. In the living room, I saw Pidge, lying on the couch with an ice pack on her temple.

"Pidge!" Ignoring my own wooziness, I ran to her side.

Her eyelids fluttered open. "Oh, Meelie." She smiled at me, reaching for my hand. Her clasp was reassuringly strong. But why was she calling me that? "I'm so happy you're back."

"No, Pidge. It's Beatrice. Your granddaughter." Did she really think I was her sister? Now this was the second time she'd gotten us confused.

"What?" She squinted at me for a minute. "Oh, I suppose you are. I'm just . . . a little shaken up. I . . . Yes. You're *Beatrice*." Her eyes showed she recognized me, and she pulled me toward her for a hug. "I don't know about you, but I'm starting to feel the slightest bit cursed."

I laughed, hugging her tighter. "Thank you," I whispered into her blouse. I didn't want to elaborate. I didn't want to think about what would've happened to us if she hadn't helped bring us out of the sky. I didn't want to give words to it.

"Who would've thought," she murmured, "that Meelie wouldn't be the only capable Earhart sister to fly."

# NINETEEN

## Sisterly Practice

Nobody knew quite what to do with us: the old woman and the young girl, covered in dirt (and, in Pidge's unfortunate case, a bit of Roscoe's throw-up), marooned on a farmstead. Of all the things one might expect to crawl out of a Kansas cornfield, I don't think anybody expected the likes of us. After the ambulance left with Roscoe, a doctor made a house call to check on Pidge and me. To the surprise of the assembled farmers and police, we were both fine—other than the whopping goose-egg bruise on the edge of Pidge's hairline.

"Is there any family we can take you ladies home to?" one of the officers asked.

Pidge started to shake her head, stopped when she remembered the ice pack and bruise, and cleared her throat. "I'm afraid we have no family in these parts. We were flying to Atchison." We had landed slightly east of Manhattan—Kansas, not New York.

"Atchison's less than two hours away," Helen offered. She'd come into the room bearing glasses of lemonade and some angel food cake. I'd already drunk two cups and eaten a slice. "Is there someone there who can drive here to fetch y'all?"

"No," Pidge said. "We were to stay in a hotel." Truthfully, we had no idea where we would stay once we got there—especially with fewer than ten dollars to our names. Maybe Amelia would have some money. Pidge and I hadn't thought that far ahead—the goal this whole time had been to get to their front yard and figure out the rest later. I suppose if we got there tonight we'd have to sleep under the stars.

"My sister was going to meet us. But she's traveling, and unreachable . . ."

I caught Pidge's worried glance. We'd survived being kicked off a train and crash-landing a plane, and we were so close, but everything kept unraveling. We *did* seem the slightest bit cursed. Pidge readjusted the ice pack to her temple and sighed with something like resignation. I couldn't stand it. Not after we came this whole way. We *had* to make it in time.

"Maybe someone could give us a lift there?" All the adults in the room stared at me, and the boldness that had allowed me pipe up faded. I shrank back into the sofa and readjusted our luggage in front of me, which someone had helpfully retrieved from the *Serendipity*. "We've been through so much," I said, bowing my head in a manner intended to create sympathy. That was a move I could picture Pidge doing.

Eventually, one of the police officers cleared his throat. "Well. I could give you a ride—but not until the morning. My wife's a nurse, and she works the night shift. I can't leave the kids." He looked up at the older officer, like he was seeking permission, and waited for his nod. "I suppose you could stay with us for the night."

Pidge perked up at that. "We would appreciate that ever so much." If we left early, we would still make it to Atchison in the morning. There was hope.

That was how we found ourselves sitting on Officer Wendell's back porch, full plates of roast chicken and potatoes in front of us. Meanwhile, his two towheaded daughters, Suzie and Sara, sat next to me, peppering us with questions.

"Why were you in the plane?"

"What was it like to crash?!"

"Where are you from?"

"Why are your ankles so dirty?"

I hunched over from a sudden wave of embarrassment—and to inspect my ankles. The skin above my no-longer-white Keds was *incredibly* dirty, but that paled in comparison to my days-unwashed hair and sweat-stained, grimy clothes. I hated to think of how I smelled.

"We have the dust of an adventure on us," Pidge said. She started telling the girls our whole story. Hearing Pidge describe everything we'd done, I curled up from my slouch.

Yes, *I* had crossed the desert and plains, in rocking trains and rolling stones and glinting silver buses and a sputtering plane. I'd seen mountains and forests and red rocks and golden fields, and I'd even passed through the clouds. I'd stood outside in the dark desert night and stared at stars brighter than the lit-up Hollywood sign. I'd been on a true adventure.

And I was *proud*.

We watched the sisters run around the yard, catching fireflies, while we finished eating. They twirled in bare feet, holding hands—looking like the sticky pipe cleaner figures of us that Sally had made me. They alternately whispered and filled the air with their peals of laughter. The scene reminded me of one of Meelie's letters, when she talked about hot summer days in Atchison when she and Pidge were kids: the happiest time of their lives. I glanced over at my grandmother and saw the mistiness in her eyes, and I knew she was making the same connection. But Pidge was smiling. Despite all the sadness she'd felt without Meelie, being a sister still made her happy.

What memories would I have, years from now, of Sally and

me? Ever since my father met Julie, I'd hated how Sally kept trying to worm her way into my life. But I had been the one to give her no other way of being a part of it than by force. Maybe I'd been wrong about seeing our family as something that couldn't come together. Maybe I should've seen the addition of a younger sister to my life as a gift—not a trial.

Whenever we got home to California, it wouldn't be too late to change that. I set down my plate, took off my shoes, and ran barefoot into the yard, where I started dancing around with the sisters. *Practice*, I told myself. I simply needed a little sisterly practice.

After baths and before we went to sleep, I reached into my knapsack to take out my adventure journal. If there was ever an adventure to write down, I think my grandmother landing a plane in the middle of a cornfield was it. But before I found the journal in the jumble of things at the bottom of my bag, my hand passed over a thin envelope. I yanked it out and waved it in the air for Pidge to see.

"Look what I found! Meelie's last letter—I must've shoved it in my knapsack when we were on the bus."

Pidge sat up in our bed—we were sharing one in the guest room, but it no longer felt weird. Not after everything we'd been through together. "Good girl! Bring it here." I handed the envelope to her, and while I wrote down in my journal every-thing that had happened, Pidge read and reread Meelie's letter. In fact, she fell asleep hugging it to her chest.

In the morning, I woke up to the scent and sizzle of bacon. Pidge was fastening a belt around her waist before I'd even pulled back the sheets. I ached all over, but especially my right shoulder. I must've bumped it during the landing. As I mas-saged it tentatively, Pidge looked at me with sympathy. The bump on her forehead had gone down, but the bruise was a deeper shade of purple.

"I wish I could let you sleep off some of the aches. But I'm afraid we need to get on the road."

Because I was so groggy, it took a minute before I remem-bered what day it was. Monday, July 24. We were supposed to be in Atchison already.

The anxious and hopeful look on Pidge's face—and the way her hands shook, maybe from nerves—gave me the push to get out of bed and hurriedly dress. I couldn't bear to go back to the stained outfit I'd worn on the train and in New Mexico, and my blue jeans were a mess. So I threw on the only other clothing I had packed, a mismatched striped skirt and top. I wrapped Neta's scarf around my neck to symbolically keep her with us for this last leg. I changed even with Pidge in the room—I wasn't so modest anymore around my grandmother. While I laced my shoes, she made the bed. Then I grabbed our bags to lug downstairs. Pidge eased her suitcase from my grip. "I know you think I'm an old lady, and it's very nice of you to try to manage all our things, but you need to watch that shoulder." She shook her head. "I shudder to think of what I've put you through the past few days."

"But it's worth it," I insisted.

The sheriff was finishing his coffee in the kitchen. His wife, Louise, was standing at the counter. She clucked at us as we shuffled into the room. "Let me fill a couple of plates. When I got home from my shift, I heard all about what happened to you two." She started heaping food onto a dish. Even though we'd eaten well the night before, I was still starving. Residual hunger, I guessed.

"That is so kind of you, but—" Pidge hesitated, and I hoped she wouldn't be rude. "I'm worried about my sister waiting for us in Atchison, without word. I'm afraid that's affected my appetite."

Louise frowned. "There's no way to give her a ring? Let her know you'll be delayed?"

Pidge shook her head. "I'm afraid not. It's my *older* sister," she added, probably hoping that they would picture hair even grayer than Pidge's and maybe a cane.

"Well, I can't let you out of my house without a proper

meal." Louise guided me, with a loving forcefulness, into a chair at the kitchen table. "I won't take no for an answer." She set another plate down across from mine, but let Pidge grudgingly seat herself. "And let me take another peek at your head." She examined Pidge's goose egg and eyes. I held my breath until she pronounced her still okay.

Pidge practically inhaled her food. I could barely keep up with her pace of eating. As soon as I got down to two glistening strips of bacon, Louise came back with the pan. More eggs and bacon piled on my plate. She topped off Pidge's coffee.

"Oh, honey." Louise turned to Officer Wendell, who was reading the paper. "Before you head out, I need you to look at the washing machine—it's on the fritz. And I have loads to do."

I thought Pidge's eyes were going to bulge out of her head. The yellow clock above the refrigerator ticked us past eight thirty. We'd already missed arriving first thing. If it took almost two hours to get to Atchison—and Officer Wendell had not been a fast driver the night before—then we were barely going to make it there while it was still morning, when Meelie's letter had said to meet. But Meelie would wait for us, right? After making Pidge wait for thirty years?

Officer Wendell wiped his mouth, stood up, and headed for the laundry room. While the washing machine got its repairs, we waited on a bench in the Wendells' front yard.

Pidge practically vibrated with nerves. Suzie came running out of the house, and I joined her on the plush grass for a demonstration on how to make dandelion chains.

"You're lucky that you get to travel around with your grandmother. I never get to go anywhere alone." As if on cue, Sara bounded out the side door. Suzie sighed. "Sara's like my shadow."

I knew that feeling. But I also had learned what it was like to miss someone. "If you didn't have your shadow any longer, you'd be really blue. Believe me."

Suzie plucked another dandelion from the grass. "Do you have a little sister?"

"I do." I twisted the chain I was almost done with. "And I kind of wish she were here right now." I wrapped the chain around my wrist, next to my elephant bracelet. My words surprised me. Especially because I meant them. "It's something my grandmother taught me—I can think of few things more important than my one and only sister."

Suzie nodded. When Sara plopped down next to her, she took her wrist and fastened a bracelet around it. There were dandelions in our yard at home. When I got back, I'd make sure Sally knew how to make jewelry out of them.

Despite our predicament, Pidge smiled as she watched us play. I was wearing a crown, two wristlets, a necklace, and Sara had applied dandelion "blush" to my cheeks. Pidge took a picture of us with my Brownie camera. I had only a few shots left.

Finally, Officer Wendell emerged from the side of the house. "I suppose we better get a move on." My wristwatch said it was almost ten. But when he smiled at us, showing no annoyance about carting an old lady and a kid almost two hours away, on his day off, it was hard to be mad about the time. How could he know that this morning was the culmination of thirty years of worrying and waiting?

We thanked Louise, who had wrapped up some sandwiches for us in case we got hungry later on, and said good-bye to the girls. Sara grinned and waved in an exuberant way that reminded me of how Sally had made a big show of saying good-bye when my family left me at Pidge's. I found myself imagining how excited Sally would be when they came back to Sun City to pick me up—and for once, I looked forward to her clinging to my waist in a hug.

I settled into the backseat. Pidge climbed in next to me. It seemed oddly fitting that we'd gone from trainhopping to hitchhiking to bussing it to flying—and now we were riding in a squad car. Officer Wendell turned on the radio, which played Johnny Cash. He hummed along from the front seat. I bounced around with excitement. *We're really going to make it to Atchison. And we just might make by noon.* All my doubts about Meelie had faded when we'd survived the flight. If an arthritic, sleep-deprived, sometimes forgetful, dehydrated grandmother could prevent a plane from crashing—the impossible really could happen.

"So where's your sister coming from?" the officer called back to Pidge. That was the question we all wanted answered.

Pidge turned her head to stare out at the azure sky. "Well, I guess you could say she's been round the world. And now she's finally back."

# TWENTY

## *Atchison*

The drive was a blur, and when we saw the sign welcoming us to Atchison, Kansas, it felt like a mirage. Or perhaps a dream come true. The sun, in the process of getting blocked by a few thick, ominous clouds, was high in the summer sky—it wasn't morning by any measure. Any dew that had been on the lawn would've been baked away. Pidge moved to the edge of her seat, nose pressed to the glass like a child. Like Sally, actually—she always sits that way when we're driving in my dad's Cadillac, and although I hate finding her gross nose smudges on the glass afterward, I have to respect the way she's intent on absorbing everything around her.

It's funny, but on this journey, I felt like finally my nose wasn't up against the glass, looking at the world outside—but like I was really a part of the world around me.

"Where should I take you ladies?" Officer Wendell asked.

"Over to Santa Fe Street, please." Pidge added, "At the intersection with Second Street." She unwound the scarf from around her neck and dropped it to her lap, where her hands wrung it.

"Over by the river. Okey-doke." Officer Wendell turned the car. Atchison didn't look like I'd always pictured it—truly, I'd imagined wooden shacks in a cornfield, based on my limited knowledge of America outside of California's golden hills. The homes in leafy downtown Atchison were stately Victorians, with turrets and stained-glass windows. Redbrick walkways led up to wide front porches. Many were honest-to-goodness mansions. I spotted a gargoyle perched on one particularly fancy stone house. It wasn't the prairie backwater I'd expected, and I felt ashamed of my assumptions. I'd learned on this trip that places could, and often did, surprise you—just like people.

"What happened to the Hotel Atchison?" Pidge asked as we drove through the downtown.

"Oh, that's been closed for a while."

Surprise flickered across Pidge's face. "My. The world just keeps turning, doesn't it? I can't imagine Atchison without that hotel." She pressed her lips together tightly. It must be strange, returning home after so many years—when the map of your memories is no longer accurate.

The squad car rolled to a gentle stop. "Here?" Officer

Wendell scratched his head, looking out the window at the nice homes on all corners of the intersection. It didn't look like a place where you'd leave a random couple of travelers.

"Yes, this is perfect," Pidge said. To me, she muttered, "I want to do the last block on my own two feet." She stayed in her seat, palm hovering above the door handle. I could see her throat bulge as she swallowed. After a few moments, she grasped the handle and pushed the door open, then climbed out. I bolted out on my side. It was time to find Meelie. I couldn't understand why Pidge wasn't already halfway to the house. Maybe she was nervous.

Officer Wendell pulled our bags out of the trunk and stood awkwardly at the curb. "Are you sure you're okay here? You two *do* have a place to stay and all?"

"I'm sure," Pidge said, struggling to control the waver in her voice. "Thank you so much, Officer. You have been too kind to us." She stared down Santa Fe Street, a twisted look on her face.

"Well, I'm grateful you ladies are safe and sound and that I could help you get home . . . or, get you wherever it is you're going." He furrowed his brows. "I don't know that I like leaving you on a street corner, even a mighty nice one like this . . ."

"We're fine, really," I said. Pidge was out of her trance and already walking away from us, dragging her suitcase. "Thank you again," I said, swinging my knapsack over my shoulder. "And to Mrs. Wendell for the delicious breakfast."

Officer Wendell didn't look convinced, but even so he tapped the hood of the car and swung himself inside. "I guess I'll be on my way. Take care, now."

"Good-bye!" Pidge turned and waved. The police car had barely pulled away before Pidge started down the street again, so quickly she was almost running. I hurried to catch up to her, lugging my battered O'Nite. It didn't look new anymore; it was covered in gunk and a few deep scratches split the exterior. But it looked like a suitcase that belonged to a real traveler. My mom would be proud when she saw it.

Pidge stopped at the corner of a street named Terrace, where she let her bags fall with a thud onto the narrow side-walk. Ahead of us was what I assumed to be the grassy banks of the Missouri River. In the corner lot in front of the river, a big house sat in the middle of a neat yard, surrounded by old trees. The white paint was peeling in a few places, but it was nice-looking, even if not quite as grand as some of the other homes we passed on our way in. The front porch looked out onto the bluffs, and so did the balcony on the second floor. Light from the afternoon sun glinted on the arched windows. An American flag fluttered in the breeze.

It was exactly the kind of scene I'd pictured from the

letters. Except it was missing a homemade roller coaster.

I whirled around, looking for Meelie. *She's here, somewhere.* But the yard was empty. There wasn't even a car parked out front. It was hot and muggy, and the whole street stood still, except for the lazy buzz of insects.

Pidge ran past the house, crossing the road and heading down the grass toward the river. I abandoned my knapsack and my suitcase next to hers but grabbed her pocketbook and slung it over my shoulder, just in case. Then I followed her down the bank, moving so fast that I thought I might tumble into a somersault. But speed wasn't necessary—I could see from the top that nobody was around. Maybe Pidge knew of some special spot in the trees, a place where they had played as children, in which Meelie would be waiting. I pictured a woman, old like Pidge but with Amelia's short hair, sitting on a smooth rock at the river's edge, watching for us and smiling. I wished with my whole heart that she would be there. I squeezed the elephant bracelet on my wrist, for luck. I murmured her name aloud. I *believed* we would see her, at any moment.

At the bottom of the incline, I stopped and sank onto the grass, letting my grandmother look on her own. I didn't want to be right behind her, breathless, adding to the pressure she must feel. *What if we failed—what if we didn't make it here in time to meet Meelie? After all that.*

Pidge emerged from the river's edge, moving more slowly. I expected her to stop and sit with me, but she walked right past. She spoke to me over her shoulder in a clipped tone. "Meelie must be waiting inside. It's so hot. It feels like it could storm." Even though Pidge wasn't looking at me, I nodded in agreement.

I followed her up the redbrick walkway to the wide front porch. She stood, perplexed, in front of the door. Then she knocked. We both were holding our breath.

*Please please please please let Meelie answer.*

Waiting for someone to come to the door felt like an eternity. Finally, it creaked open. My heart hammered in my chest. Pidge braced herself with one hand against the worn wood beside the doorframe. We stared into the widening space inside the home, at the figure emerging as the door swung open. The figure of an old woman, with close-cropped white hair. She was wearing brown pants—and a brown blouse. Her eyes were bright. I felt like I was going burst into tears.

I looked at Pidge's face, and I knew.

# TWENTY-ONE

## *There's Still Time*

Her face was stricken. It wasn't Meelie.

"Can I help you?"

Pidge's mouth opened and closed a few times like a fish's, but she was struggling for words, not air. I stepped up.

"We're looking for someone. A woman—about my grandmother's age." I didn't know whether to tell this stranger the truth. Standing on her front porch, it suddenly sounded too unbelievable.

"Well, I suppose I'm about your grandmother's age." The woman smiled. "You're not looking for me, right?" I shook my head no. "Who *are* you looking for?"

"My grandmother's . . . friend, who used to live around here. She was going to meet us, but we're late. Nobody else has been by, maybe earlier this morning? Around the time the sun came up?" I glanced nervously at Pidge. She leaned against the

281

side of the house, slouching like she was trying to curl into a ball while still standing up.

The woman shook her head. "I'm afraid not." She looked warily at Pidge, who was pale and sweaty. "It's so hot and muggy—could I get you two a glass of water or lemonade? Maybe you'd like to cool off for a few minutes." Lemonade sounded like a lifesaver.

"No," Pidge said, her voice trembling. "I'll wait outside, thank you." She whispered to me. "Meelie is so terrible about being late."

I flinched, worrying that she seemed rude. To the woman, I said, "We would love a drink, though, if you don't mind."

"Come on inside, and I'll fix you up two glasses. Ma'am, feel free to take a seat on the porch." Pidge nodded wearily and before I followed the woman into the house, I made sure she lowered herself into a worn rocking chair.

*This can't be happening.* I rubbed some sweat off my temple. *Where is Meelie?* She must have been waiting for us earlier in the day. Maybe this woman just didn't understand the situation. In the kitchen, I explained further, but cautiously. I needed answers—especially for Pidge. "The truth is, my grandmother used to live here, in this house." The woman's eyebrows raised as I continued. "She's Muriel Earhart."

"Oh, my! I'm honored to have her visit. Why didn't she say so?"

"We've had a long trip, and I think she's a bit overwhelmed."

"Did you say she was meeting a friend?"

I nodded, remembering a detail from one of the letters about their childhood days in Atchison. "An old . . . cousin, actually, whom she used to play with here. Are you *sure* nobody else has stopped by? Maybe even yesterday."

The woman shook her head. "No, but my husband and I were in Kansas City visiting our grandchildren. We only came back this morning, around ten. It's entirely possible she was here and we missed her visit."

A bud of hope bloomed in my chest. *That's it.* Meelie must have arrived before they returned home. It was so hot out—she had to go somewhere to get a drink or rest. She was old, after all. But Meelie would come back.

We carried sweating glasses outside, and the woman set one down on a tray next to Pidge's chair. "Your granddaughter told me you used to live here—I'm so pleased to meet you. May I call you Muriel? My name's Viola."

That shook Pidge out of her daze. She took a sip of the lemonade. "Nice to meet you, Viola. Yes—this was my grandparents' home. My sister and I spent a lot of time here as children. In fact, she was born here."

Viola attempted to ask Pidge questions about her childhood in Atchison—and Meelie—but Pidge only offered halfhearted answers with a growing undertone of annoyance. Viola didn't seem offended. "It's a tricky thing, to go home again," she said before heading back into the house, telling us to sit as long as we liked.

"Viola and her husband were gone this morning, Pidge," I said. "So Meelie probably arrived then, and she's taking a break from waiting in the hot sun for us. I'm sure she'll be back." Pidge nodded, not taking her eyes off the street.

Eventually I went back to the sidewalk and dragged our luggage up to the porch. Pidge stayed in the chair, rocking slowly. Sometimes she'd stand up and shade her eyes to look far off in the distance, toward the muddy river down below. As we waited, she pointed to two maple trees in the yard, telling me how Amelia named them Philemon and Baucis, after the Greek myth. "Meelie was always so creative." She took a long drink of water. "But she was not always punctual. You know, she was late to my *wedding*, among other things. She was fogged in, then suffered a busted propeller, and ended up having to catch a train. She barely made the ceremony." Pidge smiled in a sadly optimistic way that made me feel like someone had taken my heart and squeezed it in their palm. "There's still time, Beatrice."

The time passed. As we rocked on the porch, the sun moved farther beyond us, dropping lower and lower in the sky. More clouds bunched together on the horizon. Viola's husband,

Walter, came home from the store and seemed somewhat befuddled by the two strange, tired ladies occupying his porch. Viola came out late in the afternoon with fresh cookies and generous slices of watermelon. I gobbled it all up, along with the sandwiches Louise Wendell packed for us, but Pidge only nibbled at her food.

*Please please please please let Meelie stride up the river-bank.*

I wrote more in my journals. I finished describing the crash-landing in my adventure one and could hardly believe it wasn't fiction. My own words gave me goose bumps, in a good way. In my worry journal, I wrote about Pidge sitting next to me, and the way energy and hope was draining from her face as each hour passed. I took a bathroom break, thanking Viola profusely for her hospitality.

*Please please please please let Meelie walk down the street.*

Backlit storm clouds over the river turned a beautiful pink-orange, almost the color of the sherbet I ate at the Bon Voyage Diner, and the blue of the sky purpled. I wished Margo were there to paint it. I continued working on my letter to Ruth and wondered where her adventure had taken her. Somewhere in the neighborhood, a dog started barking. A light wind rustled the leaves on Baucis and Philemon. Two kids on bicycles raced down the riverfront street, dinging their bells. We waited, still. Crickets chirped. The sun went all the way down, and then Pidge started to weep.

*Please please please please let Meelie land a plane in the yard.* Even I knew that wasn't going to happen.

At first the tears fell softly, and I only noticed them because as I sneaked sideways glances at Pidge, I saw her quickly wipe one away. Then they fell faster, and soon her shoulders shook with sobs. She curled her body down until she was sitting in the brace position. This time, it was her spirit that was crashing.

"Pidge," I whispered. "I'm so sorry." I knelt at her side and, after a moment's hesitation, put my arms around her in an awkward hug. Tears formed at the corners of my own eyes as, holding onto her, I felt her ache.

Eventually her sobs quieted, but she stayed hunched over. "Pidge, what should we do now?" I whispered. She didn't respond. It was going to be night soon, and we had nowhere to go and nothing to race toward. "Pidge?" I stood. Taking care of us was now up to me.

I went inside and explained to Viola that, sadly, Pidge's cousin hadn't arrived after all. "Thanks for letting us wait here. We'll be on our way now." We could walk down to the main street and try to find a hotel that wasn't closed. Perhaps we wouldn't have to pay up front. That would at least give me the night to figure out how to get money, and how in the world we were going to get home.

"Forgive me for prying, but on your way to *where*? Do you have a place to stay?" My hesitation was all the answer Viola needed. "No, you'll stay with us—I insist. This was once your grandmother's home, and she should always feel welcome here. I'll have Walter set up two beds."

"Th-thank you." My impulse was to refuse—she'd already been so kind—but really, what other option did we have? If this journey had shown me anything, it was the unbelievable generosity of the people we'd met along the way. I made a silent promise to pay it all forward somehow.

Out on the porch, I convinced Pidge to stand. Then I led her up the stairs and to a bedroom. "N-no," she whimpered. "Not this one." It must have once been Meelie's. In the smaller second room, I helped her settle herself onto the bed. "Viola offered us dinner. Will you come downstairs for it?"

She simply rolled onto her side, facing the wall and away from me. All the fight had gone right out of her. Watching that was more alarming than realizing that we were stowaways on the train, than wandering the desert road, than thinking Pidge had disappeared from the bus station. I supposed Pidge's crash wasn't really scarier than the *Serendipity's*, but it was a different kind of scary. "I'll bring up a plate for you," I said to her back.

Downstairs, I asked Viola if I could make a phone call, and if she minded if it would be long distance. She pointed me to the phone and even said that the cord would stretch pretty far into the hallway if I'd like privacy.

I dialed the number I'd scribbled on a napkin, to some hotel in Elizabeth, New Jersey. But when I asked the operator to speak with my mother, he said that the woman by that name had already checked out. I thanked him, then hung up with a sigh. I had no choice but to phone home.

I dragged out dialing on the rotary, pausing after each digit. I let my index finger rest in the last hole almost until the dialing attempt would disconnect. Then I jerked my hand to finish the number. A few staticky clicks, and it rang. I closed my eyes and pictured what I would be interrupting in California.

An anxious female voice begged, "Hello?" But it wasn't Julie's.

I was so confused I didn't know what to say at first. "Mom?"

"Bea!" I heard the clack of one of her rings hitting the mouthpiece as she covered up the phone, and then her muffled voice calling, "Ken, it's her!"

I asked her, "What are you doing there?"

"I flew back to California yesterday, and I drove straight to Sun City to see you. When I got there, I found your stepmother and stepsister, hysterical—but not my daughter! Where are you? Are you all right?" I couldn't believe it. My mom had come home? And Julie and Sally had been at Pidge's empty house? "Bea! Talk to me. Is everything okay?"

"I'm fine. We both are. But we're in Kansas."

"Kansas! What in the world?"

"Pidge—I mean, my grandmother—wanted to go home," I said.

"Unbelievable. Can I speak with her? Or, hang on, I think your father wants to."

I shook my head, even though my mother couldn't see me. "She's . . . not okay. I mean, she's not in trouble or anything. She's upstairs resting. I—Mom, I want to come home too." My throat tightened as I said it, and I had to take a few deep breaths not to cry. *Home.* I thought I'd lost that when my parents split up, but maybe I was wrong. I was standing in a place that had been home to Pidge for years and years, but it held little for her now, without her sister and the rest of their family. Hadn't Meelie written that home, for her, became her memories of Pidge? Home could be a person, or a place and a time; it could be anywhere that held people who loved you or the memories of them. Maybe I was wrong about thinking I didn't have a true home anymore.

"Oh, baby. We'll come get you." She sniffed. "We've all been so worried."

I thought about the worry that Pidge had carried for the past thirty years. I'd given my family only a few hours of fear, but even that was too much. Voice cracking, I said, "I'm so sorry, Mom."

Next my father came on the line and asked to speak to Walter so he could figure out how to make arrangements to collect us. I walked into the kitchen and shyly handed him the phone. Viola patted my shoulder and sat me down at the table for a sloppy joe. "It'll all be okay, hon." I hoped she was right.

Later on, I brought a plate to Pidge, but she wouldn't sit up to eat it. I sat on the edge of her bed and held her hand. I didn't know what to say. The lines on her face looked deeper than this morning, like she'd aged years instead of hours. The letters had brought her decades of hope. They'd buoyed her the whole time, and now she was sinking, into a sadness and old-person-ness that she'd somehow avoided until this moment. Pidge said nothing, and didn't touch her food, but she did squeeze back as I held her hand.

After I heard Viola and Walter head up the stairs and into their room to sleep, I left Pidge. I washed my face, marveling at how tanned it had gotten in only four days. Frankly, I'd thought the suntan was just a lot of stubborn dirt whenever I'd glimpsed my face in a bathroom mirror or a window while on the road. I looked wiser, too—like every freckle was the mark of a new experience or thought I'd had on our way to this point.

The room I was sleeping in had a window with a grand view but was furnished simply, holding only a twin bed, a desk and chair, some bookshelves, and a woven rug. A few landscape paintings hung on the walls and they reminded me of the views from the *Super Chief.* A toy chest sat underneath the window, and a few stray blocks and wooden animals and trucks lay on top of the desk—for the grandchildren in Kansas City, I assumed.

I sat on the bed, overcome with a sudden tiredness. The hope and anticipation that had been fueling our desperate journey had run out. I couldn't believe that we'd made it all this way—for nothing. It was so unfair. I flopped flat on my back and closed my eyes. I couldn't stop thinking about the defeated look on Pidge's face. It haunted me.

There was a thunderclap in the distance, accompanied by the scent of impending summer rain, so I rose to close the window and pull down the shade. It was when I was pushing the gauzy curtains to the side that I saw it, sitting just inside the window-sill: another small toy. A worn wooden donkey, with joints that let it walk and move. As I picked it up, my bracelet shifted and the elephant charm tapped against my wrist. *Ellie.* Pidge's childhood elephant toy. *Donk.* Amelia had kept Donk in her flight bag for the fateful final leg of her last grand adventure. This one on the sill looked just like Donk.

*Just like Donk.* Unless—unless it *was* Donk.

# TWENTY-TWO

## *Flight Paths*

Realizing what that would mean was like being hit by the far-off lightning. *She was here!* Meelie left Donk in the house for Pidge, as a sign.

Meelie could still be out there.

I ran, as quietly as I could, to Pidge's room. I couldn't wait to watch the color, and the hope, return to her face. I pushed open the door. *"Pidge,"* I hissed.

But Pidge wasn't there. The bed was neatly made, her suitcase and pocketbook were sitting in the corner, but she was gone. *She's flying.* I raced down the stairs, not caring anymore what kind of racket I was making, and burst outside, still clutching the toy donkey. The streetlamps offered a faint bit of light, but storm clouds had hidden the moon and stars. "Pidge!" I didn't see her in the yard, so I ran across the street, toward the river. It was starting to rain, giant warm drops. Hurrying down the bank, I lost my footing and slid, tumbling over the grass and narrowly avoiding a tree. "Pidge!" I pushed myself up from the ground, scanning the dark for a sign of my grandmother. I kept running. Down by the water, thanks to a flash of distant lightning, I saw a figure. I ran faster.

She didn't move when I halted next to her, gasping and heaving. But she finally spoke again. Her voice was low and weary. "All those years—all those letters. I just wanted, so badly, for it all to be real. Oh, Beatrice, how desperately I wanted that." She was holding the remaining letter in her hands. "Meelie was determined, strong . . . to the point of being bullheaded. If anyone could ever find her way home against such incredible odds, it would have been my sister." Thunder interrupted her. It was pouring rain by then, and quickly we were both soaking wet.

"Meelie, I believed, had always been living proof that the impossible was, indeed, possible." The ink on the envelope was starting to run and darken Pidge's hands. "You and I beat the odds to make it back here, and I believed that was further proof. But, Beatrice, as much as I wish it were different, some things *are* impossible." I shook my head no, but Pidge continued. "I have to accept reality—nobody, not even Meelie, could have beaten those odds against her. For years, I've been a foolish old woman, for hoping otherwise." She brought one hand to her face, covering her mouth. "I just miss her so much. I've missed her so long. My one and only *sister*." Her voice caught in a sob. She looked down at the wet letter clutched in her other, ink-stained hand, the words streaming from the paper like her hopes being erased. Watching her, I felt my heart crack.

She waved the envelope in the air. "I could never suitably explain these letters, even to myself. But I had to make myself believe, Beatrice. You see, for people like Meelie, adventure keeps them alive. For me, it was *hope* that did." She shook her head, in sadness and shame. "And look what I've done. I took you along with me on this foolhardy journey, and I put you— my one and only granddaughter—in *danger.* Something awful could have happened to you. I'd never forgive myself. What was I thinking?" Pidge's voice lowered to a whisper. "I haven't been brave. I've been terribly, terribly selfish." Lightning flashed again, closer. "I'm sorry I dragged you all this way, and shared my false hope with you, too."

"Pidge," I urged. "It wasn't false. Look." Finally, I held out the donkey, my hand shaking.

She squinted at it. "What is that?" I moved next to her, so she could better see. "Donk?" Her voice barely crept above a whisper. She reached out and stroked the toy. "This notch, on her hind. It's from when I dropped her from a rafter in the barn." I let her take it. "It's really Donk. But—where did you find her?"

"In Meelie's old room, on the windowsill, as I was going to

294

bed." I didn't mention that there were other, similar wooden animal toys in the room. I trusted her recognition. Pidge would know Donk, or Ellie, if she saw them.

"Meelie took Donk with her on the last flight," she whispered.

I nodded. "Yes, I remember that from her letters." And even if the letters were mysterious, that was real, solid proof. None of the "cranks" that had contacted Pidge over the years knew of details like Donk. The memories that only sisters shared.

Pidge cradled the wooden animal in her arms, like it was a baby. "I don't know what this means." Her eyes were pleading. "Because Meelie's not here."

"I don't know what it means, either." Another bolt of lightning lit the sky across the river. I took a deep breath. "But maybe it's a sign. To show you—*us*—that we weren't wrong. Donk came home. Everything that's happened since we left California, all the people we've met along the way . . . it has to be more than serendipity. Maybe there's always a reason to hope, Pidge." I stood straighter as I said that. "The world is uncertain, but hope's one thing we always have."

Pidge looked at me with admiration. "You inherited my sister's wisdom, you know. After watching your courage all the way here, I think maybe you have some of her adventurous spirit, too." She reached for my hand. "I'm not alone anymore. I have another Earhart girl in my life. And I'm so thankful for that."

My eyes brimmed with tears. "I am too." Even if Pidge felt bad for taking me with her to Kansas, *I* didn't feel bad. Everything I'd seen and everyone I'd met along the way had opened up my world, and our mishaps had made me find bravery deep inside myself. I had learned about being a sister. This trip was the best thing that had ever happened to me.

Pidge hugged the donkey to her chest, protecting it from the rain. "We may never know exactly what all this means, or whatever happened to Meelie. If she's somewhere out there and if our flight paths still haven't intersected. But I know it's time to make peace with all that. It's taken thirty years. I suppose I am ready." She tucked Donk into the waistband of her pants. She let her wet hair fall loose, past her shoulders. Then she straightened and spread her arms wide into the air, like she had outside of the bus station on that desert night. They were like wings. "Come fly with us, Beatrice. One last time." In one hand, she clutched the letter. "Help me say good-bye."

I stood next to her, raising my arms into the air. We leaned back our heads and stared up at the sky. The wind teased our hair and the rain pelted our faces, washing away the tears. Thunder rumbled softly in the distance. The storm was moving on. So were we.

"I love you, Meelie. Wherever you are. It's been fun having you as a sister." Then Pidge released her grip on the letter, and it floated out of her hand. The wind twirled it around like it was a paper plane. The letter danced in the air, making loop-the-loops until it dropped into the churning river. We watched it float downstream, until it was gone. The look on Pidge's face wasn't sad anymore. It was one of relief.

On the rain-cleansed banks of the Missouri, back where it all had started, it felt like their flight paths finally crossed.

# TWENTY-THREE

## The First Grand Adventure

O n Thursday, a rental car pulled up to the house. Pidge and I were rocking on the porch again—but no longer in anxious silence. That afternoon she was regaling me with stories about when she and Meelie were kids, including the exact process by which they built that roller coaster in their yard. Viola sat with us for part of the afternoon, drinking up everything Pidge had to say about the house when she lived in it. "I might have to bring back some of the flowers you're describing—heliotrope would look divine this time of year."

That morning, Pidge had untied the donkey bracelet from her wrist. "I love this bracelet, Beatrice, and the special memory of getting it with you. But I think it would be nice if you had something to share with your sister." I liked the idea of our generation having our own Donk and Ellie. I put the bracelet safely in my pocket.

When the car arrived I jumped up from the rocker, my heart fluttering. On Monday night, I hadn't gotten into much trouble on the phone—my parents were too relieved to hear we were safe and sound. Apparently, after our last call from the diner had cut out on my dad, Julie had gotten suspicious, especially once she'd repeatedly confirmed with the management office that the phone lines were in perfect working order. The next morning, Sally had tearfully confessed to Julie that I was calling from a pay phone. (The tears were because she didn't want to get me in trouble.) Julie didn't believe her at first, but Sally insisted—she sensed something was wrong. It was because of her that Julie drove them out to Sun City to check on us and ended up discovering we were gone. I was touched that Sally, and Julie, had been the first to worry about me. But it was also kind of funny that Sally had already carried on the tradition of searching for a lost, adventuring sister.

On Tuesday night my family had boarded the train to Kansas. Now that my dad and Julie had plenty of time to absorb what Pidge and I had done, and had seen how far we'd traveled—would they be furious? We hadn't even told them about our flight on the *Serendipity* yet.

I walked to the edge of the porch, watching the car and trying to think of the right words to tell them how sorry I was for sneaking away and lying about it. I didn't want to put all the blame on Pidge. It had been my choice to go on our adventure. Meelie had written that she had no regrets from the ones she'd taken. The only regret I had was making my family worry. Well, and not packing different shoes. Mine were filthy and my feet were dotted with blisters.

First out of the car was Sally, who raced across the yard toward me. "Be-ah!" Her hug almost knocked me off my feet. I clutched her right back, breathing in the scent of my special coconut shampoo that she must've sneaked and, to my surprise, feeling grateful for it. *I can think of few things more important than my one and only sister.* I was so glad Meelie and Pidge had taught me that.

"Thanks for helping find me, Sally," I said, as she beamed up at me.

My father and Julie got out next, and then a woman wearing jeans and a paisley shirt and sunglasses, with her hair long and loose. *Mom!* My whole entire family had come to get us. I gave Sally another squeeze, then raced across the yard to greet them.

My mother wrapped me in a hug. "I missed you, Mom," I choked.

"Oh, Bea, I missed you too." She pulled back to study my face. "Look at my voyager, off on her own adventures."

"I can't wait to tell you all about them."

"I can't wait to hear!" She moved aside to make room for Julie and my dad.

He looked peeved but still held me in the longest hug. "You have no idea how concerned I was about my little girl. Well"—he cleared his throat—"my independent girl, I suppose." His voice cracked slightly. "Thank goodness you're okay. What would we do without you?" A stern talking-to was definitely in my future, but I was okay with that. I liked knowing that even if I wasn't little anymore, I was still an important part of his—*our*—mixed-up family. Because on this trip, I hadn't only proven I could be brave when everything around me was uncertain, and found my own appetite for adventure. I'd also learned what my family meant to me. Even if sometimes things weren't perfect, or I felt out of place, I didn't want to fly away from the people I loved. At least not for too long.

"So this is where my mother grew up, huh?" My dad scratched at his beard and stepped back to study the house and the view of the river. Julie stood to his side, looking unsure of herself now that my mom was there. I put my arms around her waist and embraced her.

"Thank you for worrying about us," I said, resting my head on her shoulder.

She laughed with surprise. "Of course I was worried! You gave me quite a scare," she said, hugging me back. "Because

I care about you." When she said it, I realized I cared about her too.

Viola insisted on making us all something to eat before we left for the hotel. "It's a belated birthday party," Pidge said, as we helped carry trays of food out from the kitchen. "For my sister's seventieth. Oh, I remember the summer birthday parties our family used to celebrate here. Those memories have been my home." I gave her a strange look. Those words were familiar. I'd definitely heard her say them before. Or someone had . . .

We shared a fried-chicken picnic on the riverbank, everyone sitting in the shade of Baucis and Philemon and enjoying the food and the river view and one another's company. I sat next to my mother, telling her everything that had happened between Sun City and that spot on the banks of the Missouri. I pulled out my adventure journal to read parts aloud to her. "I can't wait to show you the pictures after they're developed. I'll do that as soon as we're home." I had one last exposure to use, though.

"Bea, I'm not going back to California right away," my mother said. "I got an opportunity to go to New York, to interview with a new magazine I'd love to write for. But as soon as I get back, I want to know every detail . . ."

It stung a little, that she wouldn't be going back with me. But thanks to Meelie's letters, and my long and winding trip to Atchison, I understood better why my mother needed to go. Her adventures were important. She had been given eyes to see, as Pidge's grandfather would say. And she was using them. Even if I missed the way things used to be with her at home, I was proud of what my mom was doing.

"Here," I said, handing her my adventure journal. "It's full, anyway. I can't add more to it."

"I'm going to savor every word," my mom said, hugging it to her chest. "But wait," she reached into her bag and dug out a new notebook. "You need a fresh one, for the way back."

Before we finished our food, Viola did the honors of snapping the last picture with my Brownie—my whole family, together, picnicking in Pidge and Meelie's front yard.

When it was time to go, I ran upstairs to grab my bags. Walking into Meelie's old room, I found Pidge standing at the window, an unopened envelope in her hand. It read on the front: ALWAYS MY SISTER. I recognized the handwriting, and my chest swelled with joy.

Before I could beg her to open it, Pidge turned to me. "I wrote her back. Just in case." My shoulders dropped. Pidge propped the envelope on the sill, right where I'd found Donk waiting for us. I kept staring at the handwriting, which was so familiar. I wished I still had one of Meelie's letters to compare it to. Was the script *exactly* the same? I wasn't sure, although it would make much more sense if Meelie's and Pidge's handwriting simply had a sisterly resemblance, like their eyes and height and hair color. Maybe they also shared a way of speaking. That would explain why Pidge sometimes said things that gave me déjà vu, like I'd heard her use those exact phrases before . . . or I'd read those words already. In a letter.

Those letters had been real. I'd held each one in my hands. *Someone* had written them. But questions about them kept nagging at me. If Meelie wrote them, then why wasn't she there? And if they hadn't been written by Meelie, then who could've known all those personal things, about both her and Pidge? Only one person, like she said. When I found Pidge "flying" outside in the desert, she said she had conversations with Meelie under the night sky. She'd called them "my letters" when we left them on the bus in Salina . . . and she'd said the only writing she ever did was "correspondence." The night of the storm, out at the river, what had she told me? *I just wanted, so badly, for it all to be real.* I thought about how I wrote in my journals when I needed to sort feelings out. Pidge sometimes got confused, and once or twice mistook me for Meelie. *Could Pidge have somehow written the letters . . . and forgotten where they came from?*

I shook the thought out of my head. The letters had been sent over decades, long before Pidge wound up in Sun City.

I stared at my grandmother, who was savoring a last look out Meelie's old bedroom window. I didn't know what to think. I believed every single word in the letters. Not just the facts about Meelie, but the *feelings*—both were real. *What does it mean if I'll never be able to know where they came from—or from whom?* Pidge turned to me. A true smile spread across her face, and I knew. Explaining the letters wasn't important. Whatever the truth was about them, they had led us on a journey to this moment in Meelie's room, a moment full of more sweet than bitter. Like Meelie had written, home was more than a place. It could be memories, and it could be being with the people who loved you. Those letters had finally brought Pidge *home*, by bringing her here and by bringing us together. That was what mattered. Meelie could stay a mystery. I gave Pidge a Grandma Anna loving smile. She returned it, taking my hand and giving it one last squeeze, and then we were on our way.

We headed to the airport in Kansas City the following day, after dropping my mother off at her train bound for New York. My family had taken the *El Capitan* out, and Julie said she couldn't handle another long train trip in coach, so my dad begrudgingly bought plane tickets for all of us. I was ready to be home in California, but I'd be lying if I didn't admit to feeling nervous about going back up in a plane after our last flight.

As we were boarding, Pidge leaned over and whispered in my ear: "She'll be up there with us in the air, and she won't let anything happen. Just like the last time—Meelie helped us get the *Serendipity* safely on the ground." She smiled at me, with a touch of sadness. "And if my sister can't do it, I'll step in." I believed her. Pidge was a capable Earhart girl, after all.

My father and Julie sat next to each other, holding hands while dozing. Across the aisle from them, Pidge rested in a window seat, hugging Donk on her lap. I sat in the row behind, next to Sally. It was chilly on board, so I wrapped Snooky's scarf around my neck. As the plane started rolling down the runway, a look of terror crossed Sally's face, and she gripped the armrests until her knuckles turned white. This was her first flight. It was my job, as her big sister, to soothe her.

I reached in my pocket and pulled out the donkey bracelet. I took Sally's wrist and tied the bracelet around it. "It's a lucky charm," I said. I held up mine, so she could see that we matched. Sally smiled.

"Want to hear a story?" Sally nodded her head. I felt the shudder of the wheels lifting, as we soared up into the air. I took Sally's hand in mine.

"It all starts with my great-aunt, Amelia Earhart." I told my sister about the last grand adventure, and the first one, too—mine.

# AUTHOR'S NOTE

*The Last Grand Adventure* is a work of historical fiction—
emphasis on *fiction*. Amelia "Meelie" Earhart really did have a
younger sister, Muriel, whose childhood nickname was Pidge.
I borrowed some details from the real Earharts' childhood
(including their treasured wooden toys, Donk and Ellie), and
many more from Amelia's career and accomplishments, to create my characters and their imagined correspondence. Within
the novel, a few direct quotes from Amelia or her family members appear—they are listed later in this note. But despite the
facts and true details that are sprinkled throughout this book,
its Meelie and Pidge are fictional, as are the rest of the characters in this story.

Like all the middle-grade stories I write, *The Last Grand
Adventure* started with the things that fascinated me as a young
reader. I watched a lot of old movies and '60s-set TV shows—
and always kind of wished I could experience that era. Writing Bea's story gave me a chance to transport myself to 1967
through writing and research. I also went on a lot of family road
trips as a kid. There is something so unique about discovering
the country with the people you know and love (and backseat-
squabble with) best. One of my favorite car trips was from
the Midwest to the Southwest, kind of the reverse of Bea and

Pidge's journey—although I didn't have nearly such an adventurous experience (aside from one unexpected late snowstorm in the mountains, and a tornado warning in, yes, Kansas).

The story of Amelia Earhart's disappearance has also intrigued me since childhood. My initial plan for this book was to write about Amelia Earhart secretly being Bea's grandmother. I was inspired by my two amazing grandmothers: Margaret and Bette. Both are vivacious, independent-minded nonagenarians who have taught me a lot about living a bold and full life. I've always valued my special relationships with them and wanted to capture that in this story.

But during my initial research, I discovered the close relationship that Amelia Earhart had with her younger sister. The last lines of *Courage Is the Price*, Muriel Earhart Morrissey's biography of Amelia, are:

"I say, 'It was fun having you as a sister, Meely!' *Ave atque vale!*"

A translation for the Latin is "I salute you, and good-bye." (Note: The spelling of Amelia's childhood nickname varied in my sources, so I used "Meelie" consistently throughout the novel.)

I found myself a little heartbroken reading that farewell, especially after spending hours exploring Amelia and Muriel's experience as sisters, which was both extraordinary and ordinary. Being a younger sister myself, I was drawn to the idea of telling the story of a sibling left behind after Amelia's disappearance. And so the character Pidge came to be, along with the story of her bittersweet and adventurous farewell to her beloved Meelie.

## THE SUMMER OF '67

The sixties were a tumultuous period in American history, which the summer of 1967's two contradictory nicknames show: It's known as both the "Summer of Love"—referring to the thousands of hippies who gathered in San Francisco to celebrate music and art, and to promote anti-war views—and the "Long, Hot Summer"—a reference to the 159 civil disturbances that occurred throughout the United States, part of the ongoing struggle for civil rights and fight against racial injustice. The news at that time was full of reports about the Vietnam War (and the growing protests against it) and other international conflicts, such as the Six-Day War in the Middle East. Change was happening throughout the country: in large social and political movements related to civil rights, women's liberation, and the environment; in popular music and culture; and on a personal level for many people.

Living in a changing country can be scary—and energizing. Bea's story, I hope, provides a snapshot of what it would have been like to be a young person during that impactful summer.

Amelia Mary Earhart was born July 24, 1897, in Atchison, Kansas. As a child, she loved to read, study insects, roam the river bluffs near her grandparents' home, and build contraptions in her yard. She volunteered as a nurse during World War I and enrolled at Columbia University, but soon found her passion: aviation. She took her first flight (as a passenger) in December 1920 and knew afterward that she herself had to learn to fly. Anita "Neta" Snook taught her, and in May 1923 Amelia became the sixteenth woman to be issued a pilot's license by the international aviation organization FAI.

Amelia's career took off after she became the first woman to be flown across the Atlantic Ocean in June 1928. She left on the *Friendship* a relative unknown—and had a ticker-tape parade and White House reception upon her return. But Amelia wanted to make news for her *own* flying. She accomplished a slew of firsts, including altitude records and being the first woman to fly across North America. She raced around and across the country with other pilots in "air derbies." She joined the Ninety-Nines, a group of women pilots, and became their president in 1930. She married the publisher George Putnam, who enthusiastically supported and promoted her career. A poet and writer, Amelia published several books and edited for *Cosmopolitan* magazine. Amelia also served as a faculty member at Purdue University, where she worked to encourage women to pursue careers in aviation.

She impressed the world by being the first woman to fly solo nonstop across the Atlantic. The 1932 flight took fourteen hours and fifty-six minutes, which Amelia spent alone in a plane without modern conveniences like climate control and bathrooms—all the while battling mechanical problems and icy storms. Imagine the stamina and bravery that would take! It's no wonder she became a true celebrity afterward. In 1935 Amelia crossed the Pacific solo, from Honolulu, Hawaii, to Oakland, California. That flight was so relaxed that she listened to a broadcast of the Metropolitan Opera while in the air. She described it as "a journey of stars, not storms; of tropic loveliness instead of ice."

By 1937, Amelia was looking forward to her next accomplishment—a round-the-world flight. She wouldn't be the first person to do it, but her flight path along the equator, at 29,000 miles, would be the longest. After a disastrous takeoff ended her first attempt, Amelia was ready to try again on May 21, 1937, when she flew the first leg from Oakland to Miami. For a week in Florida, she and her team readied the plane. Then on June 1, Amelia and her navigator, Fred Noonan, departed Miami to begin their adventure. They flew southeast to South America, to Africa, and on to Asia, finally stopping in Lae, New Guinea. Three long flights across the Pacific Ocean were left. On July 2, 1937, they disappeared only 7,000 miles from home, while flying from Lae to Howland Island in the middle of the Pacific.

## WHAT REALLY HAPPENED TO AMELIA?

The short answer is that no one knows. But there are many theories about what happened to Amelia, Fred, and her Lockheed Electra plane.

The US Navy searched for them until July 18, 1937. Before the search ended, both the military and everyday people reported catching faint radio transmissions and distress calls from Amelia—suggesting that she had been able to land her plane safely somewhere on the way to Howland Island and was awaiting help. During an aerial search on July 9, spotters noticed signs of people living on Gardner Island (now called Nikumaroro). Not knowing that the island had been uninhabited for years, the searchers didn't realize that any evidence of human life could mean Amelia and Fred were there—and unfortunately, they took no photos to document what they saw.

Rumors spread about what might have happened to Amelia and Fred. People speculated that after crash-landing or ditching their plane in the ocean, they had been picked up by a fishing boat. An old photograph of people on a dock in the Marshall

Islands made news in 2017 when facial-recognition experts claimed Amelia and Fred might be pictured in it (although others insisted the photo predated their disappearance by several years). According to that theory, Amelia and Fred were later imprisoned, due to the tensions between the United States and Japan at the time. During World War II, some US soldiers wondered if her voice belonged one of the women whose English-language Japanese radio broadcasts they listened to while stationed in the Pacific. Others were convinced that Amelia was secretly a US government spy, and her disappearance was part of a top secret mission. Some even believed that Amelia had survived the flight and spent the rest of her life undercover, or with a new identity.

If Amelia and Fred were able to land on another island in the Pacific, they may have lived for a time as castaways. Researchers visiting Nikumaroro have found intriguing items and artifacts that might be related to Amelia's disappearance—such as a 1930s woman's shoe and a jar of freckle cream, which she was known to use. But definitive evidence for any of the theories has yet to be found.

With a story as incredible as Amelia's, perhaps anything is possible. People are still searching for evidence about her fate, and hopefully a groundbreaking clue will be discovered soon. Until then, Amelia's legacy remains one of great bravery, accomplishment, and mystery.

## THE EARHARTS' OWN WORDS

The following quotations adapted in *The Last Grand Adventure* are things Amelia Earhart or her family members really did say:

*"Our whole family loved the smell of a book."* Amelia's mother, Amy Otis Earhart, described her family this way.

*"Oh, Pidge, it's just like flying!"*: Amelia on riding the homemade roller coaster.

*"Your eyes were given to you to see things and I want you to see and remember"* was advice given by Amelia's grandfather, Alfred Otis.

*"Lots of times when you know what's the matter, you don't need to be afraid at all, do you?"* Amelia made this remark as a child while on a train trip.

*"The girl in brown who walks alone"* was the caption for Amelia's high school graduation photo.

*"As soon as we left the ground, I knew I myself had to fly"* and *"I'd die if I didn't"* were what Amelia remembered thinking after her first airplane flight.

*"How could I refuse such a shining adventure?"*: Amelia on accepting the offer to be the first woman flown across the Atlantic.

*"Hooray for the last grand adventure! I wish I had won, but it was worthwhile anyway."* Amelia wrote this in a good-bye letter to her father, in the event she did not return from her first Atlantic crossing.

*"All I wished to do in the world . . . was to be a vagabond—in the air."* Amelia said this after her flight in the *Friendship*.

*"I'm going because I love life and all it has to offer. I want every opportunity and adventure it can give, and I could never welch on one of them."* Amelia gave this explanation for going on her first Atlantic flight to a reporter afterward.

*"Merely for the fun of it"* was Amelia's justification for her solo Atlantic flight.

*"After midnight, the moon set, and I was alone with the stars. I have often said that the lure of flying is the lure of beauty . . ."*: Amelia describes her solo Atlantic flight.

*"WE KNEW YOU COULD DO IT AND NOW YOU HAVE STOP CHEERS CONGRATULATIONS MUCH LOVE MOTHER AND MURIEL"*: This is the text of a congratulatory telegram from Amy Otis Earhart and Muriel Earhart Morrissey.

*"The best mascot is a good mechanic!"*: Amelia on lucky charms.

*"You have scored again . . . [and] shown even the 'doubting Thomases' that aviation is a science which cannot be limited to men only"*: from a congratulatory letter from President Franklin Delano Roosevelt after Amelia's Pacific flight.

*"Dare to live"* was Amelia's advice to young women.

# SELECTED BIBLIOGRAPHY

Adler, Jerry. "The Lady Vanishes." *Smithsonian*, January 2015.

"Amelia Earhart." American Experience. PBS, 1993. http://www
.pbs.org/wgbh/americanexperience/films/earhart/.

Amelia Earhart Birthplace Museum (official website). http://www
.ameliaearhartmuseum.org.

"Amelia Earhart Plane." History Detectives, PBS, 2009. http://www
.pbs.org/opb/historydetectives/investigation/amelia-earhart-plane/.

Earhart, Amelia. *The Fun of It*. Chicago: Academy Press, 1977.

*Fleming, Candice. *Amelia Lost: The Life and Disappearance of
Amelia Earhart*. New York: Schwartz & Wade, 2011.

*Grant, R. G. *A Look at Life in the Sixties*. Austin, TX: Raintree
Steck-Vaughn Publishers, 2000.

*Hill, Laban Carrick. *America Dreaming: How Youth Changed
America in the '60s*. New York: Little, Brown and Company,
2007.

*Jerome, Kate Boehm. *Who Was Amelia Earhart?* New York: Grosset & Dunlap, 2002.

Lovell, Mary S. *The Sound of Wings: The Life of Amelia Earhart.* New York: St. Martin's Press, 1989.

Marshall, Patti. "Anita Neta Snook." HistoryNet, March 12, 2012. http://www.historynet.com/anita-neta-snook.htm.

Morrissey, Muriel Earhart. *Courage Is the Price: The Biography of Amelia Earhart.* Wichita, KS: McCormick-Armstrong, 1963.

Rockwell, John, ed. *The New York Times: The Times of the Sixties.* New York: Black Dog & Leventhal, 2014.

The Ninety-Nines, Inc (official website). http://www.ninety-nines.org.

"The Sixties." PBS. http://www.pbs.org/opb/thesixties/.

Unger, Debi and Irwin, eds. *The Times Were A Changin': The Sixties Reader.* New York: Three Rivers Press, 1998.

Wels, Susan. *Amelia Earhart: The Thrill of It.* Philadelphia: Running Press, 2009.

*Books for young readers

# FOR EDUCATORS

To find out more about this book and the history it includes, visit the Resources page at rebeccabehrens.com. Available for download are:

## *The Last Grand Adventure* Educator's Guide

An educator's guide for grades 4–7; it also provides tips for struggling readers and enrichment activities for advanced readers. Includes:

Prereading questions

Comprehension questions

Classroom activities

Bibliography for further research

## US History/Social Studies Lesson Plan

References in *The Last Grand Adventure* to the real history of the 1960s are excellent points of entry into deeper study. This lesson plan will guide students to research some of the events and movements of the summer of 1967.

## Book Club Discussion Guide

A reference with thought-provoking questions about *The Last Grand Adventure* for readers of all ages.

# ACKNOWLEDGMENTS

Writing a book is always an adventure, and on this one I was lucky to have fantastic travel companions. Many thanks to:

Alyson Heller and Tricia Lin, for helping me navigate my way through this story. Thanks to everyone at Simon & Schuster's Aladdin imprint, especially Laura Lyn DiSiena, who created the beautiful design, and Katherine Devendorf and Carla Benton, who polished these words and kept the train on time, so to speak. A special thanks to Robyn Ng, who captured this story so perfectly in the cover art and map.

Suzie Townsend, for always keeping me on the right path. Special thanks to Sara Stricker and the whole team at New Leaf Literary, for all their enthusiasm, support, and hard work.

Tara Dairman and Michelle Schusterman, for reading the earliest drafts and providing fuel in the form of encouragement and ideas.

Kim Liggett, for making this writing life a joyride.

My teachers, librarians, and booksellers, for not only putting books in my hands but words in my heart.

Elizabeth Behrens, for being my one and only sister, as well as a great friend and teacher.

My grandmothers, Bette Behrens and Margaret Simpson,

and the late Alice Stylianou, for the stories you've told me. I treasure them all.

My parents, Jim and Jane Behrens, for always believing in me. Thank you to my Behrens-Karsh family—Eyal, Ben, and Eva—and my Merriman family—Mark, Brigid, Elise, Grace, and Ben.

Always, thanks to Blake, for all the adventures shared and the many to come.

## ABOUT THE AUTHOR

Rebecca Behrens grew up in Wisconsin, studied in Chicago, and now lives with her husband in New York City. A former textbook editor, Rebecca loves writing and reading about kids full of moxie and places full of history. She is the author of the middle-grade novels *When Audrey Met Alice,* which *BookPage* called "a terrific work of blended realistic and historical fiction," and *Summer of Lost and Found*, which *Kirkus Reviews* praised as "a good find indeed." Visit her online at www.rebeccabehrens.com.